Primary Sins

A novel

By Oscar Corral

ISBN: 0988213133
ISBN-13: 978-0-9882131-3-5
Pandering Line Books, an imprint of AGITS Productions

DEDICATION

I dedicate this book to all the outgunned, outmanned, outmaneuvered journalists in the trenches seeking answers.

PROLOGUE

Blog update, January 21
First published anonymously in PoliticsRsic.com
Picked up by three major media websites
Retweeted 780 times

By: The Ghost of Mike Royko

Back in yonder years when my flesh and bones still rambled over rock and earth, a well-meaning ink-stained wretch of an editor asked me to depart my windy perch on the majestic Lake Michigan and cover the New Hampshire primaries for the Chicago Tribune. His pitch echoed the seductive spin the state puts forth in its argument to be the first-in-the-nation primary. Go cover the most important primary in the nation, my editor said, the place where the election can be decided by a few thousand voters.

I could not in good conscience contribute to the delinquency of a puny, insignificant state by climbing aboard its twisted merry-go-round, which orbits the political sun of democracy once every 4 years.

Instead, I wrote that New Hampshire should be expelled from the union. Yes: kindly removed from the United States.

In my own words: "The damage this tiny state now inflicts on the entire country far outweighs its puny contribution to the national welfare.

"There would be a point to the whole thing if New Hampshire was a barometer of national political feelings, which TV and some of the pundits try to con the rest of us into believing. But it isn't. New Hampshire isn't a typical cross-section of American voters in any way."

Today such an opinion may never make it onto the sanitized, corporate, and withering pages of a major daily newspaper. So I take my message to the people via the web.

Let's end the New Hampshire primary. We let a state half the size of Puerto Rico decide which candidate catapults into the race and which wilts. Most counties in Arizona, Wyoming and Nevada have larger populations.

How can a state that counts Loon Mountain and Fort at No. 4 Living History museum among its top five tourist attractions be our biggest influence in presidential politics? The $1,000 registration fee practically invites psychologically challenged citizens to run, like that frustrated scientist I shall not name who insisted his "Project Thor" was the answer to our global energy needs; or the other messiah wannabe I shall not name who told crowds he spoke to the Almighty through "afterlife orbs" and could solve the world's problems.

And then there's the utter absence of diversity. New Hampshire is so white – 96 percent -- the existence of blacks, Latinos and Asians remains mostly an unconfirmed rumor.

New Hampshire attracts more media to its primary than almost all other states combined. Reporters from everywhere camp out there for months. Sometimes they go "general assignment" and cover candidates as they come and go. Sometimes they are assigned directly to certain candidates, who spend progressively more time in New Hampshire as the primary nears.

This rigs the whole system into favoring candidates with biased messages that appeal to older white folks, but don't necessarily resonate with people who live in actual cities and deal with urban problems. To hell with New Hampshire State Statute 653:9, which arrogantly stipulates that the primary must take place at least seven days before any "similar election" in the United States.

Of course, my rants don't change the fact that New Hampshire's primary is still around, and still exerts undue influence on national politics. I would be doing a disservice to my readers if I didn't provide some sort of analytical insight into the race as it stands at this point. So while we wait for a constitutional assembly to come together over this issue, we must deal with the situation on the ground in the Granite State. With this one and done column from Manchester I hope to give my personal evaluation of the race, and the candidate I see as standing out in the Democratic pack, George Dimmesdale.

Sometime around early January the zeal provided a boost in the polls for Dimmesdale. Fall and winter rendered also-rans lost causes. Two dropped out around Christmas, after on-air pleas for Santa Claus to deliver electoral support went unanswered. Digital number crunching scrambled the race. Suddenly Dimmesdale led and the other candidates found themselves calling their billionaire Super-PAC pimps to mollify concerns.

The president flaunts power daily as a campaign tactic: remind the people who's in charge with a trade agreement signing here, a speech honoring fallen soldiers there, free media proving to be the supreme advantage of a man whose first four years in office have not been catastrophic as much as squarely disappointing.

From August to January, the extreme shifts in the Democratic primaries have extolled the schizophrenic nature of the American electorate. Polls have shown voters flirting with pragmatism, carousing with socialism, but falling hard for a message of optimism based on religious values, a combination a majority here in this unrepresentative state feels would be a winning mix against a popular conservative Christian incumbent.

The arc of the race has shattered any sense that establishment Democrats have a grip on their party. With Dimmesdale emerging as the front-runner, worried party bosses lament the unwelcome intrusion of religion into their once secular platform. Until now, claims of enlightenment from Above boosted Republicans but were rarely heard among Democrats. The God theme has provided powerful cover for the right. Claiming God in their corner, Republicans have made a political industry of "Christian" values. Now here's Dimmesdale ripping that page from their playbook and running with it. And it's working.

Like every presidential election, this one is framed by the candidates as the most important one in modern history. To get away with this kind of hyperbole, candidates raise the stakes in their rhetoric. They describe global hot spots as existential threats to the American way of life. They blame the incumbent and his party for inequality threatening the American economy. They warn of environmental calamity if current policies continue. They scold the incumbent for trying to return America to a pre-civil rights mentality. It sounds much like a standard presidential primary in the Democratic left. But polls show all candidates trailing the incumbent, whose four years at the bully pulpit have mesmerized half the country and made the other half feel like they're being force-fed political BS. Attacks on the president's integrity, motives and failures have bounced harmlessly into the digital void. Every time support wanes, he hits up Jesus in a speech and his numbers climb back up. He invokes Jesus to guide the nation through unprecedented gun violence; Jesus to spread grace over American allies across the world; Jesus to spare the Thanksgiving Turkey. Not since clergyman James Garfield briefly occupied the White House has religion so intruded into the political discourse.

Dimmesdale grasped the religious trend early on in this race. In interviews, he has discussed why American society now embraces it in politics. Just a few short years ago in 2015, he explained, something happened that few noticed but had the most profound implications for the remaking of world order since the collapse of the Soviet Union. That year, somewhat quietly, the price of crude oil slipped below $40 a barrel. American drivers may have noticed it with lower prices at the gasoline pump. But entire nations that depend on the commodity to fund their budgets suddenly reeled. In less than a year, the oil-exporting nations of the world, many of which are based in the Muslim Middle East, found themselves with government revenues slashed by 30 percent or more. Most of the OPEC nations need the price of oil to remain between $90-$100 a barrel to remain solvent. At $40, chaos erupted. In Iraq and Syria, governments once flush with oil cash suddenly could not fund counter-insurgency operations, and thus ISIL rose from the embers of the Arab Spring and conquered parts of both nations. Libya and Egypt were next in their crosshairs. Russia, grappling with a deep recession, invaded Crimea and Ukraine. Saudi Arabia invaded Yemen and offered part of its national oil company —by far the biggest in the world -- to investors in an unprecedented IPO. Iran buckled to international pressure and signed a nuclear deal, enabling them to export oil and exacerbate a supply glut that had its origins in American hydraulic fracturing technology. Russia occupied Syria. Turkey bombed the Kurds and defended their airspace by shooting down Russian aircraft. The United States got pulled back into Iraq and Afghanistan. And led a coalition of nations in a war in Syria. Terrorists attacked France and Russia.

The price of oil slipped further and further down as countries preferred to keep pumping to maintain market share, than cut production to boost prices.

Repeated attacks and threats to the homelands of Western nations roused once dormant Catholic and Christian fervor. Xenophobia flourished, fanned by the combustible mix of hate rhetoric and social media. Religion, once written off as a non-factor in international relations, suddenly resurged on the international stage. The incumbent had exploited it. But Democrats had resisted for the sake of plurality and unity.

Then Dimmesdale started talking about Jesus.

How does a candidate from the left embrace religion and turn it against Republicans? Dimmesdale tapped the Beatitudes. The Sermon on the Mount, Jesus Christ's instruction manual for living found in the book of Matthew, is apparently still relevant. Dimmesdale's message of humility, charity and brotherly love flies in the face of the intolerant condemnations that religion has produced among the right. The first time Dimmesdale uttered "blessed are they who are persecuted for the sake of righteousness" in a Memphis church honoring Martin Luther King and Vernon Johns, pundits praised his "subtle use of religious metaphor in a modern setting." Dimmesdale's use of religion is less overt than that of Republicans, but his focus on the Beatitudes has led news outlets to attempt to interpret them for unfamiliar audiences. What the hell are news anchors doing talking about Jesus, a name and notion virtually absent from the mainstream media? Getting the news media to talk about Jesus is something the incumbent has seldom been able to do, because his religious rhetoric is written off as opportunistic and irrelevant.

So divergent are the messages heard by Americans at Sunday services and in their nightly news that hearing their local anchors talk about Jesus contorted all expectations of messaging. What makes this message palatable coming from Dimmesdale is his immaculate liberal record. He has cut his teeth politically pushing for tax increases for the wealthy, greater labor and gay rights in his proud state of Illinois, more funding for education, and an aggressive denouncement of the privatization of prisons and hospitals. He is even pro-choice and explains that for him the issue is about having compassion for women, not controlling them.

At times it seems religion has seeped into the race out of boredom. The more the candidates warn of imminent peril, the farther away that peril seems to be. They are preaching to a nation that complains endlessly but benefits from the best standard of living in the history of mankind. Dimmesdale seems to reason that the concerns of the electorate are not existential but spiritual. With all basic needs met, people long for purpose and direction. Politics could never provide to people the same meaning as religion. One is rooted in reality, the other in myth. So Dimmesdale blends a unique cocktail combining the two, banking on the electorate's thirst for believing. His opponents are baffled. Suddenly their talking points seem stale. And when they try to catch up by finding their inner Jesus and preaching religion, it comes off as false and calculated. Democrats talking about religion are like doctors talking about art. It hangs on their walls, but they never gave it much attention. Until now.

Dimmesdale has stimulated the dormant religious zeal on the political left. His critics warn that religion has no place in American politics. And I will join that chorus. This kind of talk is empty and exploitative. Policies, not prayers, are needed to save America from impending doom. But policies are hard. Policies mean compromise and imagination. Policies are backed up by the law. Preaching and prayers are only enforceable by the obscure wrath of God.

Dimmesdale has performed an act of political judo, flipping religion to his advantage. Now, with New Hampshire's primary only weeks away, the race is his for the taking. He is suddenly at the front of the pack, his events filling and his name on the tongues of all pundits.

Dimmesdale's rise in the polls and his looming victory in New Hampshire are exhibit number one in my case to kick New Hampshire out of the United States. Let's never let another Dimmesdale rise in a primary the way he has this year. Let's vow to find another way to sift through possible leaders. Let's give voters in other states a bigger say.

I'll leave you with a few more of the words I wrote in 1979:

"We don't need this. It's bad enough that politics in this country has already become a Madison Avenue game of imagery, hype, mind bending and media manipulation. Every presidential election year shouldn't begin with TV and the pundits running amok in New Hampshire."

But they will, until we drop the fading star of New Hampshire from Old Glory.

CHAPTER 1

Early one January morning in Manchester's trendy post-industrial sector, Dimmesdale delivered a speech about the importance of technological innovation, and how the incumbent president had failed to encourage entrepreneurship because he was too focused on coddling oil companies and Wall Street firms. Dimmesdale tied entrepreneurship to Jesus by explaining that most of his disciples owned their own businesses and that Jesus' message early on was spread by entrepreneurial marketing, as per St. Paul's letters to the Corinthians.

Dimmesdale's entourage had swelled in the past few weeks. But at his side, as always, was his New Hampshire press secretary, Kristen Dunlop. Spouting religion, Dimmesdale had established a solid lead in Iowa, so his attention was focused almost entirely on New Hampshire at this point, generally a more skeptical, educated and secular state. The idea being that victories in the earliest voting states would catapult him to the nomination. New Hampshire, while one of the smallest states, is also one of the most civically engaged and politically aware.

Following his speech that morning, Dimmesdale lingered in the crowd, shaking hands and pining for votes. Kristen stood nearby, scanning the room. A small mob of patient New Englanders – eager to sniff out their own opinions of him instead of relying on the media's spin – held Dimmesdale at bay near the riser. Presidential candidates always took time after stump speeches in New Hampshire for retail politics.

Kristen seized on the moment to walk away, signaling for reporter Michael Cervantes to follow her to a corner of the room. Wonkish types and campaign goons lurked all around them, drowning any sense of privacy. Kristen opened her laptop, leaned it on a low windowsill. She clicked a video icon on her desktop. QuickTime player opened.

Michael stared at the screen. Within seconds the contents shocked him into a stupor. A cloud seemed to pass over the room, blocking out the lights.

"What?" he said smiling nervously, turning the computer screen away from the people near them. "Are you crazy?"

His stomach trembled, as adrenaline leaked into his circulatory system.

"Ok, ok, that's enough," he said, trying to close the laptop.

Kristen held it open. He let go before signs of a struggle alerted others.

"Turn it off," he said, glancing around.

Kristen stopped the video and reached into her coat pocket, fishing out a flash drive. She lifted Michael's hand and placed it in his palm.

"Here's your copy," she said, her face gleaming with calm confidence. Then she leaned in close. "Just make sure you forget what you saw in Berlin."

Michael must have blinked two or three times in the long seconds it took to process her warning. She didn't bat an eyelid.

"What is this, blackmail?" he asked, in honest naiveté.

"I own you," she said.

She closed his hand tightly around the thumb drive, folded up her computer and walked away, seeking out her boss across the cavernous room.

The whine of every voice, the shuffle of every snow boot, the rush of every reporter all hollowed out as Michael's immediate duties as a journalist lost all relevance.

Michael swallowed hard. He had to give Kristen credit for her clever deceit on a level of politics not usually associated with the street shakedown. For God's sake, Michael was a professional journalist! He was the one that shook the trees for fruits of truth to drop in sweet splats onto his notebook. He's the one that dangled scandal before the eyes of power to get answers.

11

Michael should have known months ago that trouble loomed when his two favorite sources of entertainment material became the Bible and Myporn.com. Every time he'd succumb to the corruption of the web, he'd wash away the guilt by immersing himself in the good book. From the beginning, he tried to convince himself that something good could come from this assignment. He had set out to rediscover his faith in the snowy trails of New Hampshire, wrapping himself in the inner workings of democracy by day, and recognizing God's wisdom and will at night. He even went to church a couple of Sundays early on, standing before the altar in a state of hypnosis as the priest mumbled prayers, that in hindsight, he should have listened to more closely.

Michael gazed around the auditorium, which suddenly seemed like a social wilderness of bright lights and echoes. His colleagues in the press corps scampered around the room, interviewing audience members who had braved the chill to hear the boilerplate stump speech. A couple of bloggers – those opinion hawkers who lingered between the press and the rest – were already filing updates via mobile phone. A few tweets dropped like crumbs from the scene. All the faces were blank pages of skin, their voices senseless din.

Michael knew he should have never been a political reporter. When he went into journalism, he steered clear of politics on purpose. It was the only stern warning his parents bestowed on him when he dropped the j-bomb on them in college: "Well, if you're going to be a journalist, stay away from politics," they had told him. "Just look at what Fidel did to Cuba." Michael had always found the American version of politics boring and tedious anyway, and on most days so splattered with duplicity that most people with an elementary school education would advocate imprisonment for their leaders if they paid enough attention.

Through the daze, he saw Dave, the press corps driver from the campaign, approach with his usual impatient walk, eyes darting around, his body leaning slightly forward with immediacy.

"We're out of here. Let's go," Dave said.

Michael mumbled, "I can't go. I don't feel well."

"You sure?" Dave said, already walking away.

Michael nodded.

He somehow made his way back to the hotel, the place where he had spent countless weeks ensconced from the world to inform worthy citizens of democracy's biggest event, where he had recently hatched a perfect plan to bring down a presidential candidate with the truth. Once again, he turned to the cardboard-bound brown book placed there by the Gideons. He didn't read it because he believed. The bible was the only paper book Michael, a compulsive reader, could read in every hotel room in the country without having to pack it in his crammed suitcase.

He flipped to Timothy Chapter 3, Verse 17, a passage he had marked weeks ago because it so perfectly described modern society: "This know also, that in the last days, perilous times shall come. For men shall be lovers of their own selves, covetous, boasters, proud, blasphemous, disobedient to parents, unthankful, unholy, without natural affection, truce-breakers, false accusers, incontinent, fierce, despisers of those that are good, traitors, heady, high minded... and lead captive, silly women laden with sins. Ever learning and never able to come to knowledge of the truth."

God had vacated Michael's life long ago, and the hole left by a withering faith had gone about sampling elixirs of the First Amendment in the hopes of filling up again with inner peace. No matter how many bible passages he read, Michael couldn't reconcile his idea that some clever monks drunk on Belgian ale had penned this worthy book in the dark ages and passed it as the word of God to future imbeciles. But the First Amendment and the Constitution, in his opinion, were insights proudly claimed by mere mortals, but with no less impact and worthiness than the bible. Still, the lack of spiritual context in these modern documents failed to elevate them to the level of a saving grace.

What's worse, Michael hadn't seen, touched, felt or smelled his wife in six weeks. Her only presence was now a daily squeak on the telephone, or the occasional Skype show. Michael didn't look at the digital pictures his wife sent of her with their young children, not even the ones of Glory taking her first steps. His wife had recently met an old friend at the neighborhood park where she took their kids to play and invited him over to their house for espresso to hear the story of his divorce. That simple gesture had triggered a pang of jealousy in Michael.

He stared at the hard drive in his hand and thought about the guiding principles of order in society.

Nowhere in the First Amendment or in the Ten Commandments did it say: though shall not extort with graphic footage. In fact, the bible might have encouraged these types of disciplinary methods: truth by force, truth by technology, truth by accurately recounting an occurrence with a hidden device. Yes, Michael had been one-upped by a renegade journalist, a collector of raw facts who used them to affect change. The only thing eating at Michael was the truth, the raw veracity, the fact that it was in the hands of an enemy.

But he couldn't let it end like this. He had invested too much in his life to see it torn down by a political operative with an appetite for subterfuge and vengeance. A plan melded slowly in his head. He stood up from his bed and began pacing his room. He couldn't just sit there moping, waiting for his life to implode. He had to take action.

"I need help," he said to himself as he paced his hotel room, the curtains drawn and the heater running full blast.

There was one person he could call back in Miami, a childhood friend who until then had failed to fit into the box of friendship that his adult life had designed; A person who swore allegiance to Michael as a boy, and knew more about computer hacking than a Russian computer engineering dropout.

What the fuck was Lazaro's number?

CHAPTER 2

It wasn't always like this.

Just four months ago, Michael sneaked out of St. Lucia's Church with his wife, Bianca, daughter Glory and son Iggy shortly after receiving communion, but before the priest had given the final blessing. Glory had been acting up inside the mass. Father Delgado had shot a few glances at the Cervantes family. Bianca lugged the child on her arms until they reached the front door of the church. Michael noticed her waving an embarrassed hello to an acquaintance as she stepped out.

"I think he saw me," Bianca said.

"Who?"

"The priest. He was looking right at me."

"Who cares? We have a young child. It's a free pass to leave mass early."

"The priests hate it when people do that. Remember a couple of weeks ago, when Father Herrera warned people not to leave early? He said 'until I say the mass has ended, you have to stay.' He was looking right at us when he said it."

Within seconds of exiting the church, the Cervantes crew broke a sweat in the muggy heat. Bianca opened the car and helped Glory into the seat. Their older son, Iggy, let himself into the car on the other side.

"You're paranoid," Michael said. "At least we come to mass. Most people our age don't even go to mass any more."

Bianca started the car. Michael climbed into the passenger side.

"That's really sad," she said. "How people just abandon their religion."

"People don't want their money going to pay for pedophile priests who diddle…"

Bianca slapped his arm as she backed out of the parking space. Michael glared at Iggy, who was all ears. He had started his Catechism classes recently and harbored customary childhood reverence for priests.

"I mean, some people just don't live very close to a church," Michael clarified, hoping Iggy would drop it.

"What's a pedophile?" Iggy asked from the back seat.

"Pedophile?" Michael said. "I don't know what you're talking about."

"Being Catholic is a big part of who I am," Bianca said, then turned her head toward Iggy. "You mean a "Pizza-file", nothing, it's just a dumb figure of speech for someone who enjoys pizza."

The family was on its way to Michael's in-law's house for dinner, a comforting ritual that he had considered a drag early on in their marriage, but now looked forward to with strange anticipation. He had the kind of in-laws that seemed like suburban misfits when he first met them. As happens with many married couples, differences among their families bred tension and confusion as they acclimated to new family cultures. Michael's father-in-law, Dante, wore a 1978 smoking jacket with leather elbow patches every night. It was a remnant of his glory days as a revolutionary who fled Chile to study history at New York University after Salvador Allende was overthrown by Augusto Pinochet. Bianca's mother, Alessandra, was a tall, weathered dancing queen from an Italian-American family in New Jersey. She had spent the better part of her career as a librarian at a local private school, and now spent her days caring for her aging father. Dante and Alessandra met at a New York disco in the 1980s and moved to Miami soon after when Dante landed a teaching position at the University of Miami. Today Alessandra remained regal and beautiful, but she considered music a source of headaches unless she had downed at least two stiff vodka martinis. Beneath the wackiness of Michael's in-laws lay a strangely functional marriage. Their antisocial streak and tendency to find a party in a crowd of two had endeared Michael. Sometimes Alessandra would stroke her cat with one hand and sip a stiff drink with the other, rolling her eyes at Dante's endless lectures about the perils of runaway capitalism.

Dante offered Michael a "brewsky" the moment he walked through the door but Michael politely declined. The usual whirlwind of an aproned Alessandra, trailing a scent of divine culinary undertaking, and blaring classical music enveloped them immediately.

"Hi, wait till you see what I've got cooking for you guys," she said. "I made home made sushi, down to the tempura. You're going to love it."

They all sat down to dinner soon after.

"So, do we keep looking for houses?" asked Alessandra, whose best friend was the Cervantes's realtor. Alessandra had the peculiar habit of cooking fabulous meals then being unable to eat them.

"The damn buses still run 24 hours," Bianca said. "They keep us up every night."

"Yeah, sure" Michael said. "Let's do it."

"O, I feel sorry for you guys," Dante said. "I hated shopping for houses so much that once I bought this house 30 years ago I never wanted to do it again. The only thing worse is remodeling your house. That's why my kitchen is 25 years old."

Bianca giggled. She still laughed at her father's jokes, even though they weren't always funny. Bianca was perfect like that. She humored her father and gave all the credit to her mother for everything. There is nothing more a parent needs from grown children. It took Michael a while to realize she was the same way with him, taking lightly even the bitterest remarks he made about life.

Glory erupted when Iggy pinched a rigatoni off her plate with her fork.

"Don't take her food, Iggy," Bianca scolded. "There's more pasta in the kitchen. I'll get you some."

After dinner, Bianca and her mom cleaned up. Michael took the kids into the master bedroom, helped them climb into the bed and played a movie for them.

When Michael came back into the living room, Alessandra settled into the couch, and his father-in-law helped himself to a glass of fine Chilean wine, sneaking in a night-cap. The retired History professor walked to a corner of the book shelf, lined with little plastic boxes that used to litter teenager's cars 20 years ago, and came back with a cassette tape. The collection of classical music accumulated by Dante was second to none. Most of his tapes were recorded from the radio in the 1980s and 1990s, but some were actually pirate recordings he made during the occasional classical music concert in the culturally devoid Miami Vice heyday. The tempo of the music he chose was usually in direct proportion to the amount of drinks he had in him. Vivaldi's "L'Autunno" jolted Alessandra.

"So where are you guys looking for houses?" Dante asked. "You can get a pretty good deal these days if you find something in foreclosure."

"We're looking around here, dad, as I'm sure mom already told you," Bianca said.

"She hasn't told me anything, just that you guys are looking for a new house."

Alessandra asked her husband to lower the music. Bianca walked over to the vintage Hi-Fi and turned the knob. It's not that Michael's father-in-law was opposed to MP3 or streaming technology, but after the accumulation of a generation's worth of media in a certain cassette format, their display and appreciation was not just a technical choice, it was a mark of character.

"Why don't you just get an MP3 player and transfer all your music into it?" Michael asked him.

"I like my tapes," he said. "Technology changes so fast, that in a couple of years, I will have to transfer them again. Besides when I walk into this room, I look at the tapes, and I feel rich. When I was growing up, only a rich man could have a music collection like this."

"They've got a shelf life," Michael said. "They'll only last a few more years."

He stopped searching for a certain tape and looked up.

"And so will you if you have another kid," he said. "Think veeeery hard about bringing another life into this world. With the economy the way it is."

Bianca's parents always knew what was going on in the Cervantes' lives. Family planning was not exempt. Bianca considered her parents her friends, and disclosed ordinary details of her life, which Michael might have considered private. For Michael, visiting his in-laws seemed like a parallel family dimension. His in-laws had raised his wife for 12 years as an only child until her younger brother was born a few months before she turned 13. For 12 years, she played the role of the quiet fly on the wall, soaking in all the spousal gossip, criticisms, comments and jokes within earshot. As a child, she heard talk of illness, divorce, infidelity, hypocrisy, and all intimate business of her extended family. Michael remembered the open discussion of her uncle's hemorrhoids one Friday evening soon after he started dating Bianca. Were those things to be discussed across generational lines over flan and plantain chips? By the time Bianca and Michael married, she was a world-weary young lady whose lack of shelter from an adult-themed childhood had made her both a moral rock and a secretive confidant.

For Michael, privacy was so rare growing up, that he kept secret even the most mundane details of his life. When Michael was a child, he worked hard to avoid getting sucked into any intimate discussions involving family. He was one of six children and longed for privacy from the days when he realized that his older and younger sisters didn't have testicles. The little he knew about the trials and tribulations of adulthood, the only ones that rang true because they were clearly explained, he learned from watching movies and reading books. Michael never had a "Birds and Bees" talk. He had "Anal Annie and Hung Husbands" at his friend's house after school in 6th grade. His parents had argued in front of him and his siblings, but usually over things like what temperature to set the air conditioner at night and how much money Michael's mother had spent at the groceries. His father tended to internalize his tension and issues, which surfaced with the occasional flaring temper. These blow-out fights over trivial issues made Michael think there was nothing alluring about adulthood, just endless boredom punctuated by frustration and occasional drinks. He wrapped himself in the machinations of childhood at every step, from the costumes at Halloween to his lust for the latest trinket. He discovered the adult world as he lived it, so it often blind-sided him. His wife took things in stride, with a more mature and serene outlook on all obstacles of life.

They soaked in a few sonatas then went home, ready to face another week.

Michael's job as a political reporter for the Miami Tribune defied his youthful prediction of the misery a typical job would bring. It was a great position that gave him a front row seat to one of the most intriguing political towns in American history. A savvy and ambitious ethnic group, the Cubans, had politically commandeered Miami. They had elected three U.S. congressional members, two U.S. Senators, the mayor of the county and controlled most of the big money and cultural institutions in town. The folly with Cubans in political life was that they loved to talk, so nothing remained a secret. Everyone's dirty laundry eventually aired out in public. Michael's editors allowed him maximum flexibility in scheduling and roaming, as long as he produced stories. Sometimes visiting an old friend and musician and gaining some perspective on the city and its issues from an outsider, an artistic one at that, was as useful as having lunch with a lobbyist or a local kingmaker.

After Michael had lunch with just a couple of lobbyists he got the picture. They were all too smooth and savvy for their own good. By nature, they were insecure about their positions in society, so they talked up a storm to prove their knowledge and connections. Name-dropping, rumor mongering and boasting were inherent to their work. A lobbyist was only as good as the politicians and government officials he or she had access to. So they let you know immediately whom they had on speed dial. They invited Michael to connect with them on LinkedIn, which Michael never felt comfortable doing, so the journalist could see for himself the depth of their power roster. They could be useful when they wanted to sabotage a competitor and were willing to leak valuable information for their own personal gain. Michael learned early on that a story that damages the credibility of a lobbyist's competitors was more valuable to them than a story that praised their clients. This cycle was vicious and every lobbyist played the game, so by nature they were treacherous. However, once

Michael established and accepted these things, he found that lobbyists could be quite charming. Their suave, assuring, shameless demeanor could make for excellent company, particularly in a swanky Miami restaurant where the powerful seal deals over linguini and espresso. A cunning reporter such as Michael could play one off the other in back-to-back phone calls or back-to-back meals.

Recently, editors had given Michael even more flexibility to write what he wanted and roam the city free of petty obligations. His expense account had steadily swelled, and he used it to buy information with beer, liquor and lunch. Two months ago he had written a series of stories about Miami's most powerful commissioner, linking him to graft, malfeasance, and a convicted Haitian prostitute and thief named Mal who had been giving him blowjobs after he placed her on the city's payroll for a no-show job. The commissioner had been indicted by the District Attorney's office two weeks ago on charges that stemmed from Michael's stories. A lobbyist connected to the commissioner warned Michael that the commissioner was dangerous and could seek revenge. But another lobbyist who benefited from his downfall assured Michael it was all bluster. Nevertheless, Michael had trouble sleeping, thinking a Molotov cocktail would burst through the window over his bed in the middle of the night and roast alive he and his wife. Sleep was already slack for him on account of a restless baby who awoke throughout the night. But although Michael was chronically tired, the politician's indictment had given him a renewed injection of faith in the power of the press. It was his first scalp, his first communion into the cult of the First Amendment.

Monday morning, Michael made a couple of phone calls from the office, and made a round at City Hall. Bianca had a habit of calling him an hour before he got off the clock, which was 7 p.m., and asking him if he could come home early. Sometimes he did. Bianca worked from home as a correspondent for a parenting magazine, and although she had a full time gig with a salary, she still managed to perform many of the duties that a traditional housewife performs such as laundry, cleaning, cooking etc. They had a nanny that helped with childcare, but Bianca paid as much attention as she could to Glory during the day.

Bianca was a true post-feminist trailblazer. She was one of those poor, exhausted souls who were cursed with having it all, a career, a family, a home. She would often manage to feed a child who didn't want to eat and bathe another who had soiled herself through her diaper, all during a morning conference call. Time for herself was a distant luxury. When she was done working, she took the baby. When Michael got home, she cooked or cleaned. Late at night, she'd manage to solve one clue on a crossword puzzle, her head propped up on a pillow, before she'd pass out. Michael helped with chores around the house the way a professional athlete stretched on the field before a game. It was all show, little feeling. Except for the nights when Michael would barbeque, Bianca did the cooking. She never complained, but Michael had better compliment her London broil.

Bianca did not exercise, but had incredibly maintained the same lean, curvy body she had when she married Michael several years ago. She shattered the feminist ideal in one key way: primping. Every week, her Dominican hairstylist would come over, blow dry her hair, give her a manicure and gossip or *chismear* about the latest thing she'd seen on TV. Last week, Michael had overheard her telling his wife that she had a crush on the county's State Attorney, who often appeared on Spanish language television, and she asked Michael if he could get the top prosecutor's phone number for her. He did, and the hairstylist ended up working on the State Attorney's campaign. She joked that the state attorney, who was bald and struggling to update his stale image, just hired the perfect person for a new hairdo and a makeover.

Michael felt Bianca had a charming personality when she wasn't asking him to do chores or telling him he didn't spend enough time with the family. She laughed off his harshest condemnations and insults and made him feel like a horse's ass the best way possible: through his guilty Catholic conscience.

When he came home one night, Michael's mother-in-law, Alessandra, was visiting. For months, she had been trying to convince the Cervantes to move to a house closer to her so that she could play a more central role in her grandchildren's lives. Bianca gave him a kiss.

"Where were you? You smell like smoke," she said.

"I passed by City Hall," he said. "Best place to catch up on the buzz is the smoker's area outside."

Michael lived in Little Havana, a neighborhood of Miami proper, so the house felt vulnerable to him because it was within the city limits of the commissioner he had investigated. The whole ordeal with the corrupt commissioner is what made him and Bianca seriously consider moving to a house closer to his in-laws in another section of the county. Michael's house was for sale, but the market was practically dead. They were hoping to get enough money out of it in Miami's flat-lining real estate market to move to pricey Pinecrest. The bad market cut both ways. Houses in Pinecrest were more affordable too.

The in-law stuck around for a few minutes before Michael's silence made her feel uncomfortable and prompted her to leave. After she was gone, Bianca asked Michael why he had been rude to her mother. He didn't want to argue, so he left the room without answering and took a shower. He lay with the baby on the bed afterward and horsed around, tickling her velvety belly and showing her a kid's book. Iggy showed up with his own book and stretch out next to them on the bed.

Soon, Michael smelled a feast coming from the kitchen and walked over with the kids. He sat Glory down on a high chair next to the table, which she didn't much care for, and helped set the dishes and utensils.

Over a dinner of breaded chicken, salad and mashed potatoes, Michael consulted Bianca on a rock-and-roll theory, which a source at City Hall had expounded that very afternoon. Bianca knew more about music than any other woman Michael knew, a product of her father's obsession with opera and the classics.

"Do you think rock stars still exist?"

"Yes," she said. "Of course. Look at Bono, or Mick Jagger."

"But they're old, they're from another time."

"But they're still around. Okay, look at Kurt Cobain. Well, he's dead. Look at Gwen Stefani. She's a rock star."

The rattle Michael had placed in front of Glory in the hopes of distracting her long enough to eat suddenly bored her. She began to wail. Dinnertime often became complicated, with Bianca and Michael tag-teaming baby-soothing duties. Bianca stood up and tried to calm her.

"Women can't be rock stars," Michael said.

"What? That's so sexist. Of course women can be rock stars. Look at Janice Joplin, or Grace Slick or Carly Simon."

"Do you consider Nick Jones a rock star?" Michael said, referring to the Jones Brothers lead man.

"No," she said. "He's not a rock star. He just doesn't have it in him."

"What do you mean? He's got the image with the greasy hair, and he's talented as hell, and he dresses funky and women flock to him, although he's kind of ugly. How is that not a rock star?"

Glory was not calming down. Bianca was getting frazzled. Michael got up and went to help her. She handed him the baby and sat down again to eat.

"Look," she said. "Being a rock star is like someone who gets elected to the presidency. A person running for president can have all the skills and track record and public speaking ability in the world. But she may lack that extra something that you can't put your finger on that will make her president. Without that little extra something..."

"Like mojo?" Michael said, shaking the baby lightly.

"*Je ne sais quoi.* It's a mark I can't describe. They either have it or they don't," she said. "Nick Jones walks the walk. But I just don't think he's a rock star."

The next day the Miami Tribune's managing editor, Harriet Spackler , called Michael into her office. In the three years he had been working there, Harriet had never called him into her office with pleasant news. It was usually a request to work overtime on some holiday weekend.

"Hey," she said with a smile as he walked in.

"Hi."

"Great job on the commission investigation."

"Thanks."

"I wanted to ask you something. Corporate is looking for people to cover different presidential candidates during the primaries. I've been telling them about your investigative work down here. They're impressed. We want to know if you want to cover one of the primary presidential campaigns."

Michael sat back and took a deep breath. Behind Harriett, he could see Biscayne Bay glistening underneath a passing cruise ship.

"Wow," he said. "Thanks. I'm honored that you're even asking me."

"I think you'd be good at it. You've done some incredible work here, and I think you're ready for something like this. It's the major leagues. It's a big commitment. You'd be gone from Miami most of the next few months, at least until the primaries are over."

"Don't they have people with more experience for this kind of thing?" Michael asked, squirming in his seat a bit.

"Apparently not," she said. "With all the cutbacks, each paper is hoarding its own political writer for in-depth analyses and profiles. They need people with speed and stamina for the primaries. You'd be filing early and often."

Tindle Bailey, the parent company of the Miami Tribune, owned 44 daily newspapers across the country. It was the second largest newspaper chain in the United States. Harriet told him that Tindle Bailey was taking a reporter from each of the top three papers to cover the primaries. After the primaries, they'd probably replace them with the more veteran political writers. Michael had been loosely following the campaigns. The Democrats were looking to upset the incumbent and were running to the left of the president on social and economic issues.

"Which candidate would I be covering?"

"I was thinking about Dimmesdale."

"Dimmesdale? Isn't he the front runner?"

"Not yet, but he could be."

"How did you swing that for me?"

Harriet winked.

"If you say yes, I think I can get you Dimmesdale. They are looking for someone with energy, someone who can file daily stories. And someone who will hold Dimmesdale's feet to the fire when necessary. This would really elevate your game."

Corporate speak tickled Michael. He wondered if managers took classes to say things like "elevate your game."

"You're on a great trajectory here," she said. "This will only do you good."

There she went again. 'Trajectory.' Wasn't that a word NASA used for space shuttle launches?

"I have to think about this."

"Talk it over with your wife and let me know tomorrow," she said.

That night, Michael went home and talked it over with his wife. Bianca was not one to stand in the way of his career advancement. She encouraged him to go. She insisted that she would make do just fine without him. Then, without hesitating, she cashed in on her sacrifice.

"My only thing is that I don't feel so safe in this house. It's kind of far from my parents, and the neighborhood's not that great. Then you have this deal with the corrupt commissioner. If you're going to be traveling, let's buy a house closer to my parents."

"But Pinecrest is so expensive," Michael said. "It's for rich people. We're two journalists. Isn't that against our religion or something?"

"It's not that bad, my mom's friend will help me find a good deal. She knows real estate better than anybody."

By the end of that weekend, Michael's wife and her mom identified a house, a cool half-million dollar shack smaller than the place they currently owned. Michael's first instinct was to fight the good fight and lecture his wife about the dangers of overextending themselves with debt. Then she reminded him that he was planning on skipping town for a few months to follow a politician around the country, and that she just wanted to feel safe. The clock was ticking. Michael wanted his family to feel safe too. He didn't want to be seen as the husband and father who left his family in harm's way when he went on assignment. He consented, they signed the contract, and they set up the closing for a couple of months down the road.

A few days later, Bianca packed Michael's bag and waved him off at the airport.

CHAPTER 3

The auditorium at Dufresne College rose from the middle of an icy patch, a brick bastion of warmth in this frosty land that seemed uninhabitable. Over the last week, 18 inches of snow had fallen across the state of New Hampshire, capping everything with a clean white layer that was still as thick as the moment it drifted down from the heavens. At the auditorium door, a college kid handing out Dimmesdale campaign literature directed Michael to the press seating area, a few chairs at the back of the room. He didn't know who to look for, what to ask, or even how to act. So he sat down and people-watched for a while, trying to absorb some of this New Hampshire couture, so aptly captured in the state motto "live free or die." One too many bearded New Englanders filed in, all of them taking their lead for an image from the husky lumberjack of yesteryear. The women wore no makeup. Most of them didn't even show their hair, instead keeping it tucked underneath wool hats or hoods or scarves. Their jackets and coats were all earth tone. Michael couldn't make out the quality of a single human shape, not a single hourglass figure apparent on the women. There was just too much clothes in the room in proportion to the amount of people. It buried everything. He had dropped in from Miami, where winter attire involved sunscreen and flip-flops. The only things plainly visible here were the faces, those pale, plain, severe facades hampered in their potential by the brutal cold. It's as though the climate here had retrofitted this part of American society to conform to Islamic law: women covered head to toe, men sporting Allah beards.

A few minutes later, Michael spotted a tall blond with curly hair spilling over her shoulders. He kept his gaze fixed on her. This particular woman was dressed in a black parka that reached almost to her ankles. She had just begun to undo the red scarf wrapped around her neck. She slipped the wool cap off and shook her head a bit to fluff her hair. She caught Michael staring and darted towards him. He looked away and pretended to be deeply absorbed in a sign that a Dimmesdale fan was holding up that said "All Hail Dimmesdale".

Next thing Michael knew, she was standing right next to him. She introduced herself with gloves on. His first handshake with her was memorable in that it reminded him that he did not own a pair of gloves.

"Hi, I'm Kristen Dunlop. I'm George Dimmesdale's press secretary for New Hampshire."

"Nice warm handshake," Michael said.

"Sorry," she said, and slipped off the gloves and then shook his hand again.

The temperature of her hands seemed to radiate through Michael's cold palms and up his neck. That's what struck him more than anything else about her. She had a magnetic grip, and her hand was feverishly warm. He clung on just a second or two longer than he should have in an ordinary social situation. A ridiculous thought shot through his mind of raising her hand to his lips and warming them on her skin. Ridiculous. But not really. Not for Michael. Not in this tundra of a state where ice and snow and cold were the only things to look forward to for months on end.

"I'm Michael Cervantes , from Tindle Bailey newspapers."

He had been brainwashed by corporate to tell everyone that he worked for Tindle Bailey, not the Miami Tribune. Saying it for the first time to someone from the campaign triggered a bit of an identity crisis.

"O, yeah, I remember we spoke yesterday," she said. "Glad you made it. You know, you look different than how I pictured you."

Kristen came off as remarkably confident about her intelligence, yet not without a degree of irony in her side glance. Was that a sarcastic smirk?

"O yeah, how did you picture me?" Michael asked.

"I don't know, shorter, I guess, maybe darker."

"I guess I hadn't really formed a mental picture of you," he said, not knowing how to respond.

But the awkwardness didn't last. She never smiled, not once. "Well, welcome aboard," she said as she walked away. Kristen was off in a flash, bouncing to the next person.

The place was filling up. New Hampshirites dressed in heavy gear kept shuffling through the front door. It took Michael a few moments to realize that the place was packed with young people. College students. He once went to a political rally in college at the University of Florida when Hillary Clinton was running for president, but he didn't make a habit out of it. He couldn't stand the way the candidate had talked to the crowd. Nor the way the crowd reacted with polite applause. But here, the youngsters seemed thrilled, as though they were waiting for their favorite band to start playing.

Three black women entered the room, the only black faces Michael had seen all day. New Hampshire and Vermont are the whitest states in the Union, with very little racial or ethnic diversity. One of the women sat down right next to Michael. Her skin was creamy and smooth. She wore a white parka. Michael was just beginning to think she seemed nice when she suddenly opened her mouth.

"Are you press?" she said. "If you are, you need to register with Dave and Kristen and tell them you're here."

It came off as an annoyed order, like an old teacher exasperated by her students' ignorance.

"Ok, I already met Kristen. Where's Dave?"

She pointed to a boyish little man walking into the room.

"The guy with the glasses and the clipboard."

"Thanks. I'm Michael Cervantes, by the way, from Tindle Bailey newspapers."

He stretched out his hand.

"Whitney Wordsworth," she said. "New York Herald."

Just as Michael stood up to walk to Dave, Dimmesdale entered the room and the crowd erupted. Campaign posters leapt high. Whistles punctured the artificially warm air. In a nervous hurry, Michael whipped the notebook from his pocket and began to take frantic notes, describing the scene around him, what the signs said, what the people yelled, the way Dimmesdale looked.

He scribbled into his notebook the following lines: "Crowd leaps to feet, grey-haired woman embraces Dimmesdale near front door, Dimmesdale smiles, all teeth, posters lunge toward ceiling, college kids whistle and chant "George is more, 2024", campaign staffers surround him, serious looking, no smiles, like Secret Service, scouring crowd, Dimmesdale shakes hands, nudges toward the stage, he points finger at a woman holding a sign then puts his hands over his chest, heartfelt thanks, boisterous cheers prevent him from speaking, he holds hands up just over the height of his shoulders, they don't quiet down immediately, they seem to stir his soul, he drops his hands and nods, smiling, must be his favorite part, the adulation, can see color from blood flowing into his face, his smile fades, he nods, his hands go up again, this time crowd quiets, he doesn't speak immediately, he gives the crowd a moment of contemplation, someone yells "Mr. President", he winks and points to the culprit."

Dimmesdale bestowed the proper accolades on Nashua town officials and local VIPs, then directed his attention to the college students.

"I see quite a bit of young faces in the crowd, and that's a great thing. After all, this is the most important presidential election in a generation."

More cheers. He waited for the students to quiet down again before continuing.

"Opportunity for world order presents itself to each generation disguised as a set of problems. Today, we see the challenge of Islamic extremism, the hostilities of North Korea and Iran. They are problems, yes, but we have come a long way as a nation in pursuing peace."

A college student in the crowd leapt up with a poster board that had a giant peace sign on it. "Peace on earth," he yelled.

Dimmesdale piped right in. "And good will towards men," he said looking at the student. "I like this young man."

The crowd laughed, and the young interrupter raised his arms in the air in a victorious gesture. Dimmesdale got the joke. He laughed and then his face receded into seriousness.

"The dilemma of our age was perhaps best summed up by the philosopher Immanuel Kant over a hundred years ago," Dimmesdale said. "He wrote that the world was destined for perpetual peace. It would come about either by human foresight or by a series of catastrophes that leave no other choice. Which it will be is the ultimate question the newly elected president will have to face. When I am president, I will make the right choice. Unlike our president, who is leading us in the wrong direction. Our great nation is on a course toward catastrophe, when what we need is someone to exercise a bit of human foresight. This is what I offer, my vision for a better America."

The crowd let out a collective "boo" at the mention of the incumbent. Michael struggled to get it all down on paper. He made a mental note to get himself a tape recorder. Whitney had one, and she wasn't even taking notes. She didn't seem all too interested either, as though she had heard it all before. Little did Michael know. But it was all new to him. It all sounded extremely important, a window of deep insight into Dimmesdale The Candidate. Quoting Kant, how philosophical.

Dimmesdale exhibited a serious face again.

"We've been ignoring the threat of climate change for too long. This is a critical risk to the world, and to America. But you wouldn't know it from hearing our leaders talk. They talk like if everything is honky-dorey, as though all those scientists who are warning them are amusing distractions. But we all know what's really going on. The oil industry is pulling their strings. Big Oil doesn't want us to change our habits and adapt to the realities we face. They'd rather bleed the earth dry, destroy our climate and seek higher ground with their billions when everything goes south. What they don't realize is that there will be nowhere to run. Every corner of our world will be affected. Every hemisphere, every continent, every country. We can't escape this threat. It is real, and it must be addressed. That's why I'm proposing a carbon tax that would make the oil companies pay for the damage they've done and help us transition into sustainable forms of energy."

Dimmesdale emphasized "sustainable", a buzzword his research team had told him resonated with young people. And they responded as predicted: cheers, applause, whistles. Then Dimmesdale pivoted, remembering the demographics in his audience.

"You know, my favorite campaign events are the ones at colleges," he said. "Seeing the hopeful look of the young before me reminds me of a time in my life when everyday I was confronted with decisions between right and wrong. And I like to believe that most of the time, I made the right choice. And I congratulate all of you, who hold the promise of the nation's future, for choosing right over wrong. It's never an easy choice. In fact, sometimes it's the toughest choice. But being young does not excuse you from being good and decent. Today, there are many more volunteer programs, more charities, and more non-profit clubs and organizations for college students to participate in than when I was in college. Of course, us old timers like to reminisce about the good old days in the 1960s when the young rebelled and changed the fabric of American society. Well, I'm here to remind you that you are the heirs of that rebellion and that spirit of free will and thought. And I like what you've done with it. I'm proud of you, and I'm deeply infected by your energy."

Another round of cheering. Then Dimmesdale brought down the hammer.

"But I'm not going to be another one of those candidates that stands in front of college students and talks about how the world is your oyster. I'm going to level with you, and I know this hits close to home. You're all being shafted, every single one of you. And it's not limited to you, it includes every college student around this great nation. You see, I don't only remember good times in college. I also remember how I worked through college. And how I earned enough money as a stock boy in a local grocery store to pay my tuition every semester. I worked my way through college. Try doing that today."

A college student in the front row yelled: "that's impossible."

Dimmesdale pointed at the young man: "He's absolutely right. It's impossible. It is not possible to work your way through college because you would have to be earning more than $50,000 after taxes just to cover the tuition payments in most colleges and universities. $50,000 dollars. That's not a number to scoff at. Most college graduates have to work for years to get to that salary in a professional environment. Let alone waiting tables or stocking groceries."

A woman in the second row with dreadlocks yelled: "It's not fair."

"No, it isn't fair to you at all. Most young people in your generation will graduate with elevated levels of student debt. You'll be entering a job market with suppressed wages and increased competition. Your chances of developing an entrepreneurial pursuit will be smothered by the monthly check you have to write for the next decade or two for the college degree you earned."

There was a general "boo" across the audience. Students and parents alike shook their heads.

"But it doesn't have to be this way," Dimmesdale continued. "Our country has the ability, and I feel, the responsibility, to make college more affordable and accessible to all Americans. That is why as president, I would help make community colleges free across the United States. If we did it for early childhood education, and we did it for high school a century ago, we can certainly do it for our young people today."

More cheers and whistles, more platitudes from Dimmesdale on the great impact his policy initiatives would have. The energy and momentum of Dimmesdale's candidacy seemed to grow before Michael's eyes.

"Thank you all," Dimmesdale said finally.

Dimmesdale winked, and suddenly U2's "It's a Beautiful Day" roared out of the scratchy speaker system. Dimmesdale did a little funk groove thing that somewhat resembled a dance, and then a crowd joined him on stage.

"Who's the woman standing next to him?" Michael asked Whitney.

"His wife, Shirley," she said.

Shirley was clearly Dimmesdale Fan number one, leading the crowd into applause by being the first to slap her hands together after one of Dimmesdale's momentous statements about the future of the nation. She nodded her head as he waxed philosophical: yes, George. You are right on the money, George. You are so wise, George. Your ideas must triumph, George. You are the only real choice in this campaign, George. After his speech, Dimmesdale put his right arm around Shirley and held her close, bestowing a kiss on her cheek. You are so handsome and courageous, George, her look said.

Michael finally caught up with Dave outside the auditorium. Keeping Dave's attention while Michael introduced himself was an exercise in futility. His eyes darted back and forth, as though searching the crowd. He seemed to be using massive mental effort to control his feet from carrying him away from Michael. After every pause or breath the journalist took, Dave tried to walk away. Finally, after about 30 seconds, Dave looked him straight in the eye.

"I have to go round everyone up so we can make it on time to the next campaign appearance, gotta go," he said.

As he walked away, Michael said, "Can I follow you? I don't know my way around. I have a rental car."

"Yeah, yeah, sure, whatever," he said and disappeared into the crowd.

Leave it to providence to place the press corps at the mercy of this 21-year-old dyslexic chauffer named Dave Myrtle, who couldn't read a map because of his pre-existing condition and raced to campaign events and appearances at 90 miles an hour on icy roads to compensate for getting lost. Good thing he was a religion major at Stanford, and claimed to be tight with the Gods of at least three major religions.

But he smoked Michael on the road from the beginning, gunning his Econoline, 15-passenger van across yellow lights, slamming on the brakes to make sudden tight turns, and thundering across New Hampshire in his pill-shaped speed-mobile.

Michael kept up as best he could, and abruptly worked his way into a Grand Prix routine.

CHAPTER 4

Michael's shield against the chill was a London Fog trench coat with a thin lining inside, heavy gear for Miami, but no match for the New England winter. He lacked gloves and a scarf. He cranked the heater in his rental car, and tried to keep up with Dave as he chauffeured the press van around southern New Hampshire. But it was no use. The guy drove like a maniac. Michael drove more like a Florida retiree, a symptom of having been involved in too many car accidents when he was a teenager. He'd arrive late at every campaign appearance, so he started skipping the ones he thought would be uneventful and head straight to the next ones.

It took about 4 days for Michael to meet and get to know a little bit about the other 4 press corps members. Every once in while, he'd catch a ride with them in the van and spend more time with his peers, even though he insisted on keeping the rental car. He still followed behind the van in his car more often than not. But the hours spent with his colleagues piled up as they often waited together for a late Dimmesdale to show, and gossiped about campaign event impacts while the candidate glad-handed with locals after his speeches.

Michael was the only man in the bunch. Dave didn't count. He worked for Dimmesdale. There were five members from the press corps originally covering Dimmesdale full time: three black women, an Orthodox

Catholic woman from Brooklyn, and Michael. Other reporters from big newspapers, networks and wire services would drift in and out of the press corps. But these were the constants early on.

At 38, Whitney was the oldest. She worked for the New York Herald, the national paper of record, and spent large amounts of her time transcribing every word uttered by Dimmesdale into her laptop computer, which was probably a good thing for the rest of the corps that she was so distracted. Whitney was chronically grouchy and peppered her demeanor with enough snootiness to reflect the paper she worked for. The more time she spent typing with headphones on, the less her colleagues had to hear about how narrow-minded and rigid her editors were and how she wanted assurances from Dimmesdale's staff that there would be allotted time at every campaign stop to transmit feeds. She huddled in the middle seat of the press van, and typed with her back against the side window so that anyone sitting behind her, such as Michael, wouldn't be tempted into peeking over her shoulder at the Nobel-prize winning literature she was creating. From that seat, she was the first one out of the van, the first to hold a microphone to Dimmesdale's winter-chapped lips, the first to nab him for a question. As a Harvard graduate, born and raised in New York, Whitney believed herself to be in the upper echelon of black society, and rarely stooped to discuss anything beyond Dimmesdale's latest political hiccup with the rest of the press corps. Keenly aware of the vicious and competitive nature among reporters on a national campaign, she never let her guard down. Her face was always severe, her eyes always scrutinizing as though whatever she was listening to was a lie.

Audra Tudrow was a reporter for MSNBC. At 35, she was younger than Whitney, but had a stable temperament and kind way that made her the default mother figure in the van. She rarely spoke because she had this uncanny ability to space out in the press van in this mid-consciousness just shy of sleep. It was probably cold-induced hibernation, since the press van was often a sub-freezing capsule for at least 20 minutes before it started to warm up. Audra originally hailed from Atlanta, but rented an apartment in Brooklyn, within a subway ride of MSNBC's studio in Rockefeller Center. There was never any talk from Audra of a love interest or a social life beyond her immediate job. Her favorite thing to do was hunker down with her I-device grooving to James Brown or Sade, staring out the press van window. She talked to her mom and son once a day, always in such an expert whisper that even the person sitting next to her couldn't make out the baby talk and googles she performed for her toddler. She never complained, except to ask for nourishment if the press corps had been dragged around for a day without a food stop, which happened often. During one of those hunger pangs a few weeks back, Michael offered her a Power bar, which she hungrily devoured. After that, he started carrying granola and power bars around in the van and using them as currency for brownie points, which he eventually cashed in for favors. All Audra had to say was that she was hungry, and he'd give her food. That went for anyone in the press van, including Dave, although he always politely declined.

The youngest reporter in the press corps was Mafikwa Coleman, a pretty black woman from Texas who reported for ABC and had an address in Washington, D.C. Mafikwa was the van gossip queen, the storyteller and mood-raiser who talked enough to compensate for the rest of them. After hearing Dimmesdale rant about America's doomed course, it was refreshing to hear Mafikwa talk about her blind dates, her big Houston barbeques during July 4 vacation, her latest messages on her FB account from her thousand-plus buddies. At 25, her age reflected her lifestyle and interests. She was single but had multiple suitors that kept her phone buzzing with several texts a day, some of which she shared with the press corps, but most which merely produced chuckles or grunts from her. As the third sibling in a working class family with six children, Mafikwa had clawed her way into Stanford after high school, and had clawed her way into covering a presidential campaign at her tender age. Unlike Whitney, whose Harvard education was the exclamation mark on her pedigree, Mafikwa made fun of Stanford and its forced diversity and inclusiveness.

Dimmesdale had his own cheerleading section in the press corps with Rachel Billingsworth, whose Orthodox Catholic upbringing in Brooklyn gave her an instant way to identify with Dimmesdale, himself a Conservative Christian. Rachel reported for CBS, and like Audra and Mafikwa, spent large amounts of time tinkering with digital camera downloads and haranguing her editors for playtime on the nightly news. Dimmesdale didn't need a spin-doctor from his campaign staff traveling in the press van. Rachel did the job for him. She was also young, 26, and didn't have previous experience covering a national campaign. But she hero-worshipped Dimmesdale constantly in the van, mentioning how much class he exhibited during one speech or how much backbone he had when taking a position on a controversial issue such as stem cell research or Iran. She had spent a year living in Greece, and another year living in Spain, making her fluent in Greek and Spanish. When the corps would get bored, Rachel and Michael would chew the fat in Spanish. Rachel was chatty, like Mafikwa, but instead of gossiping about her own life, Rachel seemed genuinely curious about the others in the press van, asking them about their backgrounds, their lives, their families. Because of Rachel, Michael knew certain intimate details about each press corps member. For example, under Rachel questioning, Audra revealed that she was divorced and her son was living with her mother in Atlanta; Mafikwa revealed that she was juggling two serious boyfriends; and Whitney admitted that her husband worked for former U.S. President Clinton, and was a good source for her on the campaign trail. Rachel even got Dave to reveal he had dyslexia, which actually answered some basic questions the press corps had about his competence reading a map. Rachel had an inquisitive, yet comforting nature about her, the way Barbara Walters grilled her subjects, but did so in such a nice way that it seemed perfectly normal to get them to talk about homicides, child molestations and affairs with presidents.

Dave was a religion major at Stanford, a nervous little college student that figured serving the democratic process would bring him one step closer to divine providence. During one of those long drives through the New Hampshire hinterland, Michael had heard him discussing the shortcomings of a godless mysticism with Rachel, who felt that god and spirituality should be considered separately. His authority on Eastern Orthodoxy impressed Rachel, who confessed that while she practiced it, she didn't always believe in it. Peaked with curiosity about the hodge-podge of faiths he was ferrying about, Dave asked Audra during another road trip about her religion. She told him she was Protestant and never went to Church. Whitney chimed in that she did indeed go to a Harlem church on the weekends, the same one Bill Clinton attended.

Mafikwa didn't have much to say at first about her own religion, then blurted out a hidden nugget of innocence: she was a member of the choir at her Baptist church in Texas, and considered gospel music the very sound of God's voice.

As for Michael, he stayed pretty quiet. Not that he didn't get along with everyone. But the cold and deadlines and competition weren't breeding grounds for friendship. He had his own questions about faith, and where it had gone and why. He quelled their curiosity by telling them he was raised a Catholic and attended an all-boys Jesuit school, and letting them apply all the stereotypes such a background entails. But the question of religion haunted Michael regularly.

And Dave admitted as much about his own beliefs. His Catholicism had evolved from a rulebook for living and acting into a loose guideline for navigating the tempest of society. Rachel told Dave that she believed that the New Testament was actually a guide to achieving heaven on earth. Dave disagreed, saying that only through grace can one reach heaven, and that grace can only come on Judgment Day. Neither wanted to touch the actual subject of Jesus, whether he was the son of God, whether he was divine, whether he was the Savior of the world, or just a hippie carpenter who dug hookers and pointed out to the political and economic elite of his day that their ways were evil.

"Michael, you're Catholic, what do you think?" Dave said, turning to glance at Michael.

"My mom taught me never to discuss religion and politics because nothing good can come of it," he said.

"You don't actually believe that, do you?" Mafikwa said. "I mean, that's pretty much everything Dimmesdale talks about."

"No, I know, I'm joking," he said. "Dimmesdale explains it better than I ever could. Truth is, I can't tell if Dimmesdale really believes what he's saying, or if he's just doing it for political points."

#

Like any journalist trapped in the alternate reality of a presidential campaign, Michael started lapping up the nightly gobs of analytical gibberish on television.

The talking heads and pundits had been weighing in on his candidate. Some viewed him as a dark horse, the great Christian hope, the scion of American holiness. Some saw him as too nice, too old, too decent, the ironies of modern day political weaknesses. People still committed the great error in the United States of expecting their politicians to be perfect. Of course, nobody's perfect, especially politicians, although Dimmesdale's white hair was perfectly coiffed and he never got flustered by questions, no matter how embarrassing or hostile.

Illinois Governor George Dimmesdale wanted to be President of the United States since the moment he walked the streets of Memphis with Martin Luther King as a young college graduate in the 1960s, scowling in anguished sympathy for the cameras. His plot to take the reigns of this unwieldy, boisterous, amusing nation stretched back farther than even he remembered. The press responded positively to him, albeit with a tinge of apprehension about his seeming perfection. The pundits liked him the way they liked their physical trainers. Gubernatorial peers liked him. Voters weren't sure. Michael Cervantes wasn't sure. He wasn't supposed to form grounded opinions of the people he covered, according to Journalism 101.

The melodrama Dimmesdale put forth was that there was a lot at stake: the Very Future of America. And only he could guide the country to greener pastures. This country was at a crossroads where it must either lead with conviction through Dimmesdale or continue to stray with the incumbent's heavy hand. The American nation needed new leadership to guide it through the mires of globalization, terrorism, climate change. The president had mismanaged our resources. That cheerful optimism which guided us through the dark moments of our history was fading. The country was falling apart. The president was the incarnation of incompetence.

Cervantes got it all down. It was all important, every word.

CHAPTER 5

Cervantes' first couple of weeks following Dave in his car, and covering only some of the campaign appearances – instead of every single one -- were a blur. Then Dimmesdale happened to verbally attack one of his opponents during one of the small campaign appearances Cervantes had skipped at a diner on the outskirts of Manchester. When Cervantes' editors saw it on the wires, they called him to give them a feed on the attack. Cervantes said ok, then hung up and sat in his car and wondered how he would produce copy on an event he had missed.

During the next campaign appearance that day, Cervantes explained to Kristen Dunlop that his editors wanted copy on the statements Dimmesdale made about Harold Kane. She looked at him and said "Look, you missed it. I can't help you."

"But you record everything he says. Can't you dig up the file from this morning and just let me listen to it for 5 minutes?"

Dimmesdale was shifting to another location, surrounded by press. Kristen moved with him and ignored Cervantes.

"Kristen, please," he said.

She darted her eyes back to him for a final strike.

"Look, I'm not your secretary," she said, almost whispering. "These recordings are for the campaign. Sorry."

She walked away. Actually, Cervantes thought, she was a secretary, a press secretary. He made a note to self to tell her that the next time he saw her. But for now Cervantes worried. Within the next hour, he would be receiving a phone call from his new editor and boss in Washington asking him for the whereabouts of his feed. Sweat seeped through his skin for the first time since he touched down in the tundra. He spotted Dave walking to his van with his cadre of journalists. They seemed to be in a hurry. He sprinted to them and cleared his throat as he emerged among them.

"Um, hi guys," he said loud enough for everyone walking to hear. "My editors called and they want a feed on Dimmesdale's statement from this morning about Harold Kane. But I missed the event. Will anyone here be kind enough to let me listen to the recording from this morning?"

For about five seconds, which seemed like a painful eternity, all he heard was the ice crunching under their shoes. Then one of them spoke up.

"Sure," said Audra.

"Really, thanks," Cervantes said. "Right now?"

"Yeah, when we get in the van."

"Dave, is it alright if you wait five minutes while I hear the recording?" he said.

Dave pulled a few layers of clothes up on his arm and glanced at his watch.

"Impossible. We're late as it is. We're in a huge hurry."

"Please, Dave, just five minutes?"

"He said we're late," Whitney from the New York Herald piped in. "What if we get to Dimmesdale's next appearance late and something major happens while we're not there. Who will cover it? Then we'll all get scooped by the Concord Gazette and we'll all be in trouble."

Cervantes rubbed his chin, feeling the adrenaline rush to his head for a fight with Whitney. But he contained it and the group continued their icy march to the van. Dave fired it up as the reporters climbed in the back. After the last one filed in, Whitney held both doors with her hands, ready to shut them in Michael's face. But she hesitated for a second. Dave turned around to investigate the delay.

"In or out?" Whitney said.

Michael had no choice. He climbed into the van and was off in a flash, leaving behind his rental car, which contained his computer, some food, his water, everything that he did not have in his pockets. Fortunately

Cervantes had picked up from his wife the useful habit of carrying with him everything he needed. His wife's purses were like Gypsy bags, full of useful items she might need in a given week: hair brush, makeup, checkbook, crossword puzzle, wallet, pain relievers, tampons, perfume, a spare toy and a bag of plantain chips for the baby. Rambo had a survival knife. Cervantes' wife had a survival purse. He had his notepad, his mobile phone, his wallet, a pen. Everything he needed.

As Dave raced to the next campaign appearance, Audra located Dimmesdale's morning statement about Harold Kane on her MSNBC-issued digital camera. Dimmesdale showed some fight Cervantes hadn't yet seen: "We need someone steady, with a solid track record, to lead this nation," Dimmesdale had said. "Harold Kane is a decent man. But frankly, I have questions about his experience, and his temperament."

A reporter asked, "What do you mean his temperament, Governor? Please elaborate."

"Sure. Some may refer to Harold Kane as fiery, and that's one way to look at it. I see him as volatile, and in the powder-keg world we live in, volatility is not a quality the American people need in a president."

Cervantes scribbled quickly, stopped the tape, and gave Audra a peck on the cheek when he returned her camera. He phoned Washington and told his Washington-based editor, Donald Jenkins, that he had the feed for him. He requested it via email, but Cervantes explained to him that he did not have access to a laptop, his phone was low on batteries, and that dictation would be best. Nothing annoys an editor more than taking dictation from a reporter. It reminds them of their real role: desk jockeys. It took Cervantes three minutes to read him the four paragraphs he had written up.

The rest of the day went by quickly. He made sure to listen to everything Dimmesdale had to say, and jockeyed for position against other reporters when he gave an impromptu statement or press conference, which were referred to officially as "media availabilities." Dimmesdale didn't break any new ground in his media availabilities that afternoon. But during a quickie later in the evening, Cervantes asked him a question just to let him know he existed, "Hi Governor, I'm Michael Cervantes from Tindle Bailey newspapers. I had a question about Harold Kane. Can you identify any specific instances in the past few weeks when Harold Kane showed symptoms of volatility?"

Dimmesdale smiled and extended his hand to Michael.

"Hi there, Michael, welcome aboard on the campaign. I heard you'd be joining us. You're from Miami, correct? Which is paradise at this time of year."

"Yes, sir," Cervantes said.

"It sure is," Dimmesdale said. "You know, it almost makes a

person wish the first primary was in the good ole Sunshine State."

Cervantes smiled in agreement.

"About Harold Kane , I said everything I was planning to say this morning. I have nothing to add. Sorry you weren't there, but maybe one of your colleagues can let you listen to their recording."

A few of the other reporters around Cervantes chuckled. Michael looked around and tried to play it off with a smirk. The bastard had done him good. In one quick exchange, he showed Cervantes who was boss, shined a light on his screw-up and hinted that he was out of his element. Whitney approached him on the way to the van.

"Welcome to the campaign trail," she said. "I think he likes you."

When the campaign events were over later, Dave dropped off the press at their hotel. He flat-out refused to drive Cervantes back to the college where he had left his car. Cervantes was the only reporter staying at a different hotel, a little Inn by the airport, and Dave was annoyed when Cervantes asked him to drop him off there. So Cervantes called a taxi from the hotel lobby where his fellow reporters were staying, setting him back $60. The car rescue took almost two hours. He didn't get to bed until 2 a.m.

Dave picked them up at 6:45 a.m. to make it to a 7:30 a.m. Dimmesdale event. He spent the day chasing Dave's van in his rental car, trying to make it to every event, catch every crucial phrase uttered by Dimmesdale. That night, throwing in the towel on the last remnants of independence he had, Cervantes returned his rental car and moved into the same hotel as the rest of the Dimmesdale Press Corps. It was a big trade off between logistical and personal comfort. In the little Inn by the airport, they had room service until midnight, a free breakfast beginning at 6 a.m. and free high-speed internet. In the new Merrell Courtyard, there was no room service, no in-house restaurant, no free breakfast, no free high-speed Internet.

But there was Dave and his van, every morning. And the ever pleasant press corps and the Dimmesdale campaign staff. And once he plunged into that routine, nothing stood between Cervantes and the abyss of campaign hell. The confines were so great, so perfect, that he began to feel like a scribe to an Egyptian pharaoh, at the mercy of a powerful man's whims. In the press corps, they went where Dimmesdale chose, ate when Dimmesdale's stomach growled, rested when Dimmesdale's eyelids grew heavy, and wrote what Dimmesdale said.

Dimmesdale's campaign morphed into routine before Cervantes' eyes from hotel room to hotel room, press van to press van like a mime show economizing the truth. Dimmesdale was a broken record of rhetoric, tweaking, ever so lightly, his unifying message of centrism from town to town. Often Cervantes would tune out his voice so efficiently that he'd just see jowls flapping and expressions narrating.

Dimmesdale talked all day, saying the same thing several times, and then turned in for the night with a cup of tea and a prayer.

Cervantes did his best to report on new developments. Very Important People read his dispatches from the campaign trail. They made decisions and strategized around his news reports. If he got a detail wrong, complaints poured in from readers and campaign staffers. Dimmesdale's flacks would call him to say they didn't like something, or point out errors. They never called with compliments.

Cervantes was 28. He had no experience covering national politics. And suddenly he was a political correspondent for the second biggest newspaper chain in the country. Sometimes days would go by without him talking to his editor. He didn't know if he was doing it right, but he had tried to cover up his lack of knowledge by exuding a studied projection of confidence to his bosses and peers. It was a daily struggle not to fall victim to the benign monotony and critical responsibility of babysitting a presidential candidate for weeks on end. Failing on an assignment like this would have sent signals of incompetence toward all the people who helped Cervantes get here. A bad move could have ended his career, another shooting star of journalism that burned too bright early on and fizzled before his prime.

CHAPTER 6

One gray, snowy morning, when the task of getting dressed and preparing for the day was particularly dreadful due to a hangover, Michael called Audra on her cell phone and told her to ask Dave to wait for him. He would have called Dave himself but he didn't want to talk to the bastard and hear him complain. By the time he dragged himself onto the van ten minutes later, the press corps gave him the evil eye. Dave twisted around nervously in his seat.

"Um, you really have to try to be on time," he said. "We're late. I'm not going to wait for you next time."

Michael felt like telling him that they were always late because he was a disabled dyslexic who couldn't tell north from south on a map. But he held back. Composure was king. He ground his teeth a little and the sides of his jaws bulged out.

"Sorry," he said. "Thanks for waiting."

Everything showed on an assignment like this. If you didn't shave for a day, you stood out. If you had a fight with a spouse or loved one, your face would likely give it away. If you changed your tone on a discussion you've had before, alarms went off. If you were keeping some internal strife bottled up, it would be communicated.

"You look tired," Audra said. "Did you shave?"

"I forgot," he said, rubbing his chin.

Everyone's senses were amped up to hyper-detection. There was a reason for this. The candidate had to detect the mood of different audiences, often just by looking at their faces when he walked into the room. Campaign managers and aides had to detect the effectiveness of their candidate's delivery and the energy or lack thereof of an audience before an appearance and after. They spun the media with rhetoric based on the reporter's perception. Reporters had to find something to write about, so they listened for screw-ups and changes in tone and wording and attacks on opponents veiled as self-descriptions. For example, Dimmesdale had recently said about himself at a house party in Concord: "I didn't just drop into this campaign out of nowhere, I have a 30-year-track record you can look at to see where I stand." This was obviously an attack on the opponent from his party, Harold Kane, who was vying with Dimmesdale for dominance at the polls. Kane had been the governor of Massachusetts for 4 years, and was now emerging as a force after being out of politics for two years.

The inquisitive nature of the journalist's job required the press corps to be part forensic psychologist trying to figure out a person's motives; part strategist trying to figure out where a candidate was heading with his message and campaign; part confidante earning the trust of campaign aides to milk them as sources; part critic assessing the weaknesses of the campaign.

After the first ten stump speeches they heard from the candidate, a journalist might put her notepad down, whip out a tape recorder and space out. At least they pretended to be spacing out. Then they reluctantly started picking up the nuanced messages delivered ever so subtly by the candidate. This happened whether the reporter wanted it to or not. After 20 stump speeches, the reporter began wondering why the candidate used a new word instead of the one he regularly used. After witnessing 30 stump speeches, the reporter could recite them during happy hour with other grouchy reporters in a Manchester bar.

After hearing Dimmesdale give 50 stump speeches, Michael had started conveying the same message of centrist unity to his wife when he'd call home. Michael would catch himself giving her entire excerpts of Dimmesdale's stump speech with just subtle differences injected to reflect the relationship between husband and wife.

For example, he'd say "We need to look forward from this point and know deep down that the best lies ahead for us. We need to believe in the optimism of our union. It's like Huckleberry Finn, honey, who never worried about what lay beyond the next bend in the river. We shouldn't worry about the things that lay ahead of the next bend. One of those turns will take me home."

In a way, being a husband was a lot like being President of the United States. You think you're in charge, then "the people", aka, your wife, suddenly starts flirting with the possibility of leaving you for someone else. And in many ways, a candidate running against an incumbent president is like the "other man" trying to get the forlorn wife to leave her neglectful husband for a tryst in the arms of another. Term limits are the natural death that leaves the wife free to choose another without betrayal.

This is what happened after four months on the campaign trail. Michael began to see the politics in everything, from marriage to friendships. And he began to act like a politician. That included pretending to care about the things people said but actually not hearing them as though he were wearing earplugs. And making promises to his wife that he couldn't keep, such as "I'll be home for your birthday, you can hold me to that." This happened all the time.

In the press van, Whitney spun around, "This is the second time you've been late in the past week. Is everything alright? Why don't you get a wake up call?"

Michael stared out the window without answering.

CHAPTER 7

Michael's news judgment on the campaign trail required a learning curve at first. A presidential campaign is unlike any other sort of electoral politics. There are so many moving parts, campaign managers can't keep track of them all. Neither can the journalists. The corporate mantra of promoting someone to the point of incompetence applied perfectly to Michael in this situation. Initially, he called his editor in Washington two or three times a day after Dimmesdale said something that he thought was significant. But his editor got so annoyed that he stopped taking Michael's calls and told him that unless there was an emergency, he was to communicate with him through email. So Michael lost the experienced guidance of an older editor to help him distinguish between news and gossip. How was he supposed to know that it was news if Dimmesdale criticized an opponent, but not news if he criticized the incumbent president? Or that it was news if he unveiled a new policy initiative only if none of his other opponents have done it?

If Michael called his editors daily in Miami to ask them for advice, it would affirm that he was incompetent and they'd lament their decision to provide him with this career-making opportunity. If he continued calling his Washington editor, he'd probably end up complaining to Miami that Michael was just not ready for an assignment like this. Michael couldn't call his other Tindle Bailey colleagues covering the other candidates because he was the youngest among them and didn't want them to begin gossiping about his inexperience.

He did what any intrepid reporter would do in a situation like this: he copied the pack. Some might call this herd journalism , as in a herd of sheep all frolicking in the same pasture, eating the same grass, and led in the same direction. But it's the safest bet to Cover Your Ass. If Michael copied the pack, he wouldn't get scooped by them. And therefore he'd get no frantic phone calls from editors panicking about a Dimmesdale story from AP or the New York Herald hitting the wires.

But Michael quickly discovered that herd journalism on the campaign trail was tricky. They were shadowing the candidate the entire day, listening to every word he said in public, and all of them sending feeds to editors once or twice a day. Deciphering what his press corps competitors deemed newsworthy proved complex. Those email feeds kept the editors up to date on what was going on in the campaign trail. The editors made the final decision on whether the material was actually newsworthy, or just scraps for the daily blogs and websites, or material that the public would rebuke with loud snoring were it to be published in any format, and therefore relegated to the delete pile. It was much different than the herd journalism at the White House, for example. In that case, reporters were invited to anywhere from one to three or four press conferences every day and they chatted about newsworthiness before the press conference began. By the time a White House press conference was over, they knew exactly how newsworthy a story was. Most solid White House correspondents could even predict with precision in the middle of the press conference where the story would run in the paper, from 1A to 5B to a brief.

Michael had to refine his copying tactics. He rationalized that he would only do it for a couple of weeks until he got the hang of it. For a few days, he keenly observed his colleagues in action. He learned that any time Whitney from the New York Herald thought something was newsworthy, she would take written notes, press a button on her digital recorder to mark the location of the statement, and follow up with a question on the issue during Dimmesdale's next press availability. Michael would check the NYHerald website frequently for recently released information on the Dimmesdale campaign. And sure enough, about one out of every three times that Whitney followed that pattern, a blurb on the issue would appear in the NyHerald.com political blog, and about one out of five times that she followed that pattern, a story would be published in the New York Herald. The television reporters adhered to similar routines to mark their assumption that something was newsworthy. They'd talk more amongst themselves too. Observing them for the purpose of copying them made Michael appear quieter, more contemplative. A journalistic gamble was as risky as a Vegas one: high stakes, butterflies in the stomach, a lucky kiss on the proverbial fist before rolling the dice.

It was mid-December, nearing the Holidays, and Dimmesdale had been campaigning straight through the slow period. Michael woke up one morning at 6 a.m. It was still dark when he slipped into his inadequate leather topsiders, his London Fog trench coat, and loaded his pockets for the day's work. When he went to the hotel lobby to stand by the front door, the parking lot was covered with a foot of snow. Whiteness like a blind man seeing the light for the first time extended as far as he could see through the post-dawn haze. There had already been snow on the ground. But the streets, sidewalks, tree limbs and parking lots had been clear for weeks until now.

The press van skidded to a stop in front of the hotel. Michael had learned to detest the sight of the van's tailpipe blowing warm, smoky exhaust. He and his press corps colleagues quietly loaded in, carrying copies of USA Today, which the hotel provided to residents free of charge. Michael's colleagues were bundled up, with scarves, gloves, hats, boots. He was sitting in the back seat with Rachel, with one leg up on the tire hump.

"Are those topsiders?" she said. "Aren't you cold?"

"No, I'm fine," Michael said, shrugging his shoulders.

Whitney turned around.

"You're wearing topsiders? Are you crazy?"

"Naw, they're great, the most comfortable shoes I own."

"Don't you have a scarf? Or a hat?" Rachel asked me. "It's snowing."

He shook his head. Mafikwa turned around too.

"He's from Miami," she said. "In Miami, you don't need gloves or scarves, right, Michael? I bet it's 75 degrees there right now."

"Actually, 77. My wife told me last night."

"Damn," Mafikwa said. "77 degrees. It ain't even that warm in Texas in the winter."

Even though Mafikwa was Stanford-educated and covering a presidential campaign for a major TV network, she still used words like "ain't" and "hey, girl." Michael guessed it was her way of trying to come across as a regular woman, unlike the Harvard-educated Whitney who never deviated from the Victorian vernacular. Her lips contoured in exaggerated movements with every word she uttered.

"Do yourself a favor and obtain some gloves, a scarf, and a hat," Whitney said, compressing her forehead with her eyebrows. "It will save you many moments of agony in the next few weeks."

"Thanks," he said, then echoed what Dimmesdale told every nutcase that suggested a bizarre strategy or idea to him. "I will take the advice under consideration."

It took Dave about an hour to get to Lamie's Inn, a quaint lodge in Hampton that locals packed into for maple syrup-smothered flapjacks and fresh bacon. Christmas paraphernalia dominated the place. A man dressed as Santa Clause was sitting in the reception area, and several children were waiting in a line to sit on his lap and tell him what they wanted for Christmas. Dimmesdale entered the building with his entourage and immediately walked up to Santa, who courteously extended his hand. But Dimmesdale wanted more than a handshake, children waiting in line be damned. He had his own Christmas wish to make, and quickly made himself comfortable on Santa's lap. The man behind the beard didn't know where to put the hand that usually rests on the laps of little boys and girls, so he just rested it on Dimmesdale's lap. Michael watched Whitney attack her notebook with little pen scratches. She elbowed her way as close as she could to Dimmesdale and set the voice recorder near him. She marked the spot on the tape.

"Ho, Ho, Ho," Santa said. "Merry Christmas."

"Why, Thank you Santa," Dimmesdale said. "I've been a good candidate all season and I want to make a wish. Can I make a wish?"

"Ho, Ho, Ho, Of Course," said the bearded fellow. "What can Santa get you this Holiday season?"

Dimmesdale cracked a giddy smile.

"Well Santa, I want to win the New Hampshire primary," Dimmesdale said. "And I'd like you to bring Shirley here a new fur coat."

Shirley made an awe-shucks face.

"You got it," Santa said. "And a very merry Chris…,uh, Happy Holidays to you and the Mrs. Ho, Ho, Ho!"

Dimmesdale patted Santa on the back and walked toward the press. He was dressed in a blue sweater and a white dress shirt underneath with the white collar unbuttoned. It was his casual attire.

"Governor!" yelled Rachel. "Why sit in Santa's lap? What's your wish?"

"I don't know if it was totally presidential, but it felt like the right thing to do. It can't hurt to have Santa Clause's endorsement," Dimmesdale said.

"Sir, did Santa Clause endorse you?" Whitney asked.

"I believe that today, I have won the ground-breaking endorsement of Santa Claus. So to all my opponents, I say, 'you better watch out. Santa Claus is coming to town.'"

The press corps laughed. Dimmesdale walked into the restaurant and visited each table for some retail politics, shaking hands with patrons over their locally made maple syrup. Whitney followed him and began interviewing people he had talked to, so Michael decided he'd better do the same. He approached a couple with two children that Dimmesdale had just departed, and noticed when he got closer that one of the children had Down syndrome.

"I'm sorry to interrupt your breakfast," Michael said. "I'm a reporter for a national newspaper chain covering the Dimmesdale campaign and I wanted to ask you what you thought about his visit here today and about his candidacy."

"Actually, I'm a little sickened by the whole thing," said the husky, pale father. "This guy will do anything and say anything to get elected."

"Like what?" Michael said.

"Like he just told me that if he were president, he would work to develop genetic therapy for children with chromosomal disorders. That's a bunch of crap. That science is years away. You don't say that to a family having a Sunday breakfast with their special needs son."

"Hank!" gasped the wife from across the table. "Please."

"Well, It's true," he said. "And then he sits on Santa's lap and makes a wish for Christmas. Isn't the guy going to too far?"

"Well," Michael said. "He is Christian."

"Well, whatever, politicians will stoop to the lowest levels of pandering for a vote. Anything to get elected. Unbelievable."

"That's enough, Hank," the wife said again. "I'm so sorry, he's just worked up because he's a Republican."

The couple declined to identify themselves to Michael by name, so he couldn't end up quoting them. But a couple of other diners expressed similar skepticism about Dimmesdale. Kristen Dunlop was lingering near Michael as he wrapped up his reporting. When she noticed that he had a free moment, she approached him with a rare smile.

"Hi there," she said. "So are you doing a story on this?"

"Maybe," he said. "It's fun, light, holiday fair."

"What are people saying?" she said.

"Different things," he said. "Depends on who you talk to. The Democrats say one thing. The Republicans say another."

"Are those topsiders?" she said, staring down at Michael's shoes.

"Why, yes, they are."

"I bet your feet are wet."

"A little."

"It's the snow," she said. "Boots are the best."

"Look, I gotta file a story now so I gotta run. But we're overdue for a dinner one of these nights. How about meeting up with us in the press corps for dinner and drinks soon?"

Michael used her approach to break the ice. He needed someone on the campaign he could rely on.

Kristen had been looking away, toward Dimmesdale. But when he asked her about dinner, she turned and looked him straight in the eye for a couple of long seconds, trying to interpret this surprising solicitation. Evident evaluation was taking place. She scanned his face before smiling.

"Sure," she said. "That's a good idea."

"Ok, great. I'll talk to the others and set it up."

CHAPTER 8

Michael filed a short story later that afternoon, which ended up running in every paper in the chain. The New York Herald ran a similar story. Whitney complimented his writing, and he said "ditto."

Naturally, the daily feeds to Michael's editors began to echo what his competitors were feeding their own editors. And it was perfect. Michael's editor seemed pleased with the material he was sending. During the first few weeks, a few of his articles were published in all 44 newspapers in the Tindle Bailey corporate chain. The combined national circulation of all 44 newspapers was five times bigger than the New York Herald's circulation, something which Michael's editor reminded him whenever they spoke, which had slowed to about twice a week. Most of their communication was through email or text. Michael would email him a story or a feed, and he would email back a few hours later to thank him or ask him for more information.

Through the constant, and often reluctant, study of his competitors, Michael began to get to know them all closely. The circumstances deemed it so. Trapped in a frigid van for hours and hours on end, cruising the white icy tundra of New Hampshire, conversations couldn't help but spawn daily. The permanent press corps was just the three TV women, Rachel and Michael. But on any given day, the 15-passenger van was crammed with 8 or 10 people, and sometimes it filled to capacity. Reporters from all over the country took turns observing the Dimmesdale campaign. On Monday, reporters from the Baltimore Sun and the Los Angeles Times were there. A correspondent from the Chicago Tribune, Dimmesdale's hometown paper, had tagged along with them all last week. Most of the journalists assigned to such a gig were older, crustier veterans who smelled like the coffee they'd been drinking every morning for 30 years and had such cynical attitudes about the entire political process that they were convinced Dimmesdale would implode as a candidate because he seemed too perfect.

Michael couldn't keep up with all the newcomers. Sometimes it seemed like the press corps was an amusement ride, with new faces coming in every day, enjoying the show, then filing out after it ended. Every once in a while, he'd ask one of the newcomers what they thought about Dimmesdale after they wrapped up their reporting, and he got a range of answers. The assessment that stuck with him most was from the Chicago Tribune journalist. She was an older woman, overweight, with a black wool coat and a purple scarf. She said she had known Dimmesdale since he was a state senator in Illinois, and that there was always something about him that troubled her, but she couldn't put her finger on it. While she had been following Dimmesdale's campaign, she said she still felt the same way.

Michael prodded her, "Well, what is it?"

"I don't think he's the same person behind closed doors," she said. "I think he's someone else in private. And that worries me."

"If these guys acted like themselves, no one would elect them," Michael said. "Imagine Dimmesdale farting and picking his nose through a campaign trail, telling his wife to fetch him his coffee. He'd be lynched."

"That's not it," she said. "It's that he's fake. It's like his ideas are not heartfelt. Like if he cooked them up because that's what people want to hear."

One Tuesday morning, with the 15-passenger van crammed with people, Mafikwa expressed curiosity about one of the newcomers.

"Who's that guy that's been showing up at all the Dimmesdale events? The guy with the denim jacket?"

Audra shrugged. But Rachel spoke up.

"You mean the hot guy?"

"Yeah, girl, you saw him too?"

"That's John Finnest," Rachel said. "He's with the Boston Globe."

"He's got his own car," Mafikwa said. "Maybe we can get him to take us out."

"I like that idea," said Audra. "I can't remember the last time we even ate a real dinner."

"Or had a beer," Michael said. "I could use a visit to a bar."

"I know a good place," said a voice from the front. It was Dave, their driver. "The Wild Rover. It's in downtown a few blocks from our campaign headquarters. That's where all the campaign staffers go to drink after work every night."

Audra leaned over and whispered so that Dave couldn't hear her.

"He's the last person I want to see at the end of the day," she said.

At the next campaign event, Rachel pointed out Finnest to Whitney. He was leaning against a column at a nursing home north of Concord, a notepad flipped open in his hand. A sort of hipster Bruce Springsteen. He had a thick denim jacket with the collar flipped up over his neck because he didn't have a scarf. Black faded jeans covered a pair of rugged leather snow boots. His blond hair was a mess, and his hands were halfway tucked into his sleeves because he didn't have gloves either. Michael wondered if he was also from a warm climate and was ill prepared for the elements.

Before long, the women in the press corps had met John Finnest, and had arranged to go out to dinner with him. They invited Michael along to the Olive Garden, which was in the mall near their hotel. It was six of them in his Honda Accord. Whitney sat on top of Michael in the back, and although he couldn't stand her, it felt nice to have a woman on his lap. He was suffering from serious sex deprivation.

The restaurant was packed, mostly with families, even though it was a Tuesday. They sat at a round table, and Finnest immediately asked to see the wine list.

"I never thought this place got so packed," Audra said.

"I've never been to an Olive Garden," Whitney said. "I never go to chains in New York."

Mafikwa rolled her eyes. Audra nudged her.

"There's some really good chain restaurants out there," Michael said. "They're not all bad."

"It's not that they're bad," she said. "It's that for the price, you can always get better food at an independent restaurant."

"The best donut in the world is at Krispy Kreme," Michael said. "Hot off the rack, with a glass of milk. That's a chain."

"What I wouldn't give for a Krispy Kreme donut right now," Rachel said. "Those are the best."

"No question," Mafikwa said. "You can't improve on perfection."

"I wouldn't know," Whitney said. "I don't eat donuts."

The waiter came back to take their drink and appetizer orders. After they had all ordered, John Finnest held the wine list up for the waiter and ordered two bottles of Monte Vino Italian Chianti with six glasses.

"I don't want any wine," said Whitney.

"Yeah, uh, how about asking us if we want any before ordering," Audra said.

Finnest hadn't said a word since we got to the restaurant.

"You know," he said. "Chain restaurants are about comfort, not quality. You always know what you're going to get when you sit down at one, whether it's Fridays, or Burger King, or Olive Garden. And a glass of red wine would make me comfortable right now, especially with Italian food. You don't have to drink it if you don't want to."

The waiter brought the glasses, set them down in front of everyone, and proceeded to fill them. No one stopped him. The glasses filled and emptied a couple of times over the next few minutes.

"I was talking to Kristen Dunlop a couple of days ago and she said she was open to the idea of coming to dinner with us," Michael said. "You know, like a sourcing business dinner."

Mafikwa chuckled. He looked over at her.

"What?" he said.

"Sourcing my foot," she said. "You asked her out cause you think she's hot."

"She is hot," said John Finnest.

"Dave, our driver, has a huge crush on her," Rachel said. "He told me he thought she was the 'most amazing' woman on the campaign."

"No question the woman is good looking," Michael said. "But regardless of her looks, it doesn't hurt to get to know her a little better. She's probably the person who can best help us out in any kind of jam."

"It's a good idea," said Whitney. "I think we should include her boss, Richard Dougherty, and Brian Petchell, their campaign manager."

"The more the merrier," Michael said. "So are you all in? Would you guys pick up the check with me?"

Everyone around the table shrugged and nodded.

"Great, I'll set it up."

"Just make sure to do it on Thursday or Saturday night," said Rachel. "Friday night's always a heavy deadline night for me."

"No *problema*," Michael said.

"*Gracias, Senor.*"

They talked shop through the rest of their dinner and went back to the hotel. Michael opened his laptop and searched DarkPage.com for the local escort listings. Just seeing the list of escorts available in Manchester made his heart race. He called one named Jenny who promised "an unforgettable time."

"Hello?" said a woman's voice. "Can I help you?"

"Is this Jenny?" he asked.

"Yes, what can I do for you?"

"How much do you charge for an hour?"

"Two hundred dollars," she said.

"Ok, thanks," he said, then hung up.

The wine and veal piccatta he had for dinner rose in his throat. He checked his cell phone. Three missed calls and two messages. All but one were from his wife, who had been trying to reach him all day. It was late, pushing midnight. His wife was surely asleep. Her natural clock was earlier than his own, and she slept roughly the same hours as their baby, from about 10 p.m. to 6 a.m. But he felt he had to call her. She picked up after three rings. Her voice sounded muffled, as though she were speaking through her pillow.

"Hi baby, it's me, did I wake you up?"

"No, it's okay," she said. "How are you? I've been trying to reach you for three days."

"I'm fine. I miss you like crazy. It's freezing up here."

"Really? Are your clothes warm enough?"

"Yeah, it's fine," he said. "My feet were a little cold today, but that's just because it snowed all day."

"Do you need gloves and stuff?" she said.

"I probably should get some. I'll make a trip to the mall one of these days."

"I'll send you over some clothes, don't worry," she said.

"No, no. That's not necessary. I'll take care of it."

There were a few seconds of silence. Michael thought maybe she had fallen asleep again.

"I miss you. How's Glory?"

"She fine, sleeping right here next to me," she said. "Finally. It took me a while to get her to sleep tonight."

"Is she giving you a hard time?"

"No, just the usual. She's my tiny little friend. She's been sleeping with me in my bed."

"Don't get her into that bad habit, baby. You know what they say, that it's almost impossible to get them out of your bed once you accustom them to sleeping in it."

"Don't worry, it's just while you're gone. So how's the campaign trail? Any cute girls?"

"Tons," Michael said. "You know how those Puritan types up north drive me crazy."

"Paws off," she said. "You have your little family waiting for you here."

"I know, I love you and the kids. You're my whole life."

Over the phone, Michael could hear the baby wake up and start crying. Bianca whispered goodbye, told him she loved him, and hung up. He lay back in his bed fully clothed. It had been more than a week since he had ejaculated. And the three or four times before that were his own self-abuse. He fell asleep with these depressing thoughts swirling in his head, and woke up at 6 a.m., halfway through a sex-dream involving his high school girlfriend, with a wet stain on his pants.

CHAPTER 9

They chose a trendy restaurant named Satin in Downtown Manchester for their dinner with the Dimmesdale campaign staffers. It was the hottest ticket in town, but they landed a table reserved for 10 people Thursday night by telling them they were reporters and would be extremely perturbed if they were not accommodated. Nothing spooks a high-end eatery like the prospect of bad press. The place was packed with more political operatives and news hacks than Inauguration Day on the White House lawn. Even Michael, a relative newbie to this strange scene, recognized a few of the faces. There was that guy with the bowtie from CNN, and Tom Brotraw, and the Staff from the Morning Show, which had been broadcasting from New Hampshire. One of Dimmesdale's opponents, Carrie Humboldt, was sitting at a corner table with a few older, grave-looking men in suits that looked like accountants or lawyers delivering bad news. With its light-colored maple wood, and modern hanging halogen lights, the place had a warm interior. The bar area had its own look: darker except for the actual bar, where the bottles were lined in front of a translucent pane of glass that glowed with LED lighting.

Drinks were ordered all around, and they came immediately. Chardonnay for Whitney, house merlot for Audra, Jack and Coke for Mafikwa and a Dewars on the Rocks for Michael. Rachel drank water, and looked distracted, as though she were secretly praying a Rosary.

Kristen Dunlop walked in not long after them, wrapped in her knee-length black parka and a scarlet scarf. A waiter inside immediately took her coat and scarf.

"O God," Michael said in that netherworld of audio volume between a whisper and saying something to yourself internally. She was wearing a tight, unbuttoned black cardigan, revealing a low-cut red V-neck underneath. The tiniest bit of cleavage peaked out, more woman than Michael had seen in weeks. As she strode toward them, men in the restaurant followed her with their eyes, their mouths suspended in mid-chew.

Michael was nearest to her, so she held her hand out to him. He stood up, took it, and without much thought, kissed her on the cheek. As he pulled back, a subtle trail followed of vanilla-scented perfume, which she never wore while on the campaign trail. Only when she flinched as Michael's face approached hers did he realize this type of greeting was probably taboo in these parts. In Miami, because of its Latin culture, everyone kisses on the cheek in a social setting, even co-workers and professional colleagues. Michael had been careful not to do it here.

"Well, gee, Michael, it's nice to see you too," Kristen said.

He suddenly wanted Kristen sitting next to him, badly, noting the crazy endorphin and testosterone buzz bubbling up in his head. But she sat two seats away between Audra and Rachel.

"I didn't get a kiss," said Mafikwa.

"Me neither," Rachel said.

"Yeah, what was that?" Whitney said. "Never seen that from you on the trail."

"We do that in Miami," Michael said. "I forgot the professional etiquette they follow in *these parts*," Michael uttered the last two words with a thick southern accent.

Michael walked up to each of them and planted a kiss on their cheeks.

"Thanks, I feel included now," Mafikwa said. "Anyone up for another round?"

"Was that a southern drawl" Whitney asked, looking at Michael.

"Actually I was going for hick," Michael said.

"*These parts* ain't no south," Audra said. "This is a whole other demography of racism right here."

Michael's head cocked up, noting that the topic of racism hadn't come up before on the campaign trail.

"MmmmmmHhhh," nodded Mafikwa. "Did you know that New Hampshire is one of the least diverse states? I looked it up. According to the last census, only one and a half percent of the population is black. Three percent is Hispanic. There are a few Asians. But that's it. The other night I walked into a bookstore in Keene and I might as well have held up the place. Everyone stopped what they were doing to stare at me. The woman behind the counter came out to the store and asked me if she could help me with anything."

"I hate it when people do that!" Audra interrupted.

"It happened to you too here?" Mafikwa said.

"Well, not here, but it has happened to me before."

Mafikwa nodded with eyes wide open and looked around, clearly wanting the others to hear and believe as well.

She continued: "Here I was picturing a peaceful, quiet place where I could just sit back and enjoy a warm cup of coffee and read some Essence Magazine and unwind. But the lady didn't leave me alone. She followed me around the whole store, like if I was gonna take something."

Everyone at the table shook their heads. Michael shrugged and made a disapproving face.

"Anyway, I just wanted to point out," Whitney said, pausing for effect, "That your accent could be," another pause as Whitney raised a hand and twisted the wrist side to side, "slightly offensive to someone with a Southern background if they were to hear it," Whitney said, then raised her palms. "Just saying."

The table went quiet. All eyes shot to Michael, whose face remained serious, and seemed to darken.

"Point taken," said Michael, then took a sip of his scotch. Before anyone else jumped into the conversation, he put on the same hick accent and said: "*won't happen again.*"

The table cracked up. Loud laughs. Other patrons looked. Even Whitney smiled.

Kristen jumped in, thank God!

"So we're all here together," Kristen said. "Where are you all from again?"

The conversation morphed into a series of self-introductions and soliloquies.

By the time Michael took his first bathroom break, he intended to go into a stall and masturbate, he was so worked up. But he decided against it for a variety of reasons, including the possibility of being discovered in the midst of the five-knuckle shuffle by Tom Brotraw. Before heading back out, Michael looked at himself in the mirror, wondering if his lust showed. There was no trace, as far as Michael could tell. Men are always surprised at how easy it is to disguise lust as benign interest.

Back at the table, Kristen sipped a glass of red wine. Traces of her pink lip-gloss created what Michael perceived to be erotic art at the edge of her glass. Dimmesdale's campaign manager, Brian Petchell, had arrived and was sitting in the middle of the table telling a story. He was a pudgy man in his mid 30s with black hair and light-brown eyes. Because of the loud atmosphere in the restaurant, Brian was speaking fairly loudly.

"I frankly never aspired to this job," he was saying. "There's people who get into political management and strategizing, and all they want to do from the very beginning is run a presidential campaign. It's a fine goal, I think. But it just wasn't what I got into it for."

"What happened, then?" Rachel asked. "How'd you get into it."

"About four years ago, I was in South Carolina running a mayoral campaign in Charleston. I hated the place. I'm originally from Washington State, so a place like South Carolina seemed a bit backward."

"Hey, that's not nice," said Kristen. "It's not so bad."

"Are you from there?" Michael said.

"Yup," she said. Then she apparently flipped a switch in her brain and let out a phrase with the deepest Deep South accent he had heard in years. "Good, ole South Caolinuh."

Embarrassed smiles and awe-shucks shrugs rolled like a human wave around the table. Kristen glared at Michael with a devilish smile, one of the few he had seen on her. He smiled too, looking at her, then mouthed the word "sorry."

She lifted her head higher, as though pushing her chin up for more dignity, and blew him a kiss. His smile broadened. He blew a kiss back, and Kristen did something that looked like blushing.

Whitney oozed incredulity.

Brian continued. Kristen turned her attention to Brian for a few seconds, then glanced in Michael's direction. He glanced at her at the same time. Instead of immediately looking away, Michael maintained eye contact. So did Kristen. She even swung her head gently to move blond locks away from her face, which had become serious. The look they shared did not last more than 5 seconds. Kristen looked away first, and Michael saw that her serious face again lightened into a smile as a direct result of their little moment.

Michael looked away and swallowed hard. He recognized something in Kristen's actions that also disguises itself well but reveals itself on rare, and wonderful occasions: a woman's lust. Michael reveled in it while Brian continued.

"To make a long story short, the candidate I was working for won, and soon after I met Wally Danville."

Whitney recognized the name.

"The governor of Ohio?"

"The one and only," Brian went on. "I had true believerism from the moment I met him. He just seemed like the real thing. So I plunged headlong into his campaign a couple of years ago, and the rest is history."

"You managed Wally Danville's campaign?" Whitney said. "That's incredible. His victory was a huge upset. His come from behind was legendary."

Brian beamed without saying anything.

"So, do you feel the same way about Dimmesdale?" Rachel asked. "Do you think he's the real thing?"

"I think Dimmesdale is the best candidate for the presidency. He's the only one with enough vision mixed with pragmatism to change the direction of the nation."

"But is he the real thing?" Rachel pressed him.

"This is off the record, correct?" Brian said.

"Everything we're talking about here tonight is off the record, unless otherwise stated. Remember the ground rules?" Audra said.

"Off the record, I don't think that way about candidates anymore. I realize now that the "real thing" is just another word for the one who voters choose," he said, holding up faux-quotation marks with his hand when he said 'real thing.' "That's the only thing that binds together the assortment of personalities and leadership styles in our country. They are all elected over someone else."

"Artful dodger," Rachel said. "You didn't answer the question."

"The only thing that makes anyone the real thing is getting elected," he said. "And I'm confident Dimmesdale will get elected. That's my answer."

Rachel and Brian went back and forth a bit longer. But the table-wide attention on Brian disintegrated into fragments of different conversations. In a dinner party at a restaurant, the conversations are usually never all-inclusive, unless someone is telling a gripping story, or unleashing a juicy bit of gossip that quells the talking with a spray of curiosity. Mafikwa turned to Kristen.

"So are you really from South Carolina?" she said.

"Yes, I am really from there," she said.

"I used to buy fireworks at South of the Border when I was a kid. My dad drove us to North Carolina a few summers and we'd always stop there."

"That's nice," Kristen said. "My home state is nothing but a pyromaniachal memory to you."

"You don't sound like you're from there," Audra said. "I had a professor in College from South Carolina and he had a deep southern accent."

"You mean lak this?" she said, fluttering her eyelashes in self-mockery. "I spent so much tam uh-way from mah home that I left the accent in Charleston."

"I love that," Michael said. "I love accents."

"You still have your accent," Kristen said, turning her attention to him.

"People say that. I can't detect any sort of accent in myself, but I guess that's normal. When I used to work in New York, everyone thought I was from Canada."

"Are you from Cuba?" she said.

"No, I was born and raised in Miami," Michael said. "My parents are Cuban. Spanish was my first language, so that may be the reason for the accent."

Mafikwa nodded.

"Haven't you noticed how a lot of Asians speak perfect apple-pie American even though they're first or second generation?" Mafikwa said. "My mom used to say that a person who consciously gets rid of their natural accent is insecure about their roots."

Whitney popped into the talk.

"I completely disagree agree with that," she said. "For example, the whole Ebonics phenomenon. That's just not proper English, and encouraging it in young blacks helps foster their marginalization in society as they grow older."

"That ain't true," Mafikwa said in her best Ebonics. "Us humble black folk gots prawlums that a change uh accents just won't solve."

Whitney smiled. Maybe she had a sense of humor after all. Michael piped in.

"If I wanted to, I could talk like fucking Tony Montana, meng," he said. "But I don't like it. I'm just not the bad guy."

A couple of people at the table got the joke and laughed.

"Ricky Ricardo, right," Kristen said.

"Fuck you, meng," he said. "That's from Scarface."

It's amazing what a few drops of liquor will do to a wound-up campaign crew. Cheeks began to flush red. After they ordered their dinner, lips loosened into petty gossip about campaign staffers and Dimmesdale bloopers. Brian wanted the spotlight. Every time he talked it was about himself, or about Dimmesdale. The guy was always on. The more he drank, the more he talked. There was his story about running into the former President in a Restroom at the Democratic Convention four years ago. And his tale of convincing Dimmesdale that he should not only embrace his Christianity on the campaign trail, but bring it up as often as possible. Brian explained that Americans were interested in a leader who could fill the morality vacuum perceived among Democratic candidates. Christianity should not be seen as a liability for a Democratic candidate, but a unique advantage. That was the first time Michael realized that Dimmesdale's religion was more of an issue in the campaign than they let on.

Brian talked so much that Whitney, who was sitting across the table from him, yawned. If the alcohol had made Brian chatty, it quieted Kristen. The more she drank, the more she seemed to sink into a mattress of hazy thought. She smiled or frowned during segments of conversation to keep up the appearance of interest. But her mind was somewhere else. The person between her and Michael got up to go to the restroom.

Kristen caught Michael glaring at her and pushed her hair behind her ear, so as to give him a clear view of her entire face. She looked down at his wedding ring.

"So what's your wife's name?" she said.

"Bianca," he said.

"That's a pretty name," she said.

"And you?" Michael said. "Who's the lucky man behind the woman?"

She smiled.

"There's no time for that on a campaign," she said. "In case you haven't noticed, campaigns purposely hire young, unattached workers so they can brainwash them into a total commitment that borders on obsessive love."

"So, you're brainwashed by Dimmesdale?" he asked.

"Brainwashed in the nice sense," she said. "It's more a cultivated conviction in a person than a true brainwash situation."

"Right, whatever. So how come you never come on the bus with us? I figured that since you're the New Hampshire spokeswoman, you'd be babysitting us more often so we don't stray from the Dimmesdale message."

"You'll be seeing more of me on the bus," she said. "Besides, Clipper's got his eyes on you guys. We debrief him regularly."

"Clipper?"

"Yeah, you know, Dave. We call him "clipper"."

Michael made a confused face.

"Before he drove the press van, he used to scour the newspapers in the morning hours and clip all the articles on Dimmesdale. Hence, 'Clipper.'"

The waiter showed up with two trays of steaming plates. Michael had the steak. There was a good mix of glazed pork chops, beef and seared tuna around the table. Kristen had the Satin salad, heavy on the blue cheese and bacon. When most people go about reinventing themselves for their Grand Plans in life, they usually disguise accents, or cultivate a sophisticated vocabulary, or splurge on nice clothes. But when it comes down to eating, few invest in proper etiquette. Mealtime rarely betrays true roots. Michael noticed that Mafikwa hunched over her food and shoveled it into her mouth, fists clenched around a fork and knife. It was a habit clearly left over from her childhood in Texas, where she had to eat quickly and keep her head down to compete for seconds with her other siblings. Whitney held her utensils well, but chewed with her mouth open. Rachel also fisted her utensils. Brian, who ordered a bone-in glazed pork chop, grabbed it by the bone and ate it like a caveman, shunning utensils all-together. Audra had her act together, even spreading the napkin over her lap. And Kristen also played her lady roll well, except she picked through her salad with her fork once she had eaten enough lettuce to grab the extra bacon, blue cheese and walnuts buried under the greenery. Michael ate decently. His father had denied him a fair share of meals when he was a kid for transgressions that ranged from burping to putting his elbows on the table. But he cut with his left hand instead of his right, and had the bad habit of pushing the plate a couple of inches away when he finished.

After eating, the table quieted down while blood worked its way from their brains to their stomachs.

"I know that every once in a while, there is the 7-second silence, but this is ridiculous," Rachel said. "So who here is hitched?"

A few blinks later from around the table, Rachel persisted.

"I actually broke up with my boyfriend before I started this assignment," she said. "I had done the long-distance thing before, while I studied in Spain. And it was a total mess. So I decided that instead of dragging our relationship through this period of uncertainty, I'd do the noble thing and break up with Nick. How about you, Brian, any special someone?"

Brian smiled.

"There's a couple of prospects," he said. Then he exhibited some liquid courage by glancing over at Kristen and winking.

Everyone else at the table saw it as well. So Rachel naturally turned her curiosity to Kristen.

"How about you, Kristen?"

"I'd really rather not talk about my personal life," she said. "Sorry."

"Oh, come on!" Brian said. "We're just talking here."

"Yeah," Mafikwa said. "I'll tell you straight up, I'm dating two guys at once because I frankly can't decide between them."

"You are?" Rachel said, aghast.

"Uh-huh," Mafikwa said. "Horace and Jason. They're both good people. They know about each other too. I just can't decide. They keep trying to outdo each other. See this watch."

Everyone around the table leaned in as Mafikwa peeled back her long sleeve.

"That's from Horace. When Jason saw it, he gave me this."

She pulled down her turtleneck and revealed a thin gold necklace that sparkled in the dim light.

"Maybe you can share one of em with me," said Audra. "I haven't had a boyfriend in a while."

"Why not?" Rachel asked.

"I don't know. It's just not automatic for some people," Audra said.

"That's the truth," Kristen said. "It's more complicated for some people."

"So you don't have a boyfriend?" Rachel asked.

Brian huffed from across the table.

"There is a special someone, we've just never met him," Brian said. "Right, Kristen?"

Kristen gave Brian the evil eye.

"Anyway," Whitney said. "Can't one of you talk to Dimmesdale or Dave or someone to remind them to stop somewhere for us to eat? On a good day, we make one food stop, and our hotel doesn't have room service. So…"

"Yikes," Brian said. "That's not very smart, starving the people who we're relying on for good coverage. Kristen will take care of it. Right Kristen."

"Yeah, sorry, I didn't know it had gotten so bad."

Kristen was the first to get up and leave. She announced that she would be at the Wild Rover, hanging out with whatever campaign staffers she found there. Dinner broke up soon after. Back into the cold night they walked, commenting on the former mills that lined the river, many of which had been converted into tech-centers and lofts for trendy young couples. Manchester was a study in urban revival. Broke one decade by the exodus of textile mills to the south and China, rich again the next decade with the rise of the tech boom, and primping every four years for the presidential primaries, the only American city reevaluated by the media on a regular basis. They tucked in their chins against the cold as they climbed into taxies. Whitney, Audra and Mafikwa were rambling on about food and hip-hop. As a co-founder of The Force, a Hip-Hop website and blog, Whitney spoke as though she harbored deeper information than Google on the genre.

"A black woman opposed to Ebonics yet dedicated to Hip-Hop," Mafikwa said. "Nice."

As the cab pulled out of the parking lot, Michael asked the cab driver to drop him off at the Wild Rover. That quickly shut down the conversation in the cab. Michael could feel their eyes just burning into the side of his face.

"The Wild Rover?" Rachel asked. "What are you gonna do there?"

"Have a drink," he said.

"See Kristen," Mafikwa said.

Michael looked over to her. "I haven't been out in weeks. I don't wanna go back to the hotel yet."

Whitney piped in. "Can't the man have a drink without facing the inquisition?"

"Thank you," Michael said. The taxi pulled up to the Rover, which was only a few blocks away. He opened the door and let in a gust of frigid air. "Anyone care to join me?"

"I ain't into being no third wheel," Mafikwa said.

CHAPTER 10

The Wild Rover reeked of pretentious hipster bullshit from the moment Michael walked inside. Picture a dark-wood, worn-down Irish joint where generations of factory workers sipped dime-bottle whisky and beer and grumbled about nagging wives, tyrannical bosses, and union dues. Except the people inside were nothing like that. The place oozed Urban Outfitters and American Apparel. So many people donned designer eyeglasses that for a moment, Michael thought he had walked into a Starbucks. In Soho. Ivy Leaguers never played under cover. And here they were on their worst behavior, allowing their alcohol-pumped bravado muscle conversations with three and four-syllable words just for the hell of it, their heads piled like busts above turtlenecks. Michael looked around for roughnecks with beards and red-faced lushes with tiny veins on their noses brooding over the bar. But there weren't any. The jukebox had been hijacked by drunken, over-educated amateur Djs. The songs jumped from Vampire Weekend's Cape Cod Kwassa Kwassa to Bob Marley's Three Little Birds to Maroone 5. The bar was split into two rooms. On one side was the actual bar with stools, and a few high tables along the wall. Michael didn't see Kristen there, so he walked around to the other side, a long room with tables. Hanging coats lined the walls. He spotted Kristen sitting at a table with a couple of people he recognized from the Dimmesdale campaign. He just stood next to their table until Kristen looked up from her glass of beer. He expected her to be surprised, to gesture in a welcoming way. But she just pulled back the chair next to her, which was empty and patted the seat with her hand as though telling Michael to sit there.

"Michael, Dan and Kelly. Kelly and Dan, Michael," Kristen said.

"So, is this where campaign workers come to let their hair down?" he said, trying to break into their conversation.

"Aren't you the enemy?" Dan said. "Should we even be talking to you?"

"Down, boy," Kristen said. "This whole thing is off the record, right, Michael?"

"Of course," he said. "Off the record. Just let me turn off the tape recorder I have hidden inside my shirt."

Dan and Kelly looked at him suspiciously.

"I'm kidding," he said. "There's no tape recorder."

"Michael, tell them where you're from," Kristen said.

"Miami," he said. "Born and raised."

"What on earth are you doing here?" Kelly said. "If I were from Miami, this is the last place I'd go in the winter. You're like a reverse snowbird."

"Precisely," said Dan.

Three syllables where none would have done fine, noted Michael. Typical.

"I visited Miami in college a couple of times," Dan continued, "and frankly I found the airport to be substandard in comparison to airports of similar sized cities around the country. And I found Miami to be somewhat hostile to regular Americans who don't speak the Spanish language."

"Sounds like you couldn't get some girl's attention while you were there," Michael said. "Did it happen in South Beach, or a club or both?"

"Ha," Dan said, "For your information I had traveled to South Florida to visit my girlfriend, who was attending the University of Miami, otherwise known as Suntan U. I had no intention of meeting other women there. I just found the place to be, um, I don't know, provincial."

"People often go to Miami expecting it to be like New York or Los Angeles," Michael said. "But it's not like that. The place walks to the beat of its own drum."

"I found the language barrier terribly frustrating," Dan said. "A true inconvenience to the typical American traveler."

The guy was starting to piss Michael off. Kristen noticed and redirected the subject.

"So, you speak Spanish?" she said.

"*Por supuesto,*" Michael said. "Cuban accents are very different from all other Spanish accents. For starters, Cubans speak faster than many other Latinos. And when they're talking it sounds more like an Italian than a Mexican. They're rhythmic with the language, but not necessarily melodic, like Mexicans."

"*Fue mi primer idioma,*" Michael continued in Spanish. "*Y honestamente, no me gusta cuando algun burro ignorante se pone a hablar basura de mi ciudad.*"

Three blank stares. "I said that Spanish was my first language," he translated for them, a fake severe look on his face, "and honestly, I don't like it when some ignorant ass starts talking smack about my city."

More stares. Then Michael smiled, and they laughed and broke the nervous tension, and everything was grand.

After a while, Dan got up to leave, and Kelly asked him for a ride back to her apartment, which she shared with two other campaign workers. Michael thought about asking for a ride because he didn't want to call a cab, but he figured he'd wait until Kristen left, then hit her up. But Kristen stayed sitting down. It was past midnight now, and the crowd was getting louder with every drop of booze they consumed. Kristen had been nursing the same Guinness Stout since Michael first arrived.

"Why'd you come here?" she said. "I really didn't expect to see you here."

"I wanted to have a drink," he said. "I haven't been out in weeks."

A few more Dimmesdale campaign staffers approached their table and asked Kristen to settle a bet.

"Kristen," said a drunken brunette, holding a man by the arm. "True or false, Richard Nixon removed 12 minutes from a crucial White House tape that showed he was guilty of a cover-up."

"True," Kristen said.

"You owe me a beer," the woman told the man.

"Wait a second," Michael said. "No one ever knew what was in that 12 minute gap. It's never been found."

"Sounds like you owe me a beer," the man said.

"I'll tell you what," Michael said, with alcohol-induced generosity. "I'll buy everyone a round, on me."

"Great," the girl said. "Considering we've had to forego paychecks for two weeks."

Kristen immediately gave her the kind of stare that says "shut the hell up." She skillfully changed the subject.

"One can assume that the gap in the tape contains evidence of guilt, otherwise Nixon wouldn't have removed it," Kristen said.

"How do you know Nixon removed it?" Michael said. "Maybe it was some subordinate who heard the tape and did not want to be implicated."

"Oh, my God," Kristen said, feigning a moment of surprise. "You really are Cuban. And conservative. I bet you're a registered Republican."

"Wrong, my dear, I'm a true no-party advocate. I don't care for parties."

"That's a convenient position," Kristen said. "Sit on the sidelines and watch."

"It's the only ethical position for a journalist, especially one covering politics."

"Ha, it humors me when a journalist speaks ethics," Kristen said.

"Why's that?" Michael said.

"Journalists hide behind this shield of ethics until it's no longer convenient. Then their ethics go out the window."

"Sounds like you've been burned."

Kristen pushed her hair behind her ears.

"Anyone who works as a press aide in politics has been burned. It's a right of passage. Actually, I know because I was also a reporting intern once at the Charlotte Observer. I can't say I liked it. I found journalism to be shallow and self-serving."

"Oh, you mean like politics?" Michael said.

He ordered another beer from a pretty waitress who introduced herself as Marie.

"I lived in New York for three years, and I could swear that I detect a trace of Long Island in your accent," he said.

That pushed a button. Kristen straightened up and her face soured.

"Do you have any experience covering campaign politics?" she asked. "It really seems like you don't. And don't take this the wrong way. But you haven't exactly gotten on Dimmesdale's good side. He knows all of you better than you think because he knows you are his conduits to the electorate. And you frankly haven't made a good impression on him. Your inexperience is obvious and Dimmesdale is disappointed that you were put on his campaign. You're not covering me. You're covering Dimmesdale, Ok?"

"Where did that come from?" Michael said. "I just thought you sounded like a transplanted New Yorker is all. Man, I've been up here for more than a month and I've never seen people as unglued, depressed and downright rude as I've met on this campaign. And you are the case in point. I just came in here to have a beer with you and talk because I was curious about you and I liked your perfume at dinner and you dump this crap on me. I'll see you later."

He got up to leave, grabbing his coat off the hook.

"Wait, hang on," she said. "Sit down."

He tucked his coat under his arm and looked at her, still standing.

"Well, come on, sit down. I'm sorry about what I said. It was uncalled for."

He looked around the bar. No one had noticed any commotion. Young people were still at their tables engrossed in their spheres of talk. Kristen looked up and for a brief second displayed a smile. It was clearly a smile of victory. He sat down again, leaving the coat on his lap so he wouldn't have to tug it off the wall again if he wanted to make another dramatic exit.

"You're very perceptive," she said. "I am from New York. Westbury, to be exact."

Michael didn't utter a response.

"My family moved to South Carolina when I was a senior in high school. New York is a part of my past I'd rather leave there."

Michael looked at her with anticipation. "And? What happened in New York?"

Kristen took a moment to decide whether to answer or not.

"You wouldn't believe what happened if I told you," she said.

She ordered another drink, a glass of wine.

"It was 1997, right around the time when the Internet craze really kicked in," she said.

"You don't have to tell me anything," he said. "I wasn't trying to pry. I was just making conversation with you."

"It's ok," she said. "It wasn't really about me, anyway. It was about my sister. I was a senior in high school and she was a freshman. Mulberry High. She had a crush on some guy who was in 11th grade. But my parents wouldn't let her out of the house to date him. One day at school, he tells her that he wants her to send him a picture of her so he can think about her all the time. So my sister went home that night, and she asked my youngest sister to photograph her. Except that she was naked."

Michael's eyes widened. "What?"

"She had my youngest sister take pictures of her naked, and in lingerie. In all sorts of provocative poses. That night, she emailed the pictures to the guy. And the next day in school, she notices people staring at her and whispering behind her back. By the end of that week, the pictures had been posted on a new website called "The Girls of Mullberry High" and were all over social media. The police arrested the guy on child pornography charges, but my sister's reputation was ruined. Her friends dumped her. She became the class plague. She turned to drugs. She almost overdosed. All this before homecoming. So my dad thought it was best to start over somewhere else. His bank had a big branch in Charleston, and so we moved there."

"Damn," Michael said. "Sounds like a tough time for your family. How'd your sister make out?"

"She's dead," Kristen said. "She killed herself."

Michael put down his beer, and reached across the table.

"I'm sorry," he said.

Kristen took a deep breath.

"So, what's your big, dark secret?" she said.

"I don't know," he said. "I'm really sorry about your sister. It's incredible the harm that can come from social media. These young kids just don't know any better."

"She knew better," Kristen snapped. "At that age, a girl knows exactly what she's doing."

A few awkward seconds passed. Michael tried to go light.

"Really, I thought women never really knew exactly what they were doing. It's how they deflect accountability."

Kristen looked insulted.

"You are so sexist. I hate to stereotype but that's typical Macho Latino talk."

"That's a pretty good Spanish accent," he said. "Do you speak Spanish?"

"*Un poquito,*" she said, smiling.

"Really, so you knew exactly what I was telling Dan earlier?"

"More or less," she said. "Don't worry, I can't stand that guy myself."

"You don't seem like the typical Ivy League hag around these parts."

"I'm not Ivy League. I'm an American University League."

"Same difference," Michael said.

A Pearl Jam song started playing in the background.

"I love this song," she said.

"Me too," he said.

They looked at each other and smiled. Then they just sat and listened to the music for a few minutes. The Pearl Jam song was followed by some brutal Limp Bizkit crap. The transition was too much to bear.

"I can't stand this stuff," Kristen said covering her ears. "I think

I'm gonna go. Do you need a ride?"

"I was about to ask you. Is that alright?"

"Sure, let's go."

He helped her with her coat, and they walked outside to the frozen sidewalk. Her car was parked a couple of blocks away, down a residential street. It was an old beige Volvo, the boxy type. She walked over and unlocked Michael's side first. Then he leaned over and unlocked her door from the inside. Her car was a reflection of her personality. Inside, there were boxes filled with SD cards and files. Not messy, but not quite orderly. She had a deodorizer in the shape of a Hawaiian dancer hanging from her rear view mirror. She had outfitted the voice recorder on her deck to play mp3s of the Dimmesdale campaign appearances, which she religiously recorded. There were a few scattered SD Disks near the adapter.

"Nice audio selection," Michael said, picking up an SD card with "Keene, NH, Speech 11/16" scribbled on it. "Great lyrics, but sucky melody, I bet."

Kristen laughed.

"If there's one person more tired of hearing his spiel than the press corps, it's me, trust me," she said, then she checked herself. "Maybe I shouldn't have said that."

"It's okay," Michael said. "It's off the record, remember."

On the way to his hotel, the vanilla perfume Kristen was wearing permeated the trapped air of the car. Then she said something that triggered a bout of stomach shakes in him.

"So, you like my perfume?"

A big smirk split his face. It was dark and she couldn't see him blush.

"Yes," he said. "It smells nice on you."

She was quiet again, focusing on the reflectors peering out of the snow on the highway's edge. His heart started beating against his rib cage. After a couple of minutes, she pulled into the parking lot of the Merrell Courtyard near the airport, where Dimmesdale's press corps was housed.

"So, tell me again why you went to the Wild Rover tonight," she said, shifting the car to park as she pulled in front of the hotel. Her face was turned toward him.

He took a deep breath and stared out the passenger window, knowing he could take his time with this answer. Cardiac arrest loomed, his heart beat so rapidly. His whole body lurched in spasms of nerves. When he turned to look at her straight in the eyes, which were fixed on him, he almost passed out. But he couldn't just walk out of the car like this. He unbuckled his seatbelt, leaned over the center console and kissed her mouth. Slowly. Softly. Her entire body seemed to go temporarily limp. But as he pulled back, she sprung back to life, grabbed his head and pressed her lips on his, opening her mouth and running her fingers through his hair.

"Let's go inside," he said as they took a breath. "Right now."

Kristen didn't argue. She parked her car, and he took her by the hand to the hotel's front door, through the lobby, and up the elevator to his room on the fourth floor. Outside his room, she grabbed his coat, turned him around roughly and kissed him again, rubbing her hands on his shoulders. He managed to get the card into the lock and opened the door. The maid had tidied up his room a bit, making it somewhat presentable. Before he could even place his keys on the desk, Kristen had removed her coat and her shoes. She tackled him onto the bed and started undoing his pants and his shoes. By now, lust blocked out all other signals. Michael peeled off his shirts so fast that he tore a button. As soon as the skin on his chest was exposed, Kristen glided her hands over it. Michael pulled her jeans down, then watched as she slowly removed her shirt, conscious of his attention. Michael found himself with free reign to cleavage that he had spent the night fantasizing over.

Sexual deprivation for prolonged periods does things to people. For starters, it makes them want to lick everything and anything on the human body lustfully. He hungrily licked Kristen's belly and breasts and panties, then everything underneath. And she did the same for him, tasting everything with gusto from his neck to his knees. He was somewhat surprised to feel a patch of hair between her legs, but it made for more drama that way as he groped it to find the wetness. He didn't have a condom, but she never brought up the topic. Still wearing white lace stockings that reached her knees, she pulled Michael down on top of her and wrapped her legs around him.

"Put it inside of me," she whispered.

At one point, she flipped on top of him and straddled him like a jockey, leaning over and letting most of her weight rest on him. He reached down and gripped both cheeks of her smooth ass. She leaned close to his ear, licking it and nibbling the lobe. Her long blond locks tumbled over his face.

"I've wanted this since I first saw you," she said, as she writhed on top of him.

"I went to that bar tonight because I wanted you so bad," he said.

Later, as they lay in bed, she leaned over and noticed the bible on his nightstand. He had left it out from the previous night.

"Do you read the bible?" she said.

"Sometimes," he said. "It's like a cold shower against temptation."

"Though shall not commit adultery," she said. "It's in the ten commandments."

Michael pushed her hair back behind her ears, caressing her cheeks.

"Though shall not covet your neighbor's spouse," he said.

She smiled, climbed on top of him, and they went at it again.

CHAPTER 11

Before the sun rose the next day, Kristen dressed herself and quietly left Michael's room, with not so much as a kiss goodbye. By the time daylight broke, it was time to get out of bed and get dressed. But a blanket of guilt kept Michael pressed firmly to his mattress.

All night, his cell phone buzzed at his desk. He had ignored it to focus on the lust at hand. Now alone in the room, the vibration of the cell phone, loaded with messages, brought the tender thought of his wife sharply into focus. He knew it was her who had been trying to reach him, probably worried sick that he had crashed into some snowy embankment in the hinterland.

She trusted Michael too much to suspect infidelity, he told himself. Fuck. That's the kind of marriage he had. Every night he told his wife that he loved her and she told him the same. Every night he gave her a kiss, either on her cheek, or over the sometimes-choppy connection of a telephone line. Not until last night had he ever cheated on her. He could hear the persistent buzz of the phone, alerting him to a message.

Even after a steaming shower and a shave, he couldn't bring himself to leave the hotel room. He sat on the bed and stared down at the rug, lamenting the folly of it all. The thought of walking outside the room sickened him.

He self-diagnosed himself with a major case of what Hunter S. Thompson would label The Fear. He didn't want to face this job anymore, this grueling task of untangling a campaign web and interpreting its essence for the masses, of analyzing every move Dimmesdale made, down to his sneezes and meals. He wanted to order a pizza, some porn and play solitaire in his hotel room.

But he knew he had to trudge out of that Merrell Courtyard door. He knew he had to interview Dimmesdale, tape record everything he said, mingle with turtle-necked New Englanders wanting to hear Dimmesdale's plan for Saving America over apple cider and pecan-crusted brownies. He knew more long rides loomed in the cold press van. He knew he wouldn't run into anyone familiar in the near future. He knew everything he heard, and said and did was scripted by politically correct formulas that he garnered from listening to ambitious Ivy League graduates who wanted an office in the White House. On the rare occasion when anyone stooped to ask the mere campaign scribes about their own feelings on climate change or income inequality or student debt, for example, Michael would say it's "a difficult situation without a simple solution." They might ask what it was like to grow up as a Cuban kid in Miami. He'd say "the ethnic diversity was gratifying and enlightening." On race relations, "progress has been made, but there is more to accomplish."

Everything was talked about but nothing was said. The Fear was his gut telling him this was all a lie. The Fear generated thoughts of his beautifully imperfect family, and of the folly of so much power focused on greed and wealth at all costs. The Fear told Michael he didn't matter. Neither did Dimmesdale. It was all vanity.

Dimmesdale could win this thing and enter the White House in November. Then he might matter. Voters would ultimately decide based on weird things like a candidate's hairstyle and his relationships with his wife and mother.

Michael could have written that Dimmesdale had a bastard kid from a one-night stand with a Mexican waitress. That's not true, but it would have probably earned him votes. All that Bible reading had led Michael to believe that the moral rectitude in this country had been turned on its head. He'd been infected with a bout of philosophizing on a half frozen brain. What's bad is good, and what's good is bad, sinners often portrayed as saints and saints assailed for their righteousness. Moral judgment was bending in ways the Good Book never intended, with piety and virtue equated to poison. This was a generational thing from having too much information at hand and not enough wisdom to process it. It was a byproduct of a trillion meaningless Google hits.

The madness in the press corps, so many weeks into a campaign, was becoming evident. But it manifested itself mostly in silence. For example, a few days ago, as they were winding down their day at 11 p.m., Dave announced: "we're driving to Berlin in the north of the state tomorrow at 6:45 a.m. we'll probably stay in that area two nights. See you in 7 hours." Silence was the only response from the press corps. Madness! They had to send feeds, pack their bags, take an optional shower, eat something, and check out in the next few hours. One would think a mild objection, or even a healthy curiosity was justified to resist the ordeal. But *nada*.

"Ok," they said as they shuffled off the van late that night, crunching over ice on the driveway in front of the Merrell. "See you in a few."

Hunger seized Michael in the hotel room, but he couldn't swallow another granola bar. A round of gagging and dry heaving would follow if he even smelled one. This substandard hotel had no room service. To get a meal, he'd have to slog three blocks in a sub-zero freeze that had packaged every bare tree limb in ice. The complimentary coffee in the rooms tasted like water rinsed through rancid underwear. Michael had shed 17 pounds since he began this assignment five months ago.

He turned on the television, and once again became paranoically glued to the big three: CNT, MSNBC, FXN. He couldn't miss a thing.

He had good, solid, reliable information that indicated things were getting twisted up in his life. He had a decision to make about continuing this assignment: Another week of American politics up close, or the touch of his wife and children as he disembarked a plane in his palm-lined city. All he had to do was miss the press van when Dave pulled in. No one would call and encourage him along. He'd be abandoned in Manchester, free to go any place he chose. His corporate masters, Tindle Bailey Inc., wouldn't even notice he was gone until Wednesday. It could have all ended there. No defining line had been crossed. He didn't have to do this.

Soon Dave would pull up in front of the hotel, neurotically clambering off the driver's seat and peeking his head into the lobby hurrying them along. There would be more house parties, more speeches, more applause, more promises. Another week of rhetoric and minor frostbite in sub-arctic weather lay ahead.

The Fear was telling Michael to stay in bed and take the first plane home in the morning.

CHAPTER 12

Michael called in sick and spent the day reading the bible, hoping to purge that sinister itch that had triggered infidelity. He chose to stay. The first day off from the campaign in more than 3 weeks felt like a drug-induced coma.

The next day, Dimmesdale announced that he would be moving into an apartment in Manchester for the remainder of the primary season to be closer to his campaign. He milked the story for all the publicity it was worth, inviting reporters to his new pad when he moved in, showing them the food in the refrigerator, the paintings he had hung on the wall, even the toilet in the bathroom.

"Welcome to my humble abode," he said as he escorted in the herd of journalists and cameramen who trampled the newly cleaned rug. "A priest came in and blessed every room. Even the bathroom. Can I offer anyone some Danish and coffee?"

Everyone raised their hands. Dimmesdale spent the next 10 minutes making coffee for everyone on the instant coffee machine, and distributing it in Styrofoam cups. Some nervous correspondent from the AP spilled a cup on the rug near the couch. He thought no one noticed, and stepped on the stain so Dimmesdale couldn't see it.

"So, Governor, why move in here now?" Rachel asked him.

"I want the people of New Hampshire to know that I'm not just campaigning here, I'm now living here. This way, I can understand the state, its issues, and its people better. I save time on flying and driving from Washington, and heck, I even save some money."

Also, several campaign staffers lived in the same apartment complex, including Brian, Kristen, and a couple of others. They had been waiting for a vacancy in the building to rent Dimmesdale a pad.

Dimmesdale's new neighbor walked out of her apartment to see what the commotion was about. She was wearing an AC/DC t-shirt and reeked of beer. It was only 10 a.m. A couple of the reporters interviewed her, including Whitney, but Michael felt sorry for the woman after she explained that she lived with her 6-year-old son and didn't know who she was going to vote for because she couldn't afford cable television and hadn't been keeping up with the campaign. She was a cafeteria food worker at the local high school, but had taken the day off because her son was sick. Whitney wrote a story about Dimmesdale moving in, as did Michael. Her newspaper ran the article, however, and Michael's newspaper chain did not.

A rumor ran through the press van that Dimmesdale's campaign had stopped paying campaign staffers, a confirmation of the offhand comment Michael had heard from a slightly drunken staffer at the Wild Rover.

"I haven't heard anything," Whitney said.

"Dave, they paying you?" Mafikwa said.

"I'm strictly a volunteer," Dave said, hunching forward on the steering wheel to try to get a better look at the street.

The conversation fell silent, as each of the press corps members registered the possibility that this could be big news. The sense of competition kept them all quiet. They were colleagues, the "herd". But a big news scoop for one of them could be their defining moment.

That afternoon, Michael called Dimmesdale's campaign to ask about frozen paychecks. At first, the spokesman he talked to pretended he didn't know what he was talking about. Then he said he'd have someone return his call. Within minutes, Kristen called Michael on his cell phone. Her tone was very different.

"I thought the other night was off the record," she said. "What's this about you calling regarding frozen paychecks?"

"That night *was* off the record, but I've heard the same thing again from a couple of other people. There's buzz about it in the press van. I can't just ignore it. What if the Herald scoops me on it? Then what? Didn't the other press call about it?"

There was an unsettling silence at the other end of the line for a few moments.

"Fine," she said. "If that's the way it's going to be."

"That's the way it's going to be," Michael said, his stomach turning with mixed emotions. Then he tried to go light, but it came out wrong: "So are you going to comment on your campaign running on fumes?"

"I'll call you back," she said.

Michael waited for about an hour by his laptop. He was pushing close to his deadline and needed to pounce on his keyboard as soon as he received comment from the Dimmesdale campaign.

If there's one thing campaigns hate to admit it's that they are running low on money, particularly in a primary campaign. Low funds are a sign of weakness as much in American politics as in American business. Potential campaign donors aren't sure which candidate to contribute to in a primary because they're all from the same party. So they are likely to choose the person with the most "momentum." The first indicator of momentum are poll results showing a candidate ahead of the others. In this respect, Dimmesdale was a leading contender, though not by a large margin. The second indicator is the war chest. Money in the bank represents a candidate's popularity among deep-pocketed party elites, and their ability to get out their message to a maximum amount of people. In a mass media society, where a candidate's message must be doled out in 15 and 30-second segments on television, radio, newspaper and the Internet, money evaporates like rain on a Miami sidewalk in August.

Michael never received a call back from Kristen. Instead, about an hour after talking to him, she sent out an email to the entire press corps disclosing that the Dimmesdale campaign's brilliant advertising had put them ahead of the competition in the polls, and that much of the staff had volunteered to forego paychecks for the next few weeks in order to keep the momentum going. Michael had to hand it to Kristen, she put out the fire before it went beyond the matchstick. But he lost his scoop, and found himself writing the same story as everyone else again. A couple of tweets about it circulated before he even filed his story.

The article ran in some of the Tindle Bailey newspapers. The New York Herald and some of the papers that subscribed to its news services also used it. And of course, CNT, MSNBC, and ABC, used it. Michael's editor called him to say he wanted him to do more "enterprise" stories. In other words, he wanted him to write something different than the rest of the press corps. He explained to his editor that he had the scoop on the low funds in the campaign before anyone else, but the Dimmesdale campaign burned him and sent out a press release to everyone with their spin on it right after he called them for comment.

His editor displayed little sympathy. He scolded Michael for reaching out to campaign flacks instead of the candidate himself. He said Michael should have tried to ask Dimmesdale about the low funds during a campaign appearance.

"Let this be a lesson to you," the editor told me. "Never get a comment from a spokesman on the phone, when you can get one from the politician himself in person."

Point well taken. Michael had learned his lesson.

But it didn't end there. He noticed for the next few days that Dimmesdale was completely ignoring him at all campaign appearances. He wouldn't take any of Michael's questions at the "media availabilities." He didn't say hello to Michael. And Kristen ignored him worse than ever before.

A couple of times he tried talking to her in the middle of campaign events, but he found it impossible to have any sort of intimate conversation in front of a team of reporters and campaign flacks. The most she afforded him was a sigh, a swift turn of the head in his direction, and a quick: "what do you want now?"

Frigid did not begin to describe her new demeanor. Maybe it was because they had been intimate that Michael wanted more from her. Having slept with her also caused him to pay more attention to her when she was around. Maybe she really hadn't changed. Maybe she was always like this, and he was the one who was acting cheesy and overly attentive with her. Michael's macho side also led him to believe that there was something going on between Kristen and Dimmesdale: the way she adjusted his tie – gazing straight into his eyes -- just before he went on the air for a television interview; the way she put her arm around his shoulders to guide him away from packs of rabid reporters; the way she sat with him for hours in his car as he jetted across New Hampshire, and managed to emerge from the car smiling, as though she had just been privileged to hear his latest joke.

All Michael knew was that Kristen was ignoring him, and he couldn't get a word in with her. So he resorted to texting her on her mobile phone, which he knew she carried everywhere with her. He sent her a couple of messages every day, one in the morning, and one in the evening, hoping she would melt that sheet of ice around her heart and give him a call, or maybe a booty call, or not. He wasn't sure what he wanted.

The more Michael obsessed with Kristen, the more he ignored his wife. Usually, Michael and Bianca talked at least once a day, usually at night. But lately, he had been turning off the ringer when he'd see her number on the caller ID. She also resorted to emails, in which she would first scold

Michael for not calling her, and then meticulously report the details of her day, some mundane, and some so perfectly described that he could almost feel his wife's warmth as she talked to him across her pillow in the dark.

After Michael slept with Kristen, he didn't talk to his wife for three days. He just didn't know what he would tell her. He felt love for his wife. But he also felt a deep and powerful desire to be with Kristen again. The thought of having his wife's voice annoy him because he lusted for another woman didn't sit well with him. So he just cut her off. He insisted he kept falling asleep exhausted before calling her.

Nor did Michael find solace in the pages of the Good Book. God, whatever that means, made it clear that adulterers are not welcome in his idea of paradise. On this forsaken assignment, as he browsed the books of Psalms and Jeremiah and Solomon, he noticed that warnings about fallen and wicked women abound. The Bible is one big, clear warning sign not to fuck with bad women. But the signs were so abundant in this holy book that he couldn't help but analyze the flip side of it: this kind of shit had been happening since the beginning of time.

The communication breakdown with the Dimmesdale camp went on for a week before the campaign announced a marked shift in its message delivery. Monday morning, Dimmesdale began a blitz across the granite state pushing his family values agenda – or as he put it, valuing families -- with a visit to Maxx Clothing on Bedford Street in Manchester to unveil his three point plan. He picked the spot because much of his plan leaned heavily on tax cuts and fringe benefits. His next stop was the Merrimack Valley Day Care Center in Concord, where he told parents about his new family policy that would guarantee parents four weeks paid by the government for medical leave, including stress. Later that day, at the Student Union Building in Plymouth University, Dimmesdale told college students that he planned to double the amount of money available for Pell Grants, and that he would subsidize student loans at a low interest rate for the life of the loan. His tone, so holy, was clearly a strategic shift.

By the time the nightly house party came around at the home of Randy and Maybelle Woodburn in Whitefield, Michael could sense Dimmesdale burning out for the day. His voice was hoarse, and his eyes were puffy. He was slouching. Kristen grabbed him by the elbow and led him into the kitchen, asking a few stragglers to please concede a moment of privacy to Dimmesdale to prepare for his entrance. Michael happened to be sitting in a breakfast nook with Audra, out of sight from Dimmesdale and Kristen, sipping coffee and eating an apple. They overheard parts of the conversation:

"You look great," Kristen said. "It's your last appearance for the night."

"I should have eaten dinner before coming," Dimmesdale said.

"My sugar is very low."

They heard the refrigerator door open. Audra and Michael looked at each other. They leaned over and watched Kristen as she fumbled for something inside. She pulled out a two-liter bottle of Cola, and a carrot.

"Kristen, close that refrigerator, for Pete's sake," Dimmesdale said. "We don't even know these people."

"Don't worry," Kristen said. "The woman who owns the house told me to help ourselves to anything we needed. The Coke will give you a quick sugar and caffeine rush. The carrot will hold over the growling in your stomach till we get out of here."

Kristen poured the Coke into a plastic cup and gave him the carrot. In two huge bites, he inhaled the carrot and gulped the Coke down swiftly. Then in a quick movement that initially startled Michael, Dimmesdale dropped down, his palms on the tile floor, and started doing pushups. Audra couldn't control herself.

"What's with the pushups, Governor?" she asked, showing herself from behind the wall.

Dimmesdale didn't show any surprise to hear Audra's voice. Michael also walked out from behind the wall, and stared at Kristen while Dimmesdale finished his exercise.

"It's a quick way to get my energy up," Dimmesdale said, standing back up. "It's too late for a big cup of coffee, so pushups will do the trick. Are you surprised to see a 64-year-old man drop to the floor and give you twenty?"

"Not at all," Audra said. "I'm impressed."

"Kristen," Michael said, taking a step toward her, unsure of his intentions. But before he even finished saying her name, Kristen hurried over to Dimmesdale, brushed the front of his jacket with her hands, pressed record on her voice recorder and hurried him into the crowd in the living room.

Dimmesdale charged out like a star athlete, smiling and waving and shaking hands and pointing fingers. The crowd loved him. Older women wanted a kiss from him. Younger men wanted to shake his hand and offer their services. The new campaign messaging was clearly resonating with the populace. Dimmesdale trudged across the hardwood floor, near the spot where a log roasted in the chimney.

These house parties were the ultimate challenge for candidates. Almost every night, a complete stranger would volunteer to invite Dimmesdale, his close staff, the press corps and dozens, sometimes hundreds of supporters or would-be supporters to their homes. The houses ranged from mansions in Keene to humble townhomes that needed a coat of paint in Portsmouth. One of these old houses had been a school in the 18th Century, but had been bought by yuppies and converted into an 8-

bedroom house in the country. The families usually left their homes fairly intact, including family pictures, calendars and report cards stuck with magnets to their refrigerators.

New Hampshire was the only place left in the United States where intimate, retail politics still mattered for a national candidate. The state is small enough to force candidates to rub elbows with the masses on a regular basis. In fact, it's the only real way to get elected there. In New Hampshire, usually the people who vote in a primary are educated, if not fanatical about their politics. They are less likely to decide on a candidate based on his or her advertisements, and more likely to come out to a public event to meet them and judge them for themselves.

The Woodburn house in Whitefield had a huge family portrait hanging in the kitchen, obviously shot by a professional photographer. It showed two parents with three children, one of who was a little girl with what looked like Downs Syndrome. That revelation drew tender feelings from Michael toward the family. He looked around the house for the girl, but couldn't spot her anywhere. He saw her brother and sister and parents mingling. Then suddenly Dimmesdale began to speak. Michael should have known. The Governor was standing at the front of the dining room, with his arm around the little mentally disabled girl.

"Mothers and fathers today are working more and more and seeing our kids less and less," Dimmesdale said, squeezing the little girl near. "Where has our President been while all this pressure has been building on the heart and soul of America, our families? Nowhere."

Dimmesdale continued, "every one of the Democratic candidates running for President will tell you he or she is a champion of the middle class."

"But Harold Kane and Carrie Humboldt -- two Democrats who say they want to help ordinary Americans -- would go in the complete opposite direction and actually raise taxes on the middle class," Dimmesdale said. "And though Harold Kane and others may let middle class families keep the limited relief they've gotten during the last three years, that's about it."

"I'm the only candidate who is stepping back and taking a fresh look at the whole system -- and presenting a fundamental tax reform plan," Dimmesdale said.

Dimmesdale pitched his vision: under his plan, a family of four in Whitefield that makes a combined $50,000 a year would save $300 on their tax bill compared to current law.

In contrast, Dimmesdale said that if Harold Kane gets his way, that family would pay $300 more in taxes than they would under Dimmesdale -- the same as they'll pay under current law.

"Carrie Humboldt would go even further," Dimmesdale said,

"forcing families to pay $2,000 more in taxes than they would under my plan. She's no family candidate. That's equal to about 15 college credits, about two years of home heating oil, or a substantial portion of property taxes."

"This all leads me to this beautiful little girl standing here next to me," Dimmesdale said, and he again squeezed the girl and smiled at her. The little girl, with her mouth slightly agape, looked up at Dimmesdale and then wrapped her arms tightly around his torso in a bear hug.

"Wow, what a strong girl," Dimmesdale said. "This is exactly who would benefit from the special education bill that I will do everything in my power to pass when I become president. Little Jenna here and her parents would never again have to worry about money for treatment, day care or special education. Under my plan, children with special needs would be fully covered by Medicaid with no deductions."

Jenna's parents began a cascade of applause. They elbowed their way through the crowd and hugged Dimmesdale, the mother pecking a kiss on his cheek. But as usual, a sourpuss in the crowd burst the bubble.

"Uh, that's great, Governor," said the man, clad in a plaid lumberjack shirt and a turtleneck. "But how exactly would you pay for that?"

The Governor's face turned serious. "Good question, thanks for asking. By the way, there's a job opening in the press corps if you're looking for some real fun."

The crowd laughed. "No, seriously, I would propose asking insurance companies to cover the cost of Medicaid deductibles for special needs cases and allow those companies to claim those deductibles as tax-free expenses."

"So, you would subsidize insurance companies?"

"That's not exactly it," Dimmesdale said.

"I just don't understand how this would work then," the man said. "What's the exact plan, because I believe this family has been through enough emotional turmoil to not be misled."

"Come on, cut the guy some slack, it's a great idea," said someone else in the crowd.

"Hey, don't I know you?" Dimmesdale said to the man.

Dimmesdale's two bodyguards were closing in on the guy.

"Why don't you tell the crowd about your Christian agenda," the man yelled. "Tell them how you'd make the United States a place of right wing extremists and drag us into a global war to serve the interests of the Christian extremists."

The crowd erupted into confused talk, not sure how to handle this confrontational stranger grilling the Governor. And just as Dimmesdale's bodyguards reached the man, the mother of the little girl charged over to him and slapped him good on the face.

"How dare you come into my house and cause problems? Get out before I call the police."

The bodyguards grabbed him each by one elbow.

"Ok, ok, I'm leaving peacefully," said the man. "No police brutality here, please. Don't Tase Me, Bro."

Dimmesdale shook his head as the man left the house. The crowd quieted down as he raised his arms.

"Folks, I'm sorry about the outburst. I recognized that man. He is a very active and vocal critic of Christian values and he turns up at my campaign stops every once in a while."

A woman in the crowd yelled out: "nothing to apologize for, George."

"Why thank you," Dimmesdale said. "Very nice of you."

The family moved away from Dimmesdale, giving him the entire spotlight.

"Now that the subject has come up," Dimmesdale said. "Let me clear the air about my religion and my principles, so as not to let a detractor impose his impressions of me upon you. As a people, I feel that we need to reaffirm our faith and renew the dedication of our nation and ourselves to God and God's purpose. George Washington warned us never to 'indulge the supposition that morality can be maintained without religion.' I am an American that happens to be Christian, not the other way around. Now some people might shy away from religion, thinking our founding fathers wanted it so. But not me. I never will. Even when I am president. We have practically banished religious values and religious institutions from the public square. People of faith are working to repair some of the worst effects of our damaged moral and cultural life, and because of their good works and that of others, we have made real progress in reducing teen pregnancy, youth violence, and abuse. I have never, and will never back down from my demand that Hollywood clean up content that is delivered every day in large doses to our youth. Every day, our children receive a larger dose than I believe is healthy of sexuality, violence and depravity. I'm no saint, but our leaders can do better. Our party can do better. Our country can do better."

The mother of the mentally disabled girl began to cry. She hugged Dimmesdale and told him that even though she was Catholic, she admired him for his convictions and would vote for him.

"You are a great man," the woman said.

"Thank you," Dimmesdale said. "My wife, Shirley and I are truly blessed with a wonderful marriage and family. For us, honoring our country and worshiping The Lord come second to none. That's what I'm about. That's what my presidency would be about, and that's what our country should be about."

The press corps noted the story in the next day's news cycle. Michael wrote a touching piece about Dimmesdale being grilled by an anti-Christian activist only to turn the tables on the man by going off into a discourse about morals. The rest of the week dragged on, and Dimmesdale continued pumping his righteous discourse, both in interviews on the air, with his press corps, and with crowds. He expounded his moral and religious views much more than he had been the previous months. But once Michael wrote one story about it, his editors didn't seem interested in other anecdotes about Dimmesdale preaching holiness and devotion to the electorate. Besides, the winter ice had done a fine job of freezing any ambition Michael had to do more than what was absolutely necessary.

His editor announced midweek that the correspondents would be allowed to go to their homes for the weekends. And for the rest of the week, all Michael could think of was Miami in a warm moment, a shot of Cuban coffee, a hug from his children and a kiss from his wife, and his city nursing him back to reason and virtue.

CHAPTER 13

Michael took a Continental Airlines flight from Manchester, which connected in New York's La Guardia. Normally, he disliked flying. But on this day he dreaded it like never before. His conscience felt so guilty about Kristen that he felt God might strike down the plane just to punish him. A young, attractive college student sat next to him. He was not one to show signs of panic in front of an attractive woman. She was heading to Miami to meet her family so they could go on a trip for the Holidays.

If you ever want to know how a person would write their own obituary, strike up a conversation with them on a plane. Forced to cram their entire life, its purpose and its struggles into a conversation on a three-hour flight a passenger is forced to be concise. This girl was no different. After a quick exchange in which Michael divulged that he was a professional journalist and was extremely curious about the people that inhabited this world, he urged her to tell him more about herself. He had stereotyped her as a sorority type, with a long-sleeve tight shirt, and a knee-length denim skirt. But he was wrong. It turns out she thought television was a scourge on society, she was getting married to her black boyfriend in the summer, and she was going to Spain with her family because she had read there was good rock-climbing there. At the end of the flight, he wished her luck and went his way.

Michael had decided to surprise his wife and children instead of asking them to pick him up at the airport. A cab dropped him off at his house at about 4 p.m. on Friday, and for a moment he stood there just staring. He felt like a ghost.

As soon as his key entered the lock on the front door, their dog started barking from inside. But the dog soon recognized Michael and quieted down as he pushed open the door. His wife was in their childrens' bedroom. He heard her yell.

"Who's there?"

"It's me. I'm home!"

Glory and Iggy ran to him with gleeful faces, and threw their arms around him. The dog yelped up a high-pitched storm. Bianca pecked him on the lips.

"What a great surprise," she said. "We've missed you so much. Glory, *es papi. Que bueno.*"

Michael's youngest was tugging at his pants. He picked her up and she gave him a tight hug and kiss. She looked at him as though she wasn't sure it was him. Her little hand patted down his hair, as though it were longer and thicker than she remembered. Bianca sat down on the couch, with a sad look on her face.

"What's the matter, Bianca," he said.

Glory repeated: "watsa matter Bianca?"

"It's nothing. It's just that I know you're just here for a couple of days because Dimmesdale is still a candidate. I hate that assignment. Can't you just stay?"

Michael fought back an urge to say yes. He should have stayed in this sanctuary of dirty diapers, petty arguments, baby talk, home-cooked meals and holiness. And his life would have been perfectly fine.

He sunk his head and sat next to her on the couch, putting his arm around her shoulders. He took a deep breath to speak, but nothing came out. There was nothing he could say. So he hugged her and told her he wanted to take her out to dinner somewhere.

Bianca's mom volunteered to babysit, and Michael took Bianca to a trendy Peruvian Restaurant in Coral Gables. She ordered a pink cosmopolitan, a drink she caught on to watching television. He ordered a beer. They waved hello to some acquaintances at a nearby table. Bianca's Dominican hairdresser had blow-dried her hair the day before. The soft light brought out the honey-color in her eyes. Michael asked her to tell him stories about her and Glory and Iggy the last few weeks. She relayed some anecdotes from Glory's teachers at her pre school. The teachers called his daughter "independent" and "strong-willed," two pre-K code words for stubborn and disobedient. Bianca told him about her job, her mom, her life, her cooking. Then she told him about the park.

"Poor Ken, he's all bummed out by his divorce, so I've invited him and Greg over a few times to play with Glory, and I just make Ken some coffee and he tells me all about his wife and the problems. Poor guy."

This last segment jolted Michael from the warm haze of family coziness that he was erecting with his wife's words.

"Ken?" he asked. "Ken from the park?"

"Yeah, you know, Ken from the park. His son, Greg, is Glory's age."

"Yeah, o, yeah, I know Ken."

"Yeah, you know him. Anyway, his wife is a real number. She screwed him over really bad."

"How's that?"

"She left him for some amateur actor. But that's not the worst part. She waited until Ken's father died and he inherited all this money before divorcing him so that she could get half of everything. And she wants full custody of the baby."

"Damn," he said. "Sounds harsh."

The waiter took their order and they requested more drinks.

"So, is Ken dating anybody?"

"I don't think so," she said.

"I gotta be honest with you, I don't really like him coming to my house when I'm not there."

Michael's wife stopped eating and looked at him.

"Why not?" she said.

"Because," he said, squirming a bit in his seat. "What if he tries to kill you, or takes Glory. Or what if he gets the wrong impression and tries to make a pass at you? A man in his state can do desperate things."

"So you're saying that if Ken ever made a pass at me it's because he's desperate, not because I'm a nice, attractive woman?"

"No, that's not what I meant at all. I'm saying that Ken may decide to set aside social conventions of respect for marriage in his distraught state."

"Ken has never made any passes at me, and if he ever does, I will quickly put him in his place. Because I do have respect for our marriage, okay? Now I don't want to hear any more about this. You haven't been home in weeks, then you start judging me based on who has visited my house. How about taking note that your children are healthy and happy, that your home is clean, that your bills are paid? That I call you every night, even if you don't call me back."

Fuck. Michael looked away.

That night, Michael had a deep sense that he needed to spend more time with his family. But for some inexplicable reason, he did the complete opposite. The next morning, he concocted some story for his wife that he needed to go into the Tribune building to meet with his editor, who just happened to be working Saturday coincidentally.

But he instead bee-lined for his friend's house. He got to Freddy's around 11 a.m. Freddy slumbered so deeply Michael tapped his bedroom window with his car keys for a full five minutes before he heard him curse and order whoever was knocking to go to hell. A few minutes later, Freddy opened the front door clad in boxers, his huge afro lopsided like a deflated basketball, his eyes bloodshot from a night of music and boozing.

His living room reeked of cigarettes. An overflowing ashtray graced the coffee table, accompanied by a Russian mandolin, a couple of maracas and a pothead pipe. It was dark and cold inside. Freddy had always liked to sleep with arctic AC. Michael remembered sleeping over at his house when they were kids and having to grab towels from Freddy's bathroom in the middle of the night for extra warmth. He saw one of Freddy's girlfriends slink into the hallway bathroom. JJ, his roommate, was still sleeping.

"What are you doing here so early?" he said.

"It's 11."

"That's dawn for me. Aren't you supposed to be somewhere up north, like New Haven or something New or something."

He scratched his crotch and yawned.

"Yeah, I'm on a weekend furlough from my prison assignment in New Hampshire," Michael said.

Freddy went back to his room for a few minutes, so Michael walked over to the makeshift studio Freddy and JJ had pieced together at the back of the house. It's the room where Bingos, the Latin Rock band Freddy played keyboards with, had recorded most of their Grammy-winning album. Michael stepped over a tangle of cords, pedals, amplifiers and motherboards and approached a portable USB burner with recently burned thumb drives piled on top. Freddy's keyboards and guitar were safely ensconced in a corner of the room. Michael turned on the CD player and pressed play. A song about urine came on. It was Freddy's latest studio mix. As Michael stood there pondering the not-quite-mystical lyrics about girls who tinkle during sex and boys who pee on themselves for fun, Freddy walked in.

"What do you think?"

"You're on your way to your second Grammy, bro," Michael said, not a little bit sarcastically.

"I've decided to write songs about weird fetishes."

"Like golden showers? That's not a fetish, man, it's a crime."

"Sounds like you've never partaken," Freddy said. "You're missing out."

"For some reason, the idea of peeing on a girl's tits right before I fuck her doesn't quite do it for me."

Freddy munched on a slice of pizza that Michael could only guess was left over from the previous night.

"So what brings you by here, man. It's great to see you," he said.

"Just looking for a friendly face, bro."

"You've got the wrong place. I'm recovering from a rough night."

"Man, this assignment is rough," he said. "Bianca is all depressed because of all the traveling."

"Oh come on," Freddy said. "Tell Bianca to calm down. Dude, she could have it much, much worse. For example, she could be married to me."

He lifted his shirt and rubbed his belly after finishing his breakfast. He served himself a cup of water in a dirty glass that he took from the sink.

"Besides," he said. "It's not like you're moving away for good. You'll be back here in a couple of months, right?"

"I don't know. It looks like Dimmesdale might win the primary. If he survives to run against the president, I may be covering him for the long haul."

"You mean, all the way until November? Damn. If that's the case, then I recommend that Bianca buys herself a dildo and you get yourself an inflatable doll."

"Bro, I don't know if an inflatable doll would be enough," Michael said, laughing, then paused and lowered his voice. "There's temptation over there."

"O yeah? Are you having an affair with some hottie over there? Those Washington types must be all repressed and shit."

Freddy walked back out to the living room and sat on the couch. He lit up a cigarette and opened the Venetian blinds, letting a splash of sun soak the room.

"No affair," Michael said. "Nothing like that. But yes, there are hotties."

"What's it like, covering a presidential campaign?"

"It's hectic," he said. "Very hectic. There isn't time for anything else. My brain is starting to go to mush. You want to come with me to grab a café con leche."

"Let's go."

They drove to Latin Cafe on Coral Way, the closest Cuban joint to the house. They sat at the counter inside and ordered two café con leches. The waitresses were all middle aged, thick around the waist, and overly made up. Freddy eyed their waitress and then leaned close to Michael.

"I'd fuck her," Freddy whispered.

"You're sick."

"O, you wouldn't?"

"I didn't say I wouldn't. I just wouldn't comment on something like that. It's just one of those thoughts that I'll keep to myself."

"I'm not good at keeping stuff to myself. If I don't talk about something, then I write a song about it. Either way, I express myself."

"You have to see the people up there," Michael said.

"In New Foundland?"

"New Hampshire."

"Right."

"Ivy Leaguers. Competitive as fuck. Everybody is out to screw everybody else."

"Sounds like Hamilton," he said, referring to the prep school they attended.

"Kind of, except there's no real camaraderie up there. It's all fleeting, the relationships, the events, the impact. I don't know what the fuck I'm doing up there."

"Don't worry. Sometimes I don't know what the fuck I'm doing with Bingos. Sometimes I find myself thinking that I don't deserve any of this. Usually when I'm standing on a stage just before the lights go on. I think for a second that someone out there must deserve this more than I do, or would be better at it than me. But it's not someone else up there, man, it's me. For some reason, I've been put on that stage. And kids cheer at me, and women throw their bras at me."

Michael sipped his sweet, warm drink as Freddy spoke. The steam from the cup fogged his vision. Freddy's comparison sunk in.

"I can't say that any women throw their bras at me," Michael said.

"Dude, you're the one who got married at 24. I warned you, man. I think Bianca's great and all, but you married young as fuck. Now you want to fuck a bunch of women. Which is a totally normal and healthy thing to feel at our age. You're just bound by marriage."

"Marriage doesn't come with a chastity belt. I feel that shit too. Every once in a while I meet a woman and want her so bad. I usually just settle for a little light flirtation, harmless words. Then I jerk off in the bathroom thinking about her in the middle of the night."

Freddy eyed the waitress.

"Listen, if you ask me, I say fuck as many women as you can. Just don't let your wife catch you, unless you want to get divorced. And now you've got two kids. So divorce would be messy for you."

"Who the fuck said anything about divorce?"

"Just don't fuck up," Freddy said.

"What do you mean?"

"Look, we all have our lives here in Miami. We're all doing our thing. Some of our friends are more successful than others. You're my fucking hero dude. You're the friend I talk about with other people. You're the guy I hold up as an example of someone I'm proud to know. So if you fuck up, where does that leave me?"

"Really, you talk about me that way? Do you ever mention my good looks too?"

Freddy shook his head. "You could fuck any woman you wanted to. But you chose to get married and do this journalist thing."

"It's funny, you're the guy I hold up as my successful celebrity friend to all the city hall types that want to sound hip and tuned into Miami's "real" culture," Michael said. "You've done something unique and succeeded at it. It takes balls to stick to music and reject conventional notions of success like a stable 9 to 5, a marriage and family, and two cars in your garage. That in itself makes you successful."

Freddy scratched the scalp underneath his thick afro. They both sipped away at their cafe con leches, staring at the middle-aged servers.

"What I'm saying," Freddy said breaking the silence, "is that there's a big difference between walking the path, and knowing the path. Even if you don't know the path. Walk it, bro. And keep walking."

Michael nodded and hunched over his cup.

"Deep," he said.

"I think it's from a movie," Freddy said. "Anyway, I have some pictures of my favorite groupies from Latin America in my laptop. Wanna see em?"

"Hell yeah. Let's go."

Later that night, after Glory had nodded off to sleep and her Winnie the Pooh video had been turned off, and Iggy curled up on his bed, Michael approached Bianca from behind as she washed the dishes and put his arms around her. With his imminent departure, Michael thought the occasion called for him to say something romantic.

"Let me help you with those," he said, gently pulling her away from the sink.

She didn't fight it. Michael finished the dishes, wiped the kitchen counters, put away the leftover chicken. In marriage, he had discovered, it's the little things that people do every day that really make a difference. He could buy a new car for his wife, but it wouldn't make her any happier than if he took her out to a nice dinner, held her hand in public, and capped it off with a walk from Barnes and Noble to the local shop for a Cuban coffee. And likewise, his wife was not one to pamper him. She seemed to have identified the invisible line between what he needs and what he wanted and straddled it like a trapeze. The only problem was that he hadn't been around enough to do any little things.

His wife lied down on the couch in the dark, and after finishing the dishes, Michael sat in a nearby chair. The television was off.

"Let's go to bed," he said.

"I have to shower," she said.

"Then later," he said.

"We'll see."

Bianca showered. Glory had a nightmare and burst out crying while Bianca was in the bathroom. Michael entered her room as quietly as possible and gently palmed her blond, curly hair. She calmed down almost immediately and went back to sleep. He bent down to kiss her and paused for a moment about an inch from her head to take in the smell of powder and shampoo and hair. Her little breath smelled like a milky waft of human perfection.

Bianca stepped out of the shower wrapped in a yellow towel. Michael walked to their room and lied down in their bed, watching Bianca as she dropped the towel and walked around the room. Finally, she came to bed and he immediately pounced, stroking her thighs all the way up to her waist. He kissed her neck, but she stopped him when he reached her mouth.

"Why don't you take my calls?" she asked.

"What do you mean?" he said. "We talk almost every day."

"We used to talk almost every day. But the past few weeks you don't take my calls and you don't call me back."

"Really?"

"Don't act stupid," she said. "I know that phone's buzzing away in your pants and you just ignore it."

"No, the thing is that Dimmesdale has been stepping up his night campaigning, because apparently they figured out that a lot of people aren't home during the day because they work, and at night more people can attend those house parties so they're having one almost every night."

"I hate it when I don't talk to you at night. It makes me feel totally disconnected from you. I worry about you. Sometimes I think that kid who's driving you around got in an accident or something. You know, you should have like a highway survival kit in case that guy crashes in the middle of a blizzard or something."

"Don't worry, you've been watching too much TV. We'll be fine. This is the age of the cell phone, remember? Instant emergency line," he said.

"Are there attractive women up there?"

"If you were up in New Hampshire you'd be the most beautiful woman up there."

Michael rolled back to his side of the bed and stared at the ceiling.

"Every day I curse this assignment," he said. "I wonder why God has cursed me with this work. The only thing that keeps me going every day is the thought of coming home to you and kissing you and Glory and Iggy, and sitting down to dinner with you, and making love."

But his words didn't have the effect he intended. Bianca turned on her side, facing away from him and stayed silent. She remained that way for a long while, her body turned away from Michael.

"I don't want you to leave tomorrow," she said. "I need you here."

It was Michael's turn to be quiet. He didn't know what to say. Then he remembered something Dimmesdale said often on the campaign trail. And before Michael's disgust for politics and Dimmesdale in particular gagged him, he echoed the Governor himself.

"My family means everything to me," he said. "I'd do anything for you. But not all roads lead home, and I know that you understand that. Dimmesdale may win, or Dimmesdale may not win. But whatever the outcome, it's my family that will be at my side."

"You sound like such a politician," his wife said.

"I didn't mean to," he said. "What I meant to say is that I love you guys. I hate this assignment too. But if I don't complete it, I could ruin my career."

"I know," she said. "I just wish it wasn't so long."

"It's not fair to families," Michael said. "We were such a great family."

"We still are," she said.

CHAPTER 14

Much of the snow on the ground in Manchester had begun to clear out. It hadn't snowed in a few days but it had been getting steadily colder. The temperatures consistently dipped into the teens and 20s.

So it was when Michael stepped off the plane. He didn't feel the cold for the first few minutes outside the terminal, as he waited for the shuttle from the Merrell Courtyard to pick him up. Miami's warmth still enveloped him, at least for the moment. Back at the hotel, he unpacked once again, first hanging his ironed shirts in the closet, then his sweaters and coat. Bianca convinced him to bring a pair of wool gloves and a scarf. He grumbled about it, but was happy she had sent them.

He turned on the TV and watched the political news for a while. He took the bible out of the nightstand drawer, read a few passages and fell asleep.

A few days passed that way. Another two days off for Christmas had Michael in Miami again. The New Hampshire primary loomed.

One morning, Michael was the first person from the press corps to walk into the lobby to wait for Dave to pick them up. Audra followed him soon after.

"Are you excited for Boston?" she said.

"What about Boston?" he said.

"We're going to Boston tonight," Audra said. "Dimmesdale's going to be on Chris Mathers' show. He's broadcasting from Harvard this week."

"I've never been to Boston," Michael said. "I'd like to see it."

"I love Boston," Audra said. "It's one of my favorite cities. It's very walkable. Full of small gardens and narrow streets. Very European."

"I wouldn't want to walk anywhere in this cold," he said.

"You're right," she said. "No winter cabbage is worth frostbite."

"So, what else is new," he said. "Did you go home for the weekend?"

"O yeah," Audra said. "Any chance I get I'm splitsville from this hellhole."

"I guess everybody did."

"Nope. Whitney stayed here," Audra said.

"Really, Whitney? But New York is so close. Why didn't she go home?"

"I'm not really sure. I think she was working on a story," Audra said. "She needed to get it done over the weekend."

"About what?" Michael said.

"About Dimmesdale I guess."

Mafikwa and Rachel walked out of the elevator, followed a few minutes later by Whitney. Dave pulled up at 7 and honked. He shuffled into the lobby and held the front door open for them.

Once in the van, Michael learned that Dimmesdale had been excluded from the third debate between primary candidates on a technicality and was instead planning to appear live on the Chris Mathers show on CNT. At first, Dimmesdale's staff had been furious that he would not be allowed on the debate. But Kristen offered CNT an exclusive 30-minute interview with Dimmesdale immediately following the debate, a highly coveted slate of exposure on prime time usually reserved for the front-runner. It was a win-win: Dimmesdale got eyeballs and ears tuned in on him, and CNT got a scoop with a leading White House contender.

The day went by quickly, with Dimmesdale campaigning in Manchester in the morning, then in the afternoon in Portsmouth, which lies en route to Boston. Dave informed the press corps that he himself would be driving them on the road trip. Low funds equaled no luxury bus, Michael guessed. Michael could swear Dave's driving had steadily worsened. He wasn't much looking forward to a road trip to a major American city with this hazardous chauffer behind the wheel.

It was night long before they reached Harvard. Despite the vicious cold, students in parkas and scarves packed the streets, shuffling across snowy sidewalks framed by spotlighted brick buildings. Dave dropped them off in front of the Kennedy government building, where crews were inside setting up Mather's stage in the main rotunda. Empty chairs surrounded the small, makeshift platform, as the production crew tried to give the place a town hall feel. Kristen hustled Dimmesdale into a backroom for makeup and a quick bite to eat. Students escorted the press corps to their seats: uncomfortable plastic chairs at the side of the room.

The rotunda slowly filled up with the brightest young minds in America. So brilliant, in fact, that an audience coach came out and instructed them on how to cheer when the cameras rolled. After a couple of practice runs, the quick studies were ready for Hardball.

Mathers came out and sat on a chair behind the desk. A couple of assistants quickly hooked him up to microphones and tested the equipment. After a few minutes, the place went quiet and cameras began to roll. Then Mathers belted out in his booming, obnoxious voice that he had a special guest with him today.

"A man who was excluded from today's debate, in my opinion, unjustifiably, and who is here tonight to share his views with us anyways, Governor George Dimmesdale. Governor?"

Dimmesdale walked into the room, bringing the audience to its feet. The standing ovation clearly was unscripted. Mathers quickly asked everyone to sit down.

MATHERS: Eight of the nine Democratic presidential candidates took part in a debate earlier today, so which candidate was missing? Governor George Dimmesdale. Governor Dimmesdale initially rejected the invitation, but when he learned that two other candidates would be debating via satellite, he asked to be allowed and join in via satellite himself. The DNC consulted with some other campaigns and turned him down. Well, the Democrat's loss is our gain. Governor, I'm supporting you in this effort. I think you should have been allowed in the debate. How are you, Governor?

DIMMESDALE: I'm great, Chris. Thanks a lot. And you know, I always thought the Democratic Party was the party of inclusion, but they excluded me tonight. But I got the last word because I'm on your much more highly viewed show than the other channel on which the debate is now showing.

MATHERS: That is absolutely...

DIMMESDALE: Don't turn your dials.

MATHERS: That is absolutely true. And the debate was earlier tonight. Why do you think that is, Governor? Because by far, and I have my disagreements with you and you know that...

DIMMESDALE: Sure.

MATHERS: But by far, you have been the least shrill of all of these candidates. You have been the most understanding of the need to combat Islamic extremism and do something about climate change and income inequality. Do you think politics had anything to do with your being excluded?

DIMMESDALE: It must. I mean, the first thing I didn't understand is why the Democratic National Committee polled the other candidates, to ask them whether I could be there. It set up a kind of blackball system, which was not the right thing to do. And I feel in the end that a lot of big issues were discussed and I would have taken positions that nobody else on the stage did. Strong on climate and values, I'm the only one to recommend middle class tax cuts beyond even what the president has recommended. I'm the only one who is strong on trade. So I feel that I could have added a lot to the debate, and I'm sorry they made the decision they did.

MATHERS: Here's – I watched the debate that took place tonight, Governor - and here's my problem. I'm a conservative. I'm a Republican, and I support the president. I think he's done a great job on the war on terror, and I think the economy is turning around. But here's what I've watched with the Democratic debate, and I used the word "shrill" before. I've heard your fellow candidates refer to this president as a gang leader, as a liar, as a candidate for impeachment, as a miserable failure. I've watched each and every solitary aspect of this very complicated and difficult battle against our enemies, just being pushed aside. When you hear your fellow candidates make such deeply personal attacks against our commander-in-chief, does it bother you?

DIMMESDALE: Well, look, I always say from what I know of the President that he's a good man. I'm running for president because I don't think he's been a good president. But, you know, you're absolutely right. There's one thing for making a case the voters should fire him and hire me. It's another to make him into something evil. And that hurts our politics overall. So I try not – you know, I understand a lot of Democrats are angry. I'm angry. But it takes more than anger to be the commander-in-chief. It takes some strength and experience and the ability to try to bring people together, including people of both parties. I don't get it. I don't know how the DNC and Terry McMahon ended up getting backed into a corner on that. But anyway – and as I said before, I have a point of view that I think is different than any of the other candidates, and I'm sorry I didn't get a chance to reflect it there. It wasn't the right thing to do, but there will be other debates and I'll be there.

MATHERS: Is it because – and I want to reemphasize this point – is it because your point of view is further away from the other candidates, closer to maybe the President's point of view, on certain decisions like tax cuts and conflict in the Middle East, that has the Democratic structure not in your corner?

DIMMESDALE: Well, I hope not. I mean, the DNC has been neutral, as they should be. The fact is that the strength of the Democratic Party, the strength of our country, is the diversity of points of view. And I know that I represent a great number of Democrats. I saw a poll a while ago that asked Democrats around the country to self-identify, and two-thirds self- identified as moderate or conservative. I want to speak for the independent-minded Democrats. I want to represent a center-out candidacy, which is the only kind that really can defeat the president. We're not going to do it by going too far over to the left, as the president has taken the country, with all respects, Chris, too far over to the right.

MATHERS: But not with religion, correct Governor? You believe religion should be the backbone of the American family. But how does your religion make you a better candidate in the war on climate, for example, or the economy?

DIMMESDALE: This is a battle to stop the destruction of the earth by greed and irresponsibility. Now, I'm a Bible reader. Always have been. It is clear as day in the bible: man should care for the environment and the earth, and not destroy what God has given us all. My views on religion don't run contrary to my views on the environment. They go hand in hand. As a good Christian, I think the most important thing we can do is care for this earth, create jobs that give people meaning in their life, make opportunities available for everyone. This is where that opportunity lives on, with my election to the presidency.

MATHERS: Do you think your strong religious beliefs could spark a global religious war? Do believe that in the Middle East, this may be a war of Islam versus Christianity and Judaism combined?

DIMMESDALE: Islam against — , or I should say *fanatical* Islam against Christianity, Judaism, Hinduism, every other "ism," every other religion, including every part of Islam that doesn't agree with these fanatics, is the real threat. The spread of it is real and swift. And we cannot let that happen, and it's within our power to stop it.

It is clear — and this is not imagining anything; you've just got to read and listen to what ISIS and Al Qaeda and the rest of these extremists and terrorists are saying — that that is what they desire. But it is unbelievable to think about it in the 21st century, with modern telecommunications, science, medicine, that we could be plunged back into a primitive religious conflict. Unless we defeat these extremists and create bridges to the rest of the Islamic world to show what American values are all about and help them live a better life, that could happen. The Middle East is the testing ground, and that's why we've got to make sure that victory is assured.

MATHERS: Sounds like you'd also lean on religion to pressure Hollywood and the rest of the entertainment industry, as you've done in the past, to clean up their act. How does that mesh with the First Amendment and our tolerance as a society. Doesn't your emphasis on religion trample the First Amendment in some cases

DIMMESDALE: Chris, the problem with religion and faith in this country is that many people have come to view those two things with skepticism, even suspicion. My message to the American people when I get elected will be simple: embrace the moral and ethical values that our nation was founded upon. Sometimes we forget that our forefathers drew directly from biblical lessons and values when drafting our constitution. Religion, whether it be Christianity, or Islam, or Judaism, is not something that should be shunned or feared by our mainstream institutions. It should be embraced, and resurrected as a pillar of our society.

MATHERS: But Governor...

DIMMESDALE: Let me finish. One second Chris, because I think this is important for your viewers to hear. Just as medicine tends to make society healthier, religion tends to make society more ethical. Judeo-Christian teachings are a wellspring of the civic virtues a sound democracy requires. Even Thomas Jefferson, skeptical deist that he was, considered religion "the alpha and omega of the moral law" and used government funds to underwrite the religious services held in the Capitol and other federal buildings. I have lived my life according to the teachings of God as documented in the bible. I have been loyal to my wife, my family, and my nation, always in the service of the Lord. And that is something America needs right now. A leader who is not ashamed to celebrate the wisdom and guidance of God.

MATHERS: Governor, if I wasn't on the air right now, I might ask you to bless me. But I'll settle for requesting a prayer from you in my honor. Sounds like you and the big man upstairs are on good terms.

Dimmesdale and Mathers continued chatting for a few more minutes, then it was over. The audience split in their reaction. Half of them gave Dimmesdale a standing ovation. The other half stayed seated, many of them not even clapping.

CHAPTER 15

Dimmesdale appeared on the Chris Mathers show on a Monday. Tuesday morning, as the press corps loaded back onto the van for another day of campaigning around New Hampshire, Michael's editor called him on his cell phone.

"Did you see the New York Herald this morning?" he said.

"No," Michael said. Whitney was sitting right in front of him in the press van. "Why?"

"There's a front page, top-of-the-fold, story on Dimmesdale written by a Whitney Worsdsworth. Isn't she part of Dimmesdale's press corps?"

"Yes," he said. Michael suppressed an impulse to reach over the seat in front of him and strangle Whitney. "What is it about?"

"It's about your candidate, Michael," he said. "The story basically says that Dimmesdale's religious background and morals are giving him deep traction among the nation's religious conservatives from all parties, and it could be exactly what the Democratic Party needs to overcome their image of being weak on morals."

"Shit," Michael muttered under his breath. He was trying not to let his colleagues in on what the phone call was about. Then his editor cracked the whip.

"Shit doesn't do anything for me, Michael. I sent you on that assignment expecting professional coverage of a serious presidential contender. I can't remember the last enterprise story you wrote. I don't give a flying fuck how you do it, but I want you to interview Dimmesdale, just you and him. You need to catch up on this and catch up fast. I want a centerpiece story for our Sunday papers, ready no later than Friday afternoon. On Dimmesdale's morals. If the guy's a damn saint, then we gotta write it."

Michael swallowed hard. That would give him two days to get an exclusive with what seemed to him like the busiest man on the planet, whose campaign had been giving him the run around for the past two weeks. And there went any hope of returning to Miami for the weekend.

"Um, that might be a little difficult," Michael said. "I'm not exactly on the best terms with him right now."

That was the wrong thing to say.

"Not on the best terms. Why the hell not? You haven't written anything about the guy that the press corps hasn't been all over in unison. I haven't seen a single exclusive scoop you've had on this entire assignment. I want a Dimmesdale exclusive by Friday, or you're off this assignment. *Comprende?*"

"Yes, sir. Understood."

Whitney turned around as Michael hung up. The slightest smirk appeared on her lips. Despite the freezing cold in the van, Michael actually began to sweat. Audra, who was sitting next to him, put her hand on his shoulder.

"You ok?" she said.

"Yeah," he said. "I'm fine."

He stared at the back of Whitney's head until they arrived at their next campaign stop at the Monadnock Early Learning Center in Michaelborough, New Hampshire. Michael immediately walked past a crowd of housewives and working moms and little kids and took Kristen lightly by the arm.

"Hey," he said. "I need to talk to Dimmesdale."

"He's having a press avail after this, just grab him there," she said, then started to walk away, toward Dimmesdale, who was hugging a mother.

"Wait," he said, grabbing her arm again. "Please, I need to talk to him alone."

"Impossible," she said. "He's booked through until next week."

"My editor just called me and threatened to pull me off this campaign if I don't talk to Dimmesdale."

"That sounds like your problem," Kristen said, "Not Dimmesdale's."

"Kristen, please ask him, please," he groveled as she walked away.

He pulled his phone out of his pocket and studied Dimmesdale's weekly schedule, which his campaign put out at the beginning of every day and updated daily if anything came up. As he read it, he noticed that Dimmesdale went out of his way to cross the room and talk to Whitney. They walked over to the corner alone and Dimmesdale didn't stop talking. Whitney smiled nicely at his words, as did Dimmesdale at Whitney's. When they were finished talking, Dimmesdale walked toward the stage and Michael immediately cut him off.

"Uh, Governor, Hi," Michael said.

"Hello, Michael. Keeping warm?" he said. A voter carried her baby over to Dimmesdale. He picked up the baby and held her up in front of him.

"Um, sir," Michael said as Dimmesdale kissed the baby and handed her back to her mother. "I was wondering if I could interview you alone just for a few moments in the next couple of days. It's for a story I'm working on about your morals and religious values and their role in the election, sir."

Dimmesdale thanked the mother with a smile then looked Michael in the face, his smile vanishing.

"You're late on that, Michael. Maybe you should pick up a copy of the New York Herald today."

Kristen and one of Dimmesdale's bodyguards ushered Dimmesdale toward the front of the room. "Please sir, just a few moments," he said.

"Talk to Kristen," he said.

But Kristen avoided Michael the rest of the day.

Twice that afternoon, Michael came upon the press corps chatting it up with Whitney about her story, but he couldn't bring himself to say anything. He'd walk away as she bantered on about it. During one of their legs in the press van, Audra showed him a copy of Whitney's Herald story, which she had gotten from a Dimmesdale campaign staffer. At first Michael pretended he wasn't so interested. But curiosity got the better of him and within a few seconds, he was consumed by the page.

Under the headline, "Faith and Morals help Candidate Break Away From the Pack," Whitney had written about how Dimmesdale's image as a moral, almost clerical, figure in politics was giving him the credibility he needed to challenge the Republican Party on the "God" and "morals" front. She pointed out that Dimmesdale's conservative Christianity was a unique characteristic that seemed to intrigue people more than shut them out.

Righteousness, long part of Dimmesdale's political style, is a trait that gained him national prominence when he was among the first in his party to publicly chastise President Plimpton for his affair with former intern Maggie Lapinsky. "Such behavior is not just inappropriate; it is immoral," he said then. "And it is harmful, for it sends a message of what is acceptable behavior to the larger American family, particularly to our children." Yet he also helped Plimpton by not calling for the president to resign.

In a recent interview, he said, "I felt it was never going to get better unless a Democrat spoke out about it. It was probably the hardest decision I've ever made."

While some in his party felt reassured by his moral compass following the Plimpton scandal, its place seems far less urgent and compelling today. And wearing the moralist cloak can also invite criticism over obvious contradictions. Dimmesdale has attacked the entertainment industry for excessive violence yet still takes its campaign contributions. He frequently quotes Scripture on the campaign trail yet has vigorously attacked fellow Democrats.

Still, his religious side is authentic and humble, leaving a deep impression on voters who hear him expound his views at campaign stops.

As other candidates crisscross the nation Sundays, Dimmesdale is often in Georgetown, where he and his wife, Shirley, live in a town house inside a gated community. The Governor stops for flowers on his way home as candles are lit for the Sunday pastoral celebration of Mass. Dimmesdale typically doesn't have campaign appointments on Sunday, and chooses to spend the day with his wife and 15-year-old daughter, Tara.

"An oldest child, Dimmesdale lives a more religiously observant life than either of his two brothers and sister. He said he grew more "ritualistic" with age in an effort to honor his immigrant grandmother and pass the traditions on to his children. "It's a foundation and anchor and strength for him," said Joanna, his sister.

The story included references to several interviews with Dimmesdale, some of which had to be exclusive because Michael did not remember Whitney ever asking Dimmesdale about these issues in front of the press corps. As jealous and angry as Michael was about getting scooped, a couple of things compelled him to comment to Whitney about her story. After he finished it, he put his hand on Whitney's shoulder.

"Nice story today, I just read it," he said.

"Thank you," she said, turning around.

Then, almost defensively, she continued talking about why she wrote the story now.

"He had been getting traction with talk of morals and values ever since that house party where the anti-Christian activist absolutely lambasted him," she said.

"I remember," Michael said. "So, how did you go about getting an interview with him. It looks like you had some time alone with him."

"I begged Kristen last week. She set it up for me. I interviewed him once in his car. He let me ride with him to a campaign stop. And a couple of days later, he invited me to breakfast at his apartment in Manchester."

"Breakfast?" Michael said. He was getting lightheaded with envy. He had never even broken bread in the Governor's presence. He was way, way behind.

"Breakfast?" said Audra. "So what's he like in the mornings. Is he always so chipper."

"Yeah," said Rachel, turning around. "What does he eat for breakfast?"

"And what does Shirley look like without all that makeup on?" Mafikwa said, piping in from the first row, which she had monopolized.

"Dimmesdale actually has breakfast almost every day in his apartment, at least when he's in Manchester. It's the only down time he really has," Whitney said.

The Dimmesdales had one domestic policy point, Whitney pointed out: shoes off when entering their pad. Their philosophy was that a humble home-away-from-home, even one used basically for sleep, and the occasional 11 p.m. staff gathering, should have dirt-free floors. Whitney said Dimmesdale and his wife were surprisingly candid, not afraid to show their daily living nuances as they began their start-of-the-day routines.

Dimmesdale, for example, sat at the kitchen table in an elegant blue robe and finished off a bagel with cream cheese for breakfast while Whitney peppered him with questions.

"An everyday first meal for him that he jokingly and superstitiously claims will win him votes in the Granite State," Whitney said.

Rachel laughed.

"What did you eat?"

"I settled for a bagel with cream cheese."

"A fine choice," Rachel said.

"So what about Shirley?" Mafikwa said. "I can't even picture her face without the caked-on-cosmetics."

Whitney said Shirley had not yet dressed for the day when she arrived at Dimmesdale's apartment, and she sat at the table with Dimmesdale in his robe, sipping coffee.

"She looked great without makeup, kinder," Whitney said. "Before Dimmesdale could even get a word out between final bits of bagel, Shirley shushed him because Tara, their 15-year-old, was sleeping in one of the rooms and Shirley didn't want the interview to wake her. She must have shushed him or rolled her eyes at him at least half a dozen times in the few minutes I was there."

"Uh, typical," said Mafikwa. "See, that's what I'm talking about with marriage. You're married for that long and you don't even respect each other any more."

"No, no, no," Rachel said. "That's just how old married couples are. The wife wants to control everything about her man, at least while he's in their house, because she's convinced that he's weak and inconsiderate. But the reality is that he was weakened by her throughout the course of their marriage, his resolve and backbone worn away by years of nagging."

The whole press corps turned to look at her.

"What?" she said. "I took a class on the psychology of marriage in college."

The next day, Michael approached Kristen two more times, but it was no use. It was clear to him that she wouldn't help him. By Wednesday night, the situation was so grave that he seriously considered calling his editor and telling him that he wanted out of this assignment. He stared out the window of the van as Dave drove them back to their hotel through an industrial part of Manchester, where old brick warehouses lined the streets. Bare trees provided little cover for the power lines that crisscrossed the subdivision.

As they arrived at the hotel, Dave announced that as of next week, maybe even as early as this weekend, the campaign planned to upgrade to a full-sized bus to accommodate the press because so many journalists had become interested in covering Dimmesdale after the latest poll results showed him moving up among Democrats.

Part of Michael wanted to throw in the towel and call it quits, just fuck this whole assignment. But another part, the side of him that drove him into journalism in the first place, boiled with competitive fury. Whatever happened, he had to interview Dimmesdale before Friday and write that story.

The issue was logistical more than anything else. How would Michael interview a presidential candidate exclusively without the help of his press secretary? He thought back on his days as a crime reporter at Newstime, in New York, where the latest homicide was the only assignment he had to worry about. Sometimes he had to stake out the Nassau County police station for hours, waiting for the detectives to end their shift and walk to their cars in the parking lot. Sometimes he'd approach a detective at 1 a.m. and the kind cop would let him sit in his car with the heater running and give Michael the scoop on the interrogation. Or sometimes he'd catch a dick in a bad mood and he'd threaten to arrest Michael if he kept loitering in the parking lot.

The only thing Michael could do was try.

CHAPTER 16

Temperatures overnight dipped below zero. The next morning, before Dave arrived, Michael noticed that Audra had her suitcase with her. Whitney came down with her suitcase as well.

"What's with the suitcases?" he said.

"Berlin, remember? We're spending the night in Berlin, north country." Audra said.

"I totally forgot," Michael said. "If Dave gets here tell him to wait for me."

He ran back to his room, threw all his clothes into his suitcase, sat on top of it on the bed and zippered it up. In the lobby, he checked out just as Dave pulled up in the van. In the brief time it took them to lift their suitcases into the trunk of the van, Michael's ears had turned numb and purple. Dave informed them the temperature was 16 degrees below zero. It was so cold inside the van that the windows frosted over from the inside. Only the windshield, with the defroster turned up high, had a clear view to the road. Rachel took out her press ID and scraped the frost inside the window. It cleared up for a few seconds before turning icy and translucent again.

"It's a real shame," said Rachel. "We're heading north and it's really beautiful country up there."

The drive north took three hours. They followed Dimmesdale's car. The roads were frozen in parts, but Dimmesdale's driver sped the whole way through, at one point hitting 90. Careful not to lose Dimmesdale's car, Dave kept pace in the van, barreling down country roads.

Berlin looked like Main Street, U.S.A. after the apocalypse. Not a soul present when they pulled in. Not a car on the streets. Not a pedestrian on the sidewalks. The traffic lights were out. Darkness filled most of the shops and cafes. One of the store owners explained that the low temperatures had frozen tree limbs, which in turn had collapsed over the main power line into town. Dimmesdale shook hands with the few brave voters who straggled into his campaign appearances.

In the early afternoon, Michael's editor called.

"How's that Dimmesdale weekender coming along?" he asked.

"Great so far."

"Have you interviewed him yet?"

"Um, well, not yet, but I've got something set up."

"For when? I need the story tomorrow afternoon," he said.

"I'm supposed to get some time with him in the morning."

"I expect that story by 5 tomorrow."

"You'll have it."

"Good. We'll talk then."

The sun was gone by 4 p.m., leaving Berlin enveloped in a frosty darkness that smothered the still night with a deadly silence. Dimmesdale ended the campaign day at a town hall meeting in Berlin's community center, which was flanked by a bar/pizzeria named the Grey Wolf Saloon. Dimmesdale had taken a detour to take phone calls, and the press van arrived before him. More people than Michael had seen all day packed the place. Men in felt shirts and thick coats and beards, the kind you see in commercials and television shows depicting cliché woods-dwellers, shuttled between the hall and the bar with slices of pizza and cups of beer. Dimmesdale didn't arrive until after 9 p.m. and by that time, restlessness and booze had infected the audience.

Dimmesdale, seemingly energized, walked into the hall, which had been outfitted with a formal stage and a podium with a microphone. But Dimmesdale decided to forego the microphone and just talk to people from the floor, getting as close as possible. Everyone quieted down as Dimmesdale began his diatribe about the faltering economy and income inequality. Michael had heard it all before, so he headed to the bar and ordered a pizza. Audra and Rachel joined him.

"Where are we sleeping tonight? Are there even hotels here?" Audra asked.

"From what I understand, there's a single outfit in town decent enough for Dimmesdale to sleep in, it's called the Crystal Inn," Rachel said. ""Dave told me they're canceling the meet and greet at the factory tomorrow morning because of the cold front."

"Can we sleep in?" Audra asked. "I'm drained."

"I think we're starting the day at 9 instead of 6:45 now," Rachel said. "But who knows they might add something else into the schedule at the last minute. Something indoors."

The pizza wasn't bad for the middle of the tundra. Kristen stopped by and ordered two diet colas, one for her and one for Dimmesdale. She had removed her long, thick parka. Underneath, she was wearing a tight, pink turtleneck sweater that hugged her torso, a pair of beige slacks, also tight, and brown boots. She seemed more chipper than usual.

"Hey," she said. "Long day, huh?"

"Very," Michael said. He knew Rachel and Audra were listening. But he didn't care.

"You look great," he said.

Kristen acted like she didn't hear him.

"So any word from your editor?" she said.

"On what?" Michael said.

"On getting reassigned," she said.

"You're getting reassigned?" Rachel said, jumping into the conversation.

"No," he said, looking at Kristen. "Not yet."

"Anyway," Kristen said, turning her face fully toward his. The slightest trace of empathy brushed across her face. "I hope you stay."

She walked away with her drinks. Kristen must have understood that whether Michael's editor pulled him off the assignment or not relied heavily on whether she was willing to help him. Michael was still hoping she would change her mind, grant him some sort of interview with Dimmesdale.

"What was that all about?" Rachel asked Michael.

"Nothing," he said. "Just talking."

Audra didn't say anything, but he saw her expression. One side of her mouth was twisted up, her lips pursed, as though she knew exactly what was going on but was saying it all through her face.

"U-huh," Audra said.

"I'm going to listen in on Dimmesdale," he said and he walked after Kristen.

She was standing near the entrance of the room with the drinks in her hand.

"Can you help me talk to Dimmesdale by tomorrow?" Michael pleaded.

"Look, I want to help you, but there's no time."

"How about tomorrow morning. The morning event's cancelled. We're starting the day later."

"He can't. He's doing conference calls and phone time instead from his room. His fundraising is through the roof in the last week."

"Can't I be one of those calls? I only need him 5 minutes."

"I really can't," Kristen said. "He needs his time in the morning."

The audience grilled Dimmesdale with questions about everything from abortion to tax cuts to religion. They were more aggressive and eager than most crowds. So the event went on longer than Dimmesdale intended.

"Please, how about tonight, after this event?"

"No way. Listen to him. His voice is beginning to go hoarse. He's been talking all day. He's exhausted."

"Have you gotten my emails?" Michael said.

"Yes," she said. "You shouldn't have sent those emails to me."

"Why not, I meant what I said."

"I know. It's just that…"

"What?"

"You put it in writing."

"Well, I put things in writing for a living."

"An old boss I worked for had a saying: Don't write what you can phone. Don't phone what you can talk. Don't talk what you can whisper. And don't whisper what you can wink."

Then she gazed into Michael's eyes and performed a slow, beautiful, subtle wink, touched his upper arm with hers and walked away to give Dimmesdale his drink. Michael's confusion about Kristen's intentions was absolute. Dimmesdale finished speaking and people started applauding. Michael attempted to approach the governor after the event.

"Governor, I'm working on an article about your religious values," Michael half-shouted past a heavy-set hunter-type with a beard. "Governor, two minutes. That's all I need."

"We're all wrapped up for the day," Dimmesdale said, addressing no one in particular as he took a step toward his bodyguard.

Dimmesdale bounced past a couple of voters then took shelter between his bodyguards and Kristen and walked outside. Michael followed them. Dimmesdale's car, with the chauffer behind the wheel, idled near the front door. As Dimmesdale's bodyguard pulled the door open for the governor to get in, Michael tried one last time.

"Can I ride along to the hotel, governor? I would really appreciate it."

Dimmesdale, already sitting inside, looked up at Michael.

"Let's leave it for another day," he said. "Good night."

The campaign party pulled into the Crystal Inn just past 11 p.m. The place was tiny, only 40 rooms in the motel split into two separate buildings. The lights were out in all the rooms, and the only things glowing outside were a neon sign in the window of the office building, and a light above the door threshold. Thank God there was power, Michael thought to himself. The two buildings were divided by a black parking lot lined with piles of snow that had been cleared out by a plough.

Michael watched from across the parking lot as Dimmesdale's driver parked his car next to one of the buildings and Dimmesdale, Kristen and another two aides climbed out. The two aides walked off to the office building, but Dimmesdale and Kristen walked inside the building where the rooms were housed. A few moments later, the lights turned on in two rooms upstairs almost simultaneously. And almost in unison, Kristen walked to the window of her room and closed the curtain, and Dimmesdale did the same in his own room.

The campaign housed the press corps in the other building. Dave confirmed before parting from them for the night that they could sleep in because the first morning event had been canceled and they didn't have to get going until 9 a.m. Michael's room was next to Mafikwa's. He collapsed onto his bed and grabbed the remote control, switching the TV to the news. Within seconds he heard a knock on the wall behind him.

"Michael?"

It was Mafikwa, talking through the wall from the room next door.

"Yeah?" he said.

"Can you put the TV down a little? I want to get to sleep."

"Yeah, sure sorry. I can't believe you can hear that."

"These walls are pretty thin," she said. "So what's this about you getting reassigned?"

"Oh, that's just talk. Not true. Maybe it's wishful thinking from the Dimmesdale campaign."

Michael lowered his TV. He could barely hear it.

"Is that ok with the TV?" he said.

"Yeah," Mafikwa said. "Just don't fart too loud tonight."

"I can't make any promises. Good night."

"Good night."

Michael set his alarm for 4 am.

CHAPTER 17

The cold sliced into Michael's face like sharkskin on a bare thigh when he walked outside long before dawn. The whole earth resembled a tomb: the sky starless and black, the ground covered in snow. He walked to the building where Dimmesdale and his staff slumbered away.

The outside door to enter the building was locked. The other way into the building was through the lobby, but Michael didn't want to attract any attention from the night clerk. Michael took a credit card out of his wallet, jammed it between the door and the frame and slid it down several times before the lock popped and the door creaked open. There were no modern electronic locks at the Crystal Inn. It wasn't technically breaking-and-entering, Michael rationalized, because he was a guest there. He looked over his shoulder one more time before he pushed the door open and entered. He unlocked the door from the inside to cover his tracks and took the stairs to the second floor, quietly tiptoeing to the door of Dimmesdale's room. The old wood floor creaked a bit beneath the worn-down carpeting.

He sat on the floor next to a column about five feet down the hall from Dimmesdale's front door. He turned on his side, so that his legs were spread out along the wall of Dimmesdale's room, and he pressed his ear against the wall, listening for signs of life inside. He would wait until he heard movement inside before knocking, so as not to wake Dimmesdale. When he heard nothing, he leaned back against the column and rested his head against it. The dim lamps along the wall cast circles of light down the hallway, which was wallpapered in a peeling lavender. Only the faint sound of the electric buzz from the exit sign near the stairs broke the silence.

His plan was simple: knock on the door when he heard Dimmesdale waking up and ask him to talk to him, if only for a quote or two.

Michael must have dozed off, because the chirping sound of a phone alarm going off in Dimmesdale's room jolted him awake at about 6 a.m. He heard Dimmesdale's voice, but he couldn't make out what he was saying. Michael figured he was on the phone with someone. Then he heard footsteps and a few seconds later, he heard Dimmesdale groaning. Michael pictured Dimmesdale doing some sort of morning exercise such as pushups. But then he heard a second voice coming from inside the room.

It was Kristen.

"Look at that fat boy standing up so early," she said.

Michael jammed his ear against the wall. Kristen clearly moaned as squeaking bedsprings from inside started a rhythmic pulse. Michael began to breathe heavily. His heart raced. He braced the wall with both arms, as though trying to pull the sound closer. Kristen's voice filled the room with ooohs and aaaahs. She sounded much different with Dimmesdale than she sounded with Michael. He stood up and got lightheaded, fighting an impulse to flee back to his room. But he couldn't resist and glued his ear to the wall again.

"I was worried you'd put your panties back on last night," Dimmesdale said.

Michael unconsciously took his notebook out of his back pocket and started taking down every word he heard them say. He pressed record on his digital voice recorder and held it against the wall.

"You wanna go another round now?"

"You know I'm a better candidate when I get some in the morning. Just lift your ass in the air a little. "

There was a pause.

"Like this?"

"That's perfect."

"Ohhh!"

A few seconds passed. Skin slapped against skin.

"You're so wet."

"I was dreaming about you fucking me and eating my ass."

"Oh, were you?"

Bed springs rattled. Sheets ruffled.

"Uh! You are so dirty. My God, if people only knew where your smile had been. If you keep that up I'm going to come right now."

It was Kristen's voice, but it didn't sound like her. When Michael had been with her, she had made few sounds, and talked even less.

Kristen's moaning built to a crescendo. Suddenly the sound of skin slapping together started up again at a furious pace. The moaning turned to low shrieks briefly before it all died down abruptly. Dimmesdale was a true four-minute man.

Michael's heart thumped away in his chest. He wasn't sure what to do.

He followed the impulse to flee, tip-toeing toward the exit. His hand rested on the doorknob that led downstairs. Deep breaths. Adrenaline asked: fight or flight? Michael had come here for a quote about moral values. He hadn't expected this. But he needed that goddamned quote so he could tell his editor it came from an "exclusive interview" with Dimmesdale. He turned around and charged back. He stood next to the column, so that he couldn't be seen from Dimmesdale's room unless someone popped their head out into the hallway. A few moments later he heard footsteps inside Dimmesdale's room, the ringing of a loose belt buckle, water running, more talking. The lock on Dimmesdale's front door clicked. The knob turned. The door opened.

"Yeah, I'm just gonna get some fresh clothes on. I'll be right back."

Michael stepped out from behind the column. Dimmesdale's left hand was holding open the door and his right arm slithered around Kristen's waist. He wore a blue bathrobe, and Kristen wore a long T-Shirt and fluffy slippers. Their lips were locked in an open-mouthed kiss.

Michael cleared his throat. Dimmesdale saw him first. He yanked his face away from Kristen's, his startled eyes open so wide Michael thought they'd pop right out of his skull. Kristen spun around.

"Michael? What the hell are you doing here?" she said.

"I need to interview the Governor about his morals and religious values," Michael said. "What's going on?"

For once, the Governor's hair was a tangled mess of white wires shooting out in all directions like a fiber-optic cable nest. White socks reached his knees, pulled up tautly over his hairy shins. His untied robe began to come undone and he immediately grabbed both sides and wrapped it around his torso. He composed himself enough to answer.

"Uh, nothing's going on, Michael," Dimmesdale said. "Kristen just came over to pick up some papers."

Michael felt the slap. It hit him hard. Dimmesdale's arrogance had never been more biting.

"That's not what it looked like to me," Michael said, emboldened by the Governor's vulnerable appearance. "I saw you two kissing."

"Come on, now," Dimmesdale said, kicking into damage-control mode despite his disheveled look. "It's early, you imagined it. If you give me a few minutes I'll freshen up and you can get your interview. I'll tell you all about my morals and values. Come on."

Sometimes the road before a person suddenly and unexpectedly splits down two divergent paths, just as Robert Frost said. One lane is usually lined with the familiar and predictable sights that bring comfort and security, if not boredom. In autumn, the leaves turn deep hues of red, yellow, brown. The seasons spin an endless cycle of rejuvenation and cleansing, new seasons of sitcoms and football. Death and life are bookends of an otherwise pleasant, if timid, existence.

A clusterfuck of mines and trap doors and neon signs lines the other route.

Michael's first option: nod his head and say, "you're probably right, Governor. I couldn't really see what was going on." Dimmesdale would have given him the exclusive interview he needed to finish his weekender. Michael would have shuffled onto the press van and continued covering the presidential campaign of George Dimmesdale. And later that year, he'd return to his family and job in Miami, get a promotion, and look back on this assignment as a great learning experience and a resume builder.

Michael could feel the mosaic of his world shatter as he uttered his next words.

"What morals, Governor?" he said. "You're an adulterer. I have it all on tape right here."

"Now listen here," Dimmesdale said. "You're creating an entire fiction out of this. You didn't get any sleep last night."

Michael rewound his tape recorder and pressed play, his eyes locked with Dimmesdale's. But nothing came out, not a sound. He fast-forwarded and pressed play again. Nothing. He rewound and pressed it again. Not the slightest noise had been engraved in the fucking machine.

"Bah!" Kristen said, and stormed by him toward her own room, as though everything had been resolved.

"I've been here this whole time," he said. "I heard everything in your room."

"Heard what?" Dimmesdale said. "You didn't hear a thing."

Kristen unlocked her own door. "You didn't hear anything, Michael, because there was nothing to hear."

"You two are having an affair," he said. "Admit it."

"Ok, that's it. You can forget about any interviews," Dimmesdale said. "This conversation is over."

Dimmesdale slammed his door shut. Michael knocked on it a few times, but he wouldn't open. Then he knocked on Kristen's door but she ignored him as well. One of Dimmesdale's guards suddenly appeared in the hallway and asked him what he was doing there.

"I'm waiting to interview the Governor," he said.

"The Governor isn't doing any interviews this morning," he said. "How did you get into this building?"

"What do you mean how did I get in? The door was unlocked," he said.

"I locked that door myself last night before I went to bed," he said, walking toward him. "Don't give me that."

Michael glanced at the door of Dimmesdale's room one more time just as the guard reached him. He grabbed Michael's elbow, but he pulled his arm from the guard's hand and walked down the stairs in a huff.

The home phone number of Michael's editor, Donald, was programmed into his cell phone. He had never had a reason to use it until now. The phone rang before he even entered his own building at the Crystal Inn. It was just past 6.

After about 10 rings, Donald answered in a raspy voice.

"Donald, Hi, It's Michael Cervantes. I'm sorry to wake you but I need to talk to you right away. It's an emergency."

Michael could hear the sound of sheets on the other end of the line.

"Ok, what is it?" he said.

"It's Dimmesdale. I was sitting outside his hotel room this morning so that I could interview him first thing. And next thing I know, there's a fuckfest going on in his room. I could hear it through the wall."

"A fuckfest?" Donald said, his voice getting sharper and quicker. "What do you mean?"

"I heard Dimmesdale having sex with his press secretary, Kristen Dunlop."

"Are you sure?" Donald said.

"I'm positive. I even tried to record it, but I guess my machine couldn't pick up the sound through the walls. I have notes though."

"Well," Donald said, speechless. "So you heard fucking. Are you sure it was Dimmesdale?"

"I stuck around in the hallway until the door opened and I busted Dimmesdale and his press secretary sucking each other's faces. Big-time French kissing."

A loud thud came over the line as though Michael's editor had fallen off his bed.

"You saw them kissing?!" It was the first time Michael had ever heard Donald get excited about anything he said.

"Yes," he said. "With lots of tongue."

"What did they say?" Donald said. "Did they even realize you saw them?"

"Yeah, I cleared my throat and Dimmesdale nearly shitted his pants. She was dressed in a long t-shirt and slippers, and he was in his robe. So they were very nervous. But they denied that they were doing anything wrong. Dimmesdale just said she had come over to pick up some papers. I don't know what to do."

"You can forget about the morals story, that's for sure," Donald said. "This could be huge. This could cost Dimmesdale his career."

"I know. I'm a little freaked out."

"Alright, just hang in there. Don't freak out on me. I'm going to have to talk to a couple of people about this and call you back. Keep your phone on, and let me know if anything else happens with Dimmesdale."

Donald didn't call Michael back for more than two hours. They seemed like the longest two hours of his life. He laid down in his bed, staring at the ceiling of the Crystal Inn room. Sweat trickled from his armpit to his back underneath his coat and sweater. He turned on the television, tuning in to CNT and FXN. On FXN, they showed the latest primary polls. Dimmesdale had begun to break away from the pack, taking a 4-point lead over Carrie Humboldt and a 7-point lead over Harold Kane.

Michael paced the room backwards and forwards, wall to wall, bathroom to front door. He scoured his tape recorder for any bits of sound that may have been engraved. But it recorded almost nothing. The only thing it preserved was the encounter Michael had after he saw them kissing, and there was nothing self-incriminating about what they had said. He took out his laptop and began transcribing the notes he wrote in his notebook while he was listening through the walls outside Dimmesdale's room. Not quite material for a family newspaper.

KRISTEN: "Look at that fat boy standing up so early!"

DIMMESDALE: "I was worried you'd put your panties back on last night."

KRISTEN: "You wanna go another round now?"

DIMMESDALE: "You know I'm a better candidate when I get some in the morning. Just lift your ass in the air a little. "

KRISTEN: "Like this?"

DIMMESDALE: "That's perfect."

KRISTEN: "Ohhh!"

DIMMESDALE: "You're so wet."

KRISTEN: "I was dreaming about you fucking me and eating my ass."

DIMMESDALE: "Oh, were you?"

KRISTEN: "Uh! You are so dirty. My God, if people only knew where you smile had been. If you keep that up I'm going to come right now."

Dave knocked on Michael's door at 9 a.m. sharp.

"Let's go, we're rolling," he said.

"Where's Dimmesdale?" he said, looking around for Dimmesdale's car in the parking lot. "Is he gone?"

"He left a while ago, to make some time for Manchester," Dave said. "We'll catch up with them later."

It was even colder than the day before outside. The press corps, however, seemed rested, happy to have had an extra couple of hours of sleep. Dave had been running the engine and the heater in the van for about 10 minutes before they got inside. But it hadn't even bumped the thermostat a notch up.

"How long will it be before we get to Manchester?" Michael asked Dave.

"Probably between two and three hours, depending on whether I want to jeopardize everyone's life or just plain speed."

"But we're still going there today, right, we're going to see Dimmesdale later, right?"

"Uh, yeah. I talked to Kristen before she left and she told me to meet them at the lunch event."

"Intense morning, Michael?" Mafikwa said from the front seat.

He didn't answer. After about 10 minutes in the van, Donald called him back. Finally.

"I can't really talk right now, but I can listen," he told him.

"Ok, here's the deal," Donald said. "We don't want you to write a daily story just yet. But I'm going to give you a few days to nail this thing down tight. The ideal would be to find at least two people to either confirm a relationship between Dimmesdale and his press secretary, or at least verbalize deep suspicions about it because of what they've seen or heard. Right now, you have something, but we need a little more meat to make it credible."

"Um, I think that's a mistake," Michael said.

Whitney, who was once again sitting in front of Michael, turned around half way, as though aiming her ear at him. Audra was also quietly hanging on every word he said.

"We should do it today, you know, just to get it out of the way," Michael said.

"I know what you mean, but I talked it over with corporate and this is what we decided together. This is not your run of the mill sex scandal. This is the front-runner in the campaign for the U.S. presidency.

We better have all our Ts crossed and our I's dotted before we run with it."

Michael took a deep breath.

"Ok," he said. "I'll do it. No problem."

"You don't have to worry about following Dimmesdale's campaign for the next few days. We can pick up wire copy from the other correspondents. Just focus on this and see what you get. Keep me posted."

CHAPTER 18

As soon as they arrived in Manchester, Michael asked Dave to drop him off at the Merrell. But he wouldn't do it because it was out of the way. The van pulled into Roger's Diner in downtown a few minutes later. Dimmesdale's car was parked out front. The place was packed, standing room only. Dimmesdale and his entourage hopped from table to table shaking hands, chatting it up with patrons and asking for votes. Dimmesdale's wife, Shirley, was standing next to him. Kristen spotted Michael and gave him an icy look. Dimmesdale came over and greeted the press corps, addressing them all, including Michael, by their first names. He acted as though nothing had happened, which only increased Michael's suspicions of him.

As the event winded down and Dimmesdale climbed into his car, Dave herded the press corps toward the front door. Michael took a seat at the counter and ordered coffee and a pastrami sandwich. Audra hurried over.

"We're leaving," she said.

"I know. I'm not going."

"What do you mean? You're just gonna stay here?"

"Yeah, my editor wants me to start exploring a story right away. I'm just gonna get something to eat and catch a cab to the hotel. Tell Dave."

"Yeah sure," Audra said. "Everything ok?"

"Everything's gravy," he said. "It's a welcome change for me."

Michael holed up at the Merrell that afternoon. His first step was to scour the web, including Lexis Nexis, for anything and everything that had ever been written about Dimmesdale and women. There wasn't much. For a guy that had spent 25 years in public service, his record seemed relatively unblemished. There were a few notes in the Illinois newspapers over the last 20 years about women in midlevel positions who had resigned or been fired from his senate office, all pretty routine stuff.

But one note written two years ago caught his attention. It was a small story about a woman named Terry Gagnon who filed a lawsuit against Dimmesdale for sexual harassment after she worked on his campaign for reelection in Illinois. The story said the suit was filed in court in Chicago, and said one of the chairs of Dimmesdale's campaign, a lobbyist named Frederick Newton, was also named in the suit. He Googled both their names, and got just two hits on Gagnon: the Illinois story on the lawsuit, and an announcement from Northwestern University's website that she had won a prestigious scholarship to Oxford. But Google mined a shitload of hits on Newton. A high-powered Chicago lobbyist who was once Dimmesdale's Chief of Staff, Newton was now a big fundraiser for the campaign of Dimmesdale's competitor, Carrie Humboldt.

It wasn't much, but at least it was a starting point.

He booked a flight to Chicago and boarded the plane at 8 p.m. A blizzard in the Chicago area delayed the plane's arrival for an hour. It was midnight when he checked into the Merrell on Michigan Avenue, just a couple of blocks up the street from Tribune Tower, one of his favorite newspapers in the country, where he had interned in college.

First thing in the morning, he drove his rental car to the Cook County Civil Courthouse, a dreary beige block of a building with tiny windows and smog-stained columns. It wasn't as cold as in New Hampshire, but the wind bit deep here. Soon enough, he had the sexual harassment lawsuit documents in hand and quickly flipped through them. The file was thin. Terry Gagnon had dropped the suit after Dimmesdale settled just a couple of months after she filed it. According to the paperwork, Gagnon claimed that Dimmesdale had asked Frederick Newton, a close associate of his, to allow Gagnon to volunteer on his campaign as a field director after he had met her at one of his campaign luncheons. At the time, Gagnon was an intern at Newton's lobbying firm and Newton agreed to let her volunteer for Dimmesdale at no cost to the campaign. Soon after, Dimmesdale began inviting Gagnon to dinner and spending time alone with her. Gagnon said in the suit that she rebuffed his sexual advances in the back seat of a car one night after Dimmesdale gave a speech. Dimmesdale allegedly rubbed her knee and tried to push his hand up her skirt, while trying to kiss her neck, but she stopped him. The next day, the suit said, Dimmesdale called Terry Gagnon into his office and told her that if she wanted to get ahead with him, she had to "play ball." She quit on the spot. As part of the settlement, Gagnon had to recant her accusations and agree to a gag order, so the press didn't touch the story.

The folder included an address for Gagnon, an apartment in Evanston, and an address for Newton, a condo on the Gold Coast not far from Michael's hotel. Through his background-checking database, he confirmed their current addresses. They both still lived in the same place.

He tried Gagnon's apartment first. She lived in a small, three-story brick building about four blocks from Northwestern University. The front door downstairs was locked, forcing Michael to wait in the cold for 10 minutes before a tenant on his way out let him in. No one answered the door when he knocked, so he decided to just sit there on the tile floor and wait. One of the neighbors confirmed that a young woman lived there, but wasn't sure of her name. Seven torturous hours ticked by. He played so many video games on his phone that he killed the battery, which had been fully charged. Halfway through a game of paper/rock/scissor with himself, he heard footsteps on the stairs. A tall, blond woman, her head covered with a red wool hat, trudged up the last two steps. Snowflakes, not yet thawed by the warm air in the building, covered her shoulders and head. Startled to see Michael sitting next to her front door, she dropped the keys. He picked them up for her.

"Hi, are you Terry Gagnon?" he said, handing her the keys.

"Yes," she said hesitantly. "Who are you?"

"I'm Michael Cervantes, I'm a reporter for Tindle Bailey newspapers. I've been waiting here most of the day for you. So I'm just glad to finally see you."

He smiled.

"What do you want?" she said.

"I want to talk to you about George Dimmesdale," he said. "I'm covering his presidential campaign and I'm trying to reach out to some of the people who have had any sort of conflicts with him. I read about the sexual harassment lawsuit you filed against him a couple of years ago and I just wanted to reach out to you."

Gagnon walked to her front door, her keys in hand.

"So, you're just a reporter interested in a sleazy sex tale is that it?" she said.

"No, it's not like that at all," he said. "I flew here all the way from New Hampshire to talk to you. I just want to know what happened, how you feel about Dimmesdale."

"Oh, God," she said, shaking her head. "The media is so disgusting. Why don't you do some real journalism instead of trying to dig up people's past. If the media did some real journalism, we'd live in a better world. I can't believe your company wasted their money to send you here. That's pathetic. And this is all off the record!"

"Wait, I know Dimmesdale's not a saint. I know about Newton. I just need some help putting it all together."

"Goodbye" Gagnon said, letting herself into her apartment. Before Michael could say anything else, she slammed the door in his face.

Michael wrote her a note on his pad: "I know Dimmesdale is having an affair with one of his staffers, Kristen Dunlop. I know he isn't a saint. Please call me to talk. We can talk off the record if you want. Call me 305-555-8827."

He slipped the note and his business card under her door.

Next came Frederick Newton's place, a whole other level of Chicago society. He lived in the penthouse of a massive high-rise on Lake Shore Drive overlooking Lake Michigan. Michael entered the building through the street-level door downstairs into a majestic lobby covered in marble. A huge chandelier hanging from a 30-foot high rotunda cast a soft light that shimmered off the polished oak floors. Two guards manned a desk in the center of the lobby, where leather couches, Persian rugs and coffee tables created islands of comfort for guests and residents.

He asked one of the guards to please connect him to Frederick Newton's apartment.

"Is he expecting you?" the guard asked.

"No, I'm just dropping in," Michael said.

The guard phoned upstairs and spoke to someone.

"The butler says he isn't home yet," the guard said.

"Aw, well, I guess I'll wait a little while," he said. "Can you let him know I'm here when he comes in?"

"Sure," he said. "What your name?"

"Michael Cervantes."

About two hours later, as Michael meditated on Terry Gagnon's harsh attack on the media, a short, pudgy man in an overcoat burst into the lobby with a swish that let in a burst of blizzard. Another man in a black coat followed close behind. The building guard greeted them and pointed to Michael, who stood up and walked toward the man.

"Hi, Frederick Newton?"

"Yes," he said. "Who are you?"

"I'm Michael Cervantes, a reporter from Tindle Bailey newspapers, can I have a moment of your time."

Newton turned to the building security guards.

"Is this the kind of security you guys have here, you just let a reporter sit here and wait for me?"

Both guards immediately stood up and walked around the desk, standing on either side of Michael. The man who had followed Newton into the building now stepped between Michael and Newton.

"Sorry, sir, he made it sound like he was a friend of yours," one of the building guards said. Then he turned to Michael, "sir, please leave the property immediately."

"Ok," he said, "no problem. I just wanted to ask Mr. Newton some questions."

"Not here you won't."

The guards grabbed him each by one arm to escort him out.

"I just wanted to talk to you about Dimmesdale's sexual appetites. They're coming back to haunt him. I know all about Terry Gagnon and the others."

"Wait, wait, wait, just one second," Newton said, forcing the guards to stop. "What others? What are you talking about?"

His breath reeked of Scotch.

"Give me five minutes of your time and I'll tell you, just five minutes. You don't have to say anything, just listen."

Newton gestured at his black-coated companion with his hand, a signal that his personal guard took as a cue to act.

"Do you have ID?" the man said.

"This is my personal security chief, Ivan," Newton said. "This won't hurt a bit."

Michael showed Ivan his press credentials. He snatched them and eyed them closely for a few seconds. Then he handed the ID back to Michael and asked him to raise his arms for a pat down.

"Are you carrying any weapons?" Ivan asked with an Eastern European or Russian accent.

"No," Michael said. "Just my notepad and my recorder."

"Ivan, is that Russian?" Michael asked.

Ivan looked up, insulted. "No, Chechnyan. Not Russian."

Michael nodded apologetically, "oh, cool."

"Alright, let him go," Newton told the guards, including Ivan. "Let's go to one of those couches. This is all off the record unless otherwise stated, clear?"

"Clear," Michael said.

Newton removed his overcoat, revealing a custom-tailored suit and Versace shoes. He directed Michael to one of the couches in the middle of the lobby.

"So what is this about Dimmesdale?" he said. "What do you got?"

"I've been covering his presidential campaign for the past few months," Michael said. "As you've probably noticed, he's pulling ahead of the pack, basically because of his image as a religious, moral candidate."

Newton snorted sarcastically. "Moral my ass."

"Well, exactly," Michael said. "I'm working on a story about an extra-marital relationship he's having."

Newton's eyebrows lifted his forehead into a wrinkled patch.

"You mean currently," Newton said. "With who?"

"Well, look, that's the problem. I know who he's having an affair with. But my editors want me to try to confirm it through a couple of different channels before we run with the story."

"I don't understand," Newton said. "Either he's fucking somebody or he isn't."

"I know. That's how I feel about it too. But my editors feel differently. They want me to try to confirm it through other people."

"I hope you don't mean me. I haven't spoken to Dimmesdale in two years, ever since he ostracized me to make some sort of statement for that Gagnon scrape. I lost a lot of business because of that."

"I know you're fundraising for Carrie Humboldt," Michael said. "I figured you might talk pretty openly to me about Dimmesdale."

"I won't say shit on the record. But off the record, the guy chased tale a few times. I wouldn't go as far as to call him a panting dog or a panty chaser but he fucked around. The Gagnon shit was the one time it blew up in his face."

"Do you still have any connections in Dimmesdale's office, or his campaign?"

"Listen, just because he banned me from his office didn't mean I didn't stay friends with people there. So are you gonna tell me who he's fucking or what?"

"Well, I need you to help me."

"How?" he said.

"Find out through your connections if anyone knows about Dimmesdale's current girlfriend."

"Not a chance," he said. "Dimmesdale was a lot of things, but he wasn't sloppy. He kept his women on the lowdown. Almost no one knew about it. There's no guarantee anyone on his staff even knows about it. And what if it gets back to Dimmesdale that I'm inquiring about his sex life?

Then what?"

"It won't come to that. Look, you were close to Dimmesdale. Closer than most people. You know things about him that the American public should know too. I'm not telling you to find out anything I don't already know. I just need to know if anyone knows or suspects that he has a girlfriend."

"I can't do it, sorry."

"Ok," Michael said, standing up. "Fine. You go back to raising money for Dimmesdale's competitor. Just remember, you could help Carrie Humboldt a lot more by just helping me report the simple truth."

Newton stayed quiet. Michael turned around to walk away.

"Hey, hang on a second. Hang on. Look, I can make a couple of phone calls. See what turns up."

"Can you make them now?"

"Now?! Geez, you are a pushy one."

"Why not," he said. "Now's when everyone's either drinking at bars or in bed watching Fallon. Best time of the day for gossip."

Newton smiled.

"Wait here, I'll come back down in a few."

An hour later, Newton exited the elevator in the lobby. Before he even reached the couch where Michael was sitting, he blurted out "Kristen Dunlop. Am I right or am I right?"

Michael's expression of amazement said it all.

"On the money. How did you do that?"

"Like I said, kid, I have connections. Apparently, the people who travel with Dimmesdale on the campaign have big mouths. They've heard the moaning through the thin walls at all those motels and inns. Its fairly well-rumored in the inner circles that Kristen's his girl."

Michael got up to walk out the lobby, feeling as though he were walking on air.

"Hey, hang on a second," Newton said. "Here's my card. Call me if you need anything else. And remember, this is all off the record."

"Yeah, no problem, thanks for your help."

He made his way to the front of the lobby.

"Hey," Newton yelled out. "Is this Kristen girl hot?"

Michael stopped and turned around with a smile.

"Gorgeous," he said. "Drop dead."

"He always knew how to pick em," Newton said.

Michael returned to his hotel and called Donald, his editor, at home. It was late but at this point he figured Donald didn't care what time it was. He wanted to hear the news. He was old school like that: home phone number, newspapers delivered to his house every day. Sure, he rode the desk and probably flirted with heart disease and anxiety at every meal, but hot news still fluttered his ticker.

It rang a few times before Donald's wife picked up. She put him on the phone.

"I got Newton to confirm on background that Kristen is Dimmesdale's woman. Apparently, a couple of people around the campaign office know about it."

"You need another source," Donald said.

"We're wasting time," Michael said, suddenly growing a pair of balls with Donald. "We should get this story out there before someone else beats us to it."

"Something this sensitive needs to be backed up. Just get one more source."

Just one more source? Who the hell else would or could confirm a thing like that? It's not like he could call Dimmesdale's press secretary and ask her to confirm his affair. When he hung up the phone he felt like slamming it against the hotel door. His energy spiked along with his temper.

Michael called The Miami Tribune's head researcher, Monique Goombley, a Jamaican immigrant who could dig up anything on anyone. Her cell rang twice before she picked up.

"Monique, it's Michael Cervantes, how've you been?"

"Well, Mr. Presidential journalist, how are you?" she said.

"All great. Thanks Monique. Sorry to call so late."

"It's ok, I was just watching TV with my boys."

"I really need your help on something. I need background information on three people, as much as you can give me. This is high priority. It comes from corporate in D.C."

"Ok, who are they?"

"First is Terry Gagnon, second is Frederick Newton, third is Kristen Dunlop," Michael said, giving Monique their dates of birth and what little background he knew.

"Where are they from?"

"Gagnon and Newton are in Illinois," Michael said. "Dunlop is in New Hampshire. But her family lives in South Carolina. She used to live in New York, but went to Duke. I'm not 100% confirmed on all those details."

"Whoa, a real nomad," Monique said. "So what am I looking for?"

"I need friends, criminal and civil records, where they've worked," Michael said.

"How soon do you need it by?"

"As soon as you can," he said.

"May take a day or two," she said. "Things are crazy around here. They laid off Sherry two weeks ago and dumped all her work on me."

"Ok, thanks Monique. Do what you can. Email me what you find."

Michael's flight wasn't scheduled until the next day. He had hours to waste, time burning a hole in his moral fortitude. Wasn't Chicago the backbone of jazz? The city glimmering on the shores of Lake Michigan, embracing with outstretched arms and big shoulders the immigrant traditions of the old world? He checked the drawers in his nightstand: the Bible in one, the phone book in the other. Ah, Chicago, with lust-filled alleys promoting anxiety-busting massages. Beautiful Chicago, a Catholic city built on the sweat of Poles and Italian and Irish laborers. Chicago hawked a bar and a virtuoso busker at every corner.

He bundled up for the frosty walk up Michigan and into the Loop, with the hypnotic sounds of brass instruments surfing the wind.

CHAPTER 19

"Dave, ole buddy," Michael said, slapping their young driver on the back at a campaign appearance back in New Hampshire, "It's great to be back. I missed this place. I missed this assignment. What did I miss these last few days?"

Dave was so happy just to be liked and appreciated that he didn't view Michael's uncharacteristic warmth with suspicion. There was now a full-size Greyhound-style bus tailing Dave everywhere, the invasion of the leading candidate's press corps.

"Not much, really," he said. "After you left, Audra took a day off too, and so did Rachel."

"How about with Dimmesdale? What did I miss?"

He twisted his lips and scrunched his nose, shaking his head slowly. "Nothing," he said. "Stump speeches. Breakfast with Dimmesdale."

His demeanor was so casual that Michael figured he didn't know anything about his interruption of Dimmesdale's sexscapade at the Crystal Inn. He'd be treating Michael like a nuclear waste site if he knew. Just being seen exchanging hellos with Michael at this stage in the game could be enough for Kristen to fire Dave. But the campaign didn't seem like it was in damage control mode, with spinners handling media availabilities, and a flurry of talk-show appearances. Michael made sure Kristen was busy holding a microphone to Dimmesdale's mouth when he talked to Dave.

"You know what I did these last few days? I went to church," Michael told Dave, lowering his voice and bending his head toward the ground in apparent humility. "I felt I needed a dose of God."

Dave's confession to Mafikwa weeks ago that he sometimes fantasized about joining a Trappist Monastery in the spirit of Thomas Merton, to be "liberated by the four walls of freedom" that Merton had so joyfully written about, was fresh in Michael's mind. He could almost picture Dave in a brown Franciscan habit, a white rope wrapped around his waist, the back of his head bald for piety. He carried a clerical astuteness, as though common-folk distractions such as women and hunger were voided by the trappings of his service.

"I crave that all the time," Dave said. "I wish I could go to church more often. God knows I need the spiritual reinforcement on this job."

"You know, I really admire you, Dave. You're a hardworking guy, and you never complain. You're almost stoic in your disposition. How do you do it?"

Dave adjusted his glasses nervously, unused to compliments.

"I don't really think about it," he said. "These last few months have just been a big blur."

"Jeez, me too," Michael said. "Hey do you still go drinking at the Rover every once in a while?"

"We're there like every night," he said. "You should drop by one night. Rachel stopped in a couple of weeks ago."

"Yeah, ok," Michael said. "I was actually thinking of someplace more quiet. After going to Church this week, I started thinking about that conversation we had a few weeks ago about Jesus, and whether his guidance can actually lead us to heaven on earth, or whether his grace can only be received when we die."

Dave looked surprised.

"So, what was your conclusion?"

Michael shrugged. "Still working on it."

"That's a quagmire that even St. Thomas Aquinas struggled to get through. Some think earth is heaven. Some think it's hell. Some think it's a gateway to both."

"I can't really explain how I feel in two minutes. You wanna grab a burger and beer tonight? I could use the company."

"Sure," he said. "The whole crew?"

"Nah," Michael said. "I don't really feel comfortable talking about this kind of thing with the others around. You know."

"Cool, alright," he said. "I can use a change of scenery myself."

Michael made sure to avoid Dave the rest of the day, so as not to attract unwanted attention. He even managed to make eye contact with Kristen at a house party in the early evening. She was standing next to Dimmesdale, her arms and digital voice recorder hanging limply by her side. She stared at him for a moment, letting her head hang slightly to one side, and almost seemed to smile. She wasn't recording Dimmesdale's words because he was just making small talk with cider-sipping voters.

"And it's all about reaching out to the people we've alienated in the world," Dimmesdale was saying. "Our nation is stronger and deeper than any single president. Our ties to our allies and our friends can't be broken by the whims of one poor leader. Just as the bible points out in Deuteronomy, chapter 17, 'do not turn aside from what they tell you, to the right, or to the left.' I believe our president has chosen to alienate half his country and half the world by taking a hard turn to the right at the expense of moderation."

Dimmesdale unexpectedly turned, running into Michael. He quickly shed the serious look Michael's presence triggered, and smiled.

"Hi there, Michael," he said. "We missed you these last couple of days. Welcome back."

"Thank you, Governor, it's great to be back," he said.

"Good, good, GREAT!" he said, then quickly embraced the hand of the man standing next to Michael.

Later in the van, Michael threw a question out there.

"Do any of you ever wonder whether Dimmesdale likes you?" he said.

Rachel, who was sitting in the front seat, turned around.

"I think he does," she said. "He recognizes that we have a job to do and treats us with relative respect."

"Respect?" Mafikwa said. "That's not what I call hauling us around all day without a food stop."

"That's not his fault," Rachel said. "Blame his campaign people, not him."

Audra lifted her head from the seat, where it had been resting.

"Why do you ask, Michael?" Audra said. "You think Dimmesdale doesn't like you?"

"No, it's not that," he said. "It's just that I noticed he treats everybody exactly the same. So I find it impossible to read his judgment of people."

Mafikwa shook her head.

"Dimmesdale definitely does not treat everybody the same," Mafikwa said. "If he did, we'd all have exclusive interviews with him, we'd all be invited to breakfast at his apartment. We'd all get pulled aside by him at campaign appearances and thanked for stories."

Whitney stopped her incessant typing.

"Yeah, but that doesn't mean Dimmesdale likes you or doesn't," Whitney said. "He's just behaving in relation to the power or influence each of us wields at a given moment."

"That's definitely part of it, but Mafikwa's right," Audra said. "He definitely has favorites. I can tell when Dimmesdale likes somebody. Like for example, I think he loves you, Rachel."

"Really? I don't feel that way."

"Oh, come on," Mafikwa said. "He nudges you affectionately when he walks by you. He chats it up in Latin with you. Remember the time he gave you a box of chocolates?"

"Yeah, but that's just because we have a common culture," she said. "That's all."

"Even people who look like they act the same with everybody really don't," said Audra. "You might not notice right at the beginning, but they drop small signals of how they really feel. With Dimmesdale, I can tell he doesn't like somebody when he hogs the conversation without coming up for air because he doesn't want to hear what the other person is saying. Like remember that time when a guy at a house party asked him whether the Israeli military should be considered a state-sponsored terrorist organization, and Dimmesdale just talked and talked and talked until he spun around and took another question?"

"Yeah, yeah, now that you mention it," Michael said. "I see some of the subtlety."

Dave piped in from the drivers seat.

"I feel the same way Michael does," he said. "I can't tell if Dimmesdale likes someone or not. I think all you women are at an advantage because you possess the ever-insightful women's intuition and tend to be better interpreters of facial expressions and voice tones. That goes right over most guy's heads."

"Damn, Dave, you been reading your Cosmo," Mafikwa said. "Gloria Steinem couldn't have said it better herself."

"So let's give it up for women journalists on the trail," Rachel said, doing a little celebratory dance.

By the time Dave pulled into the hotel entrance, the conversation had died down and everyone seemed tired. They quietly filed out of the van. Michael was the last one out because he had been sitting in the back row. He waited for the women to walk away. Then Dave spoke up before he said anything.

"Hey, uh, are you tired, or you still wanna go grab that burger?" he said.

"Well, I am kind of tired, but what the heck, let's do it. Go park over there while I put my stuff away inside. I'll be right out."

He caught up with the rest of the press corps in the elevator. Audra asked about eating.

"Anybody wanna grab a bite?" she said.

"I'd love to, but I just don't want to walk in this weather," Whitney said.

"Let's order a pizza or something," Rachel said.

The elevator door opened on the second floor. Michael got out without saying a word. Rachel, who was staying on his floor, got out too.

"I'll call you," Rachel said.

"Good night, Michael," Audra said.

He nodded a swift goodbye. Silence is the best defense. He dropped his laptop on the bed, waited to make sure Rachel was in her room, then quickly exited and dashed for the stairs. The lobby was empty as he made his way back to the van.

"Did the others say anything about coming along?" Dave said.

"It never came up."

"Cool. You have anyplace in mind?"

"I hear Fritz and Franz has a mean beer burger."

"You know, I've been wanting to try that place."

CHAPTER 20

Fritz and Franz smelled and sounded like a true beer joint. Cigarette smoke from the bar area gave the room a hazy glow. Polka music and rock and roll took turns scribbling out of the speakers. All the blue collar Joes who dodged the preppies and political wonks at the Rover during campaign season seemed to have gravitated here: lots of bandanas on balding heads and mid-height, steel-toed boots. Plumbers, tile layers, factory grunts.

"What do you think?" Dave said, nervously eyeing the crowd.

"Perfect," Michael said.

Dave, who always seemed invisible to Michael, suddenly stood out in the crowd. As did Michael. So they picked a table off to the side, in a darker part of the bar, away from the boozed up hustlers shooting eight ball. A middle-aged waitress with her hair in a bun and her buns in a skirt two sizes too tight took their order.

"I'll have a scotch," Michael said. "Single malt, if you've got it."

Dave jerked his head back, as though Michael had reached across the table to slap him.

"Wow, that's the heavy stuff."

"It was Thomas Merton's drink of choice. Pure. Mythical. I would even say biblical."

Dave smiled wickedly, his eyebrows nudged up a couple of times, his way of sending a message that he was about to do something crazy.

"I'll have the same," he said, without breaking eye contact with Michael, still brandishing that devilish smile.

The waitress brought the first round.

"To Merton," Michael said.

"Indeed," Dave said.

They drank in unison.

"I didn't realize you were familiar with Merton," Dave said. "He's a fascinating figure."

"Which part?" he said. "The four walls of his new freedom? Or his wayward youth?"

"Merton is one of my inspirations for studying religion," Dave said. "Not so much because I'm such a devout Roman Catholic. But because his passion for seeking an inner truth led him to such an extreme. You know, he said that the more you try to avoid suffering, the more you suffer, because smaller and more insignificant things begin to torture you, in proportion to your fear of being hurt. The one who does the most to avoid suffering is, in the end, the one who suffers most."

"That's just Buddhist revisionism, "Michael said. "In Buddhism, desire and ignorance lie at the root of suffering."

Dave let it sink in for a moment, sipping his single-malt rather confidently.

"Buddhists refer to craving pleasure, material goods, and immortality, all of which are wants that can never be satisfied. And so they can only bring suffering."

Michael thought of the Buddhism an ex-girlfriend practiced. She had turned him on to Kerouac in college.

"Ignorance is worse than desire," Michael said. "Because it means you don't see the world as it actually is. Without the ability to focus and look inward, one's mind is left undeveloped. So vices, like greed, envy hatred, anger. They all come from this ignorance. Without ignorance, politicians wouldn't be able to lie to people and get away with it, like they do every day. The world would be a better place."

"Merton said political problems aren't solved by love and mercy. Besides,' his lasting legacy is his incredible retreat from the world to live a pious, thoughtful life. I mean, I couldn't do it."

"What, you don't fantasize about dropping out of this great world we live in and hiding out in a Trappist monastery for a couple of years?" Michael said.

"He wasn't hiding. That's the whole point. It was self-discovery."

"There are many ways to skin that cat, my friend. And most of them don't require a vow of silence and poverty."

Dave paused for a moment, and swished the whiskey around in his glass.

"I guess what's alluring is that Merton sacrificed everything for his beliefs."

"Not if you consider the fame his book brought him, and how his self-discovery functioned as a tool to propel him to literary stardom. Who wouldn't sacrifice a couple of years with monks for that kind of reward?"

Dave laughed. Michael did to.

"Right?"

"Well, he didn't do it for the fame. He struggled with it his whole life. You know he used to get fan mail, and he would dutifully answer each letter?"

The waitress returned to check on them.

"I'll have another."

Dave nodded, "yep."

"Do you think life today is any more complicated than it was back then?" Dave asked.

"Yes I do," Michael said. "The way Dimmesdale makes it sound, we're facing the apocalypse."

Dave shook his head.

"Back when Merton decided to enter the monastery, World War II was raging. Communism and Fascism were spreading across the globe. Democracy was under serious attack, the very concept that our nation was founded on. Our president was severely handicapped. We were at the tail end of an economic depression. Today, things are not that bad."

"It depends on how you look at it. We are now the only superpower on the planet. Which means that by default, we are the enemy. We've never faced a planet where we weren't the underdog."

"What's so great about being the underdog?"

"People root for the underdog. They help the underdog. The world always conspires against power."

"Not if the power is benevolent. Not if it's for the greater good."

"There's a few million Iraqis who would argue that we are not acting for the greater good," Michael said.

Dave didn't answer. His eyes were wandering away, toward a moving object behind Michael. He turned around to see a woman removing a thick parka, and stamping the snow out of her feet. When he looked back at Dave, he raised his eyebrows in acknowledgement of her beauty.

"How do you think Merton coped with that," Michael said, tilting his head toward the woman.

"I don't know," Dave said.

"I bet he jerked off so much he grew hair on his palms."

Dave laughed. "Sometimes I feel like I'm better off being away from women. It doesn't seem so strange to me that Merton could handle that."

"Not me," Michael said. "I love my wife. I love women. Everything about them. I don't think I could handle a year or two away from women. Maybe Merton was gay."

Dave was incensed.

"He wasn't gay!" Dave snorted. "He was a womanizer before he converted to Catholicism, a philistine."

"Well, that's what he claimed anyway. Did anybody ever concur that?"

"Hey, what, do you think I'm gay because I'm religious?" Dave asked.

"No, of course not," Michael said. "Why, are you?"

"NO!"

Pure indignation brushed over Dave's face.

"I know you're not, I know. I've seen you checking out the hottie interns."

Dave eased up and smiled.

"I figure you can take your pick of them. A good-looking guy like you who's in charge of the press corps? I bet the interns think you're a stud."

The waitress came back and they ordered another round, this time with a beer chaser. After that, Michael felt buzzed. Dave, who was barely half his size, must have been feeling it too. They downed that round, then another, until Michael sensed Dave was slurring his speech. They hadn't ordered any dinner.

"So who would you bang on Dimmesdale's staff?" Michael asked.

Dave shrugged.

"Oh, come on," he said. "How about that chick, Vicky? She's pretty hot."

"Yeah, she is kinda cute, but she's got a boyfriend."

"I'm not asking if you'd marry her, man."

After a few drinks, the Miami slang came back to Michael. He was calling Dave "man" and "bro" every few sentences. But Dave was so sauced he didn't pick up on it.

"You know who's hot?" Michael said. "Kristen. She is fine."

Dave nodded but didn't say anything.

"Don't you think?"

"O yeah," Dave said. "She is beautiful. But…"

"What, she's got a boyfriend too?"

Dave chuckled and took a sip of his whiskey. His eyebrows shot up again.

"Something like that," he said.

"You don't have to be so mysterious, man, everybody knows she's the boss's lady."

Any evidence of a buzz that Dave exhibited suddenly flushed out of his system. He grew very nervous and started rubbing his palms on his knees. He didn't know what to say.

"What?" he said.

"Everybody knows they go at it in the motels. Come on. The walls are thin, man. People hear shit. Everybody knows. All these candidates fuck around. You should hear what the say about Kane. I hear he likes boys."

Dave shook his head, as though Michael had just broken the news to him that his mother had passed away.

"They think it's a big secret," Dave said. "I thought I was the only one who heard them."

Michael used every remote trace of willpower to keep his eyes and face from giving away his excitement. He swallowed and steadied his breath.

"Are you kidding?" he said, shrugging his shoulders as though it was old news. "I heard a motel maid heard em. And later on someone else. Anyway, who cares. Whatever. I don't think it matters. You spend enough time in one of these campaigns, and you'll chase whatever tail crosses in front of you."

Dave looked like he had tears in his eyes. He dry-heaved.

"Hey, hey, the bathroom's right over there," Michael said.

Dave sprung up and dashed across the bar. Michael tossed a 50 on the table and waited for Dave to come out.

"I'm okay," he said, as he exited the bathroom a few minutes later. "I just get sick when I think about how stupid he is."

"Who, Dimmesdale?" Michael asked, as they shuffled out of the joint.

"He's got everything going for him," Dave said. "I didn't want to believe the sounds I heard. I thought he had cramps or they were doing exercise. That's what I kept telling myself. Please, don't tell anybody about this conversation."

Michael didn't respond. As he exited, Michael heard Dave call his name.

"Michael," he said. "Please."

CHAPTER 21

"And he said it on the record?" Donald asked again.

"Well, he said it in a casual conversation. It wasn't a formal interview."

"Where'd you get him to talk?"

Michael hesitated, not sure of how Donald would react to the setting of his conversation with Dave.

"At a bar," he said. "We had been drinking."

Michael heard a distant hoot on the other end of the line, as though Donald had held the phone away to yell for his favorite team scoring a touchdown.

"O my God," he said. "That is just incredible. Does he realize you're going to quote him?"

"He asked me not to later on, but I didn't commit to anything."

"And you said this guy is 23."

"Yep."

"Well, he can kiss his job goodbye. Poor kid will never work another campaign again."

"Um, Donald, I gotta ask you something, because it's kind of gnawing at me."

"What is it?"

"Do we really have to do this? I mean, does it really matter?"

"Of course it matters," he said. "This man is running on a platform of virtuosity and righteousness, which will now be debunked. If we don't break this story, somebody else will, with that kid blabbing all over town about it."

Michael muttered something in defense of Dave, but Donald was already on to the next order of business.

"I'm calling a meeting with Tindle-Bailey executives this afternoon. I think it's necessary to brace them for what's coming."

Call waiting buzzed Michael's phone. He looked. It was his wife calling. He ignored it.

"What's next for me?" he asked.

"Write your story immediately, without the quotes from the girl and Dimmesdale. Then, you gotta interview them. My advice is to talk to Dimmesdale first because you don't want this girl to tip him off. Then you plug in the quotes and we run with it. If it's no comment then no comment. ASAP."

Call waiting buzzed again. He blew it off.

"Hey, can you get a picture of this girl? What does she look like?"

"I don't know, she's pretty good looking. About 35 years his junior. Maybe I can snap a shot without raising suspicions."

"So she's a looker?"

"I guess that's fair to say. I'll keep you posted."

Michael was in his Manchester hotel room. He had blown off the press van to make the phone call to Donald in the morning, but now he had to catch up to them. Once again claiming his independence, he rented a car and located the campaign around noon at a local bakery where Dimmesdale was scheduled to wax on "kitchen table economics" with emphasis on small business owners.

The place was packed. People had jammed up against the door from the outside, even in the bitter cold, to hear what Dimmesdale had to say.

Parked nearby, Michael waited in his car until the crowd started dispersing, then he approached the front of the store. Almost immediately, Dimmesdale walked out and shook hands with a woman standing right next to him. He avoided eye contact with Michael and turned to someone else in the crowd. Michael's stomach clenched up and he felt a slight jolt of nervous nausea jitter him from the inside. This was it.

"Governor!" he started, taking a step forward.

In the crowd, Dimmesdale strategically squeezed between a father and son and stood behind them, using them as a buffer. Michael tried to push past the boy, but the boy elbowed him near the crotch.

"Michael, hey, where've you been, man? You missed it."

It was Mafikwa. She patted Michael on the shoulder.

"Hey, you ok? You look pale."

"Fine," Michael said, his eyes fixed on Dimmesdale.

"Dimmesdale bought everyone bagels," she said. "Really good."

Audra followed close behind. She walked around and stood next to Michael.

"Are you sweating?" Audra asked.

"No, I'm fine."

More people gravitated toward Dimmesdale, competing with Michael for his attention. There was no way to get to Dimmesdale without physically pushing people out of the way. Whitney walked out, her audio recorder in her hand. Dimmesdale contorted around a large housewife just as his ride pulled up a few feet away. A campaign staffer put his arm around Dimmesdale and shielded him. Michael pushed against the few people that stood between them, bumping a man on the back of his arm, and another woman on her breast. Michael prepared to shout his questions, even at the great cost of alerting his competitors to the scoop. He put the notebook down by his side, and arched his back, his chin tipping skyward.

"Governor!" he yelled. "Governor, a quick question."

But there was no reaction from Dimmesdale, who pretended not to hear him. The governor cut off the exalting praise that some soccer mom was bestowing on him just as Michael pushed around the last two people between them.

"Governor, we're running a story about your relationship with Kristen Dunlop," Michael managed to half-yell. "Governor what do you have to say about it?"

The governor's bodyguard stood next to him. Dimmesdale used him as a body check and ducked into his car, with Michael right behind him.

"Governor! Governor! Is that a no-comment?"

The door slammed. The transmission clicked into drive. The engine rumbled. Michael's story eluded him in a grind of ice and a belch of steam from the exhaust.

"FUCK!" Michael said, swinging the notebook at the street.

The others in the press corps were nearby, but apparently had not heard Michael.

"It's been crazy today," Whitney said, suspicion in her eyes. "Kristen called in sick, so we're dealing with some neophyte flack. What was that all about?"

Michael ignored Whitney and glanced around, his teeth clenched and his hand crushing his notepad.

Dave walked out of the store and seemed surprised to see Michael.

"So, you decided to join us?" he said.

"Where's Kristen?" Michael said.

"Out sick," Dave said. "Family emergency."

What bullshit! Michael spun around and hurried back to his car.

CHAPTER 22

Michael left two messages on Kristen's cell phone. As he sped toward Dimmesdale's next campaign spot, his phone rang. Kristen's name appeared on the screen. He held the phone to his chest and let it ring a few times. He answered it while still in that position, and slowly raised the phone to his ear. It occurred to Michael that he never planned how to talk to Kristen during this interview. He turned into the first side street and swerved the car against the curb, parking it under the varicose limbs of an elm. A bundled-up housewife walking a cocker spaniel on the sidewalk frowned at him.

"Hey," Michael said, answering the call. "I have to talk to you."

"I called in sick today because I had to take care of some personal things. Do you remember where I live?"

"Um, don't you live in the same apartment complex as Dimmesdale?"

"Yes, unit 319. It's 12:30 now. Come over at 2:30 so we can talk."

"Kristen, I have to ask you a few things right now. I just pulled my car over to talk to you."

"Michael. Look. I know I've been a little cold to you lately. I haven't exactly treated you fairly. I promise I'll give you the time you need this afternoon. I promise. We need to bury the hatchet."

"But Kristen."

Michael heard a click on the line.

"Michael, I'm getting another call," Kristen said. "I gotta go. 2:30. My place!"

The heat had kicked in, washing Michael's face with warm air. He shut off the engine and sat in the suburban stillness, staring straight ahead. As soon as the engine stopped, the air began to turn icy. Kristen's proposition had created a complication for Michael. Dimmesdale's next event was in Concord, the state capital, which was about 45 minutes away. A round-trip would consume an hour and a half plus the length of the event. Dimmesdale always showed up a few minutes late and never fielded questions until after he was done speaking. If Michael went after Dimmesdale, he risked losing Kristen at 2:30.

Instead of chasing Dimmesdale, Michael decided to play it safe and return to the hotel. He opened his closet, ransacking it for the dressiest shirt he could find. He had three dress shirts, including the one he was wearing. The blue and white-striped Brooks Brothers shirt was wrinkled and badly needed dry-cleaning. The only other choice was a white Calvin Klein with double-button cuffs that fit Michael snug around the neck. It would have to do. He laid it out on the bed, and stretched a striped Hugo Boss tie, which was blue and brown, next to it. He showered, combed his hair, and changed into the fresh clothes.

He flipped on the television. CNT was broadcasting live from the Dimmesdale event. Few candidates received live coverage of events. Only the front-runners, and only during the lull of the news cycle. There were at least 200 people crammed into the small auditorium of Helmsley Private Academy, where Dimmesdale planned to deliver another "values" speech.

As Michael tugged his socks back on, Dimmesdale started talking. A few formalities later, he got to the point.

"And just where is this country heading? We must ask ourselves this question, so that we can see the answer clearly. Our constitution and our founding fathers separated religion and politics, and rightly so. But that doesn't mean that our Christian values cannot be a guiding light for us in these turbulent times. Just as Christian values were a guiding principle for our nation's founders as they drafted and wrangled over the document that would become our guiding principle, they must now be a pillar on which we lean for support.

"When I was growing up, my father taught me the importance of faith. It helped him through his own challenges, and he explained that it would do the same for me. I ask you, when a president must reflect and seek spiritual guidance, where do you want him to turn? To a background of confusion and religious ambiguity, or to a solid Christian belief, with Jesus at the center, and his teachings as the guide?"

This was the most overtly religious speech that Dimmesdale had given yet. It would make for a mention in the news, Michael suspected.

"Our faith should not be viewed as a threat, but rather as a blessing. Our faith preaches tolerance, and I embrace that. There are some who have hijacked the teachings of Jesus for their own political gain, who have used their Christian platforms to create division among Americans, and polarize people along fault lines of morality. But I am not one of those people. To me, the Christ of the bible was a radical, revolutionary figure. The tent he pitched for his religion was all-inclusive. He brought in the prostitutes and tax collectors, the fishermen and the farmers. Jesus forgave and healed. He offered a path forward in a dark world. Who else would you have your president turn to for guidance and answers? I am running for office as a man who happens to be Christian. To me that means family first, making sure the underprivileged are treated fairly and given the same opportunities as others. Defending our country against our enemies, who hate us as much for our religion as our politics. This campaign is about serving the American people with a little humility. Not the arrogance and elitism which Washington offers up again and again. It's about going back to our roots, our faith, and our values."

Michael clicked off the television and left his hotel room. His phone rang as he got into his rental car: Monique, the researcher from The Miami Tribune.

"Monique, what's up?"

"Ok, I've got some information for you, Michael. It seems Terry Gagnon and Kristen Dunlop both have some sort of sealed criminal records. Gagnon's is in Cook County, Chicago. Dunlop's is in Washington D.C. She was tough to find. I had to do a national background check on her. And here's the catch: Newton was both of their attorneys for their criminal cases."

"Newton was their attorney?" Michael said. "What were the charges?"

"The only way to get those is to either go through the FBI, or ask them," Monique said. "The courthouse won't unseal a file. Listen, there's more on Newton."

"Ok, what?"

"He's former Army intelligence, served two tours in Vietnam. I got that little doozy from an alumni archive at the University of Chicago. He's a lawyer and lobbyist. He has his own firm called SilverLake. His big clients are the oil and gas industries, the big polluters. And he's one of the biggest fundraisers for the Democratic Party. There's an anonymous blogger called "The Ghost of Mike Royko" and some people think it's Newton. I've read some of his posts, mostly political rants. His last one bashes Dimmesdale."

Michael pulled up in front of Kristen's apartment.

"Thank Monique, this is great. I gotta go."

"Check your email," she said. "I sent you a bunch of material."

Michael knocked on Kristen's door at 2:28. He had a notebook in his left pocket, and an audio recorder in his right. The lock on the front door clicked, and Kristen pushed the door slightly ajar.

"Come in, I'm watching the end of the Concord event," she said, walking down the short hallway and into her living room, where she paused in front of the television, one hand on her hip, and the other clutching the remote control.

Michael pushed open the front door and watched Kristen walk away. She didn't so much as glance back. With a single sniff of the air inside her apartment, his mission tumbled into confusion. The infamous vanilla perfume that had played so central a role in Michael's earlier moral hiccup hit him like a neurotoxin. He ambled inside, his mouth beginning to salivate, a nauseating knot forming deep in his gut. Kristen was wearing a baby pink, cable knit hoody jacket made of what looked like Cashmere wool. From the angle she was standing, Michael could see that the sweater was V-necked, with kangaroo pockets and ribbing along the trim. And toward the bottom of the V, that unmistakable insignia of temptation: a sliver of cleavage. Kristen's hair was loose and hanging down on her shoulders. Her white skirt hugged the shape of her body and reached her knees. Strapped to her feet at the bottom were a pair of red Belicia slide sandals, sans socks, evidence that she was not planning on leaving her apartment anytime soon.

"You think this will make news?" she said, watching the footage of Dimmesdale shaking hands with voters.

That snapped Michael back to the business at hand. He joined her in the living room and stood next to her, his eyes now fixed on the television.

"I think so," he said. "I stopped watching it after the first couple of minutes, but from what I remember, his speech had more religious overtones than usual."

Kristen shut off the television, but remained looking forward. Suddenly, there was no more distraction or small talk. She placed the remote control gingerly on top of the entertainment unit. She turned toward Michael and slowly raised her eyes toward him.

"I, um, I'm sorry about the way I've been treating you," she said.

The resolve that had carried him over the last few days vanished.

This was a side of Kristen he had never seen before. Her tone was so quiet, so surrendered, so incredibly feminine. Almost a whisper. She raised one forearm across her sternum, elbow bent, and grabbed her other arm with her hand, squeezing her chest tightly together, a salient stimuli.

"It's ok," Michael said. "I understand."

"I have real feelings for you, Michael," she said. "I...I made a mistake."

She whimpered the word "mistake". Her lower lip quivered as she opened her mouth to speak again. But only a weak sigh escaped. She hung her head and raised her left hand up to rub and support her forehead. Her right hand was supporting her left elbow, squeezing her chest together again.

Hearing the sigh, Michael stepped forward and gently embraced Kristen. His hands caressed her back and he pressed her against his chest. Her scent quickly corroded his last professional defenses, sending million-year-old evolution-triggered signals racing from his nostrils to his amygdala.

Soon there was no professional mission at hand for Michael. Kristen hugged him back, slithering her arms underneath his coat. He caressed her hair, so soft and lush. He felt her breasts acutely against his ribcage. She tilted her head to look up at Michael's face, and a moment later he kissed her softly. Her lips were softer than the last time they had kissed, a consequence Michael attributed to true emotion and warmth. Suddenly she pulled back.

"Michael, what are we doing? We shouldn't."

By this time, Michael's brain had been hijacked by natural impulses. The blood had rushed below his waist.

"I can't control my feelings for you," he said. "You're all I think about. Day and night."

"But Michael, you're married. This is wrong."

Dimmesdale was married too, Michael almost blurted out. But instead, he stepped toward Kristen again, taking her by the hand. She didn't resist.

"I don't think about my wife when I'm with you," he said. "I watch you when you're working, the way you push your hair behind one ear when you're stressed, the way you walk, the way you glance over at me when you think I'm not looking."

She locked eyes with him again.

"I don't want you to know that I care about you. But I do."

Michael tugged her hand toward him, and placed another kiss on her mouth when she lurched forward. He grabbed her by the back of the head, and pressed her face into his. Her mouth opened slightly for the first time, her tongue brushing Michael's upper lip with hot saliva. Michael instinctively opened his own mouth and their kiss became deeper.

The hand behind Kristen's head made its way down to her neck. Kristen pushed back Michael's coat and removed it without breaking the kiss. Once the coat dropped on the floor behind Michael, his hands clasped her waist. He spun Kristen around and moved his hands up her sweater from behind, his lips coming to rest on the neck just below her ear. A hand slid into the V of Kristen's sweater and Michael's middle finger passed over her nipple, which swelled to his touch. She exhaled loudly and pulled Michael's head into her neck, the apparent source of the perfume. Michael pulled Kristen's sweater over her head.

She sat down on the couch and pulled Michael over by the belt buckle, undoing it quickly in front of her. Still standing, Michael kicked off his shoes and dropped his pants, giving her access.

After a few minutes, she led Michael by the hand to her bedroom. He followed her fully erect, and stood next to the bed as she went down on him from a seated position. He bent her over, pushing her panties aside, and licking her from behind. Kristen stopped for a moment, and moved over about 3 feet to the center of her bed. This gave her a chance to remove her panties and show Michael a clear target. She glared at Michael, and he responded. He pounded her for about six minutes on her back, then she climbed on top of him and grinded him to oblivion, her hair and breasts hanging over his face. It ended with a sloppy pull-out and semen exploding all over Kristen's ass and thighs.

She collapsed onto the bed and the two of them stared at the ceiling, catching their breath.

Michael spoke first. The spell had been broken.

"I came to talk to you about Dimmesdale," he said.

Kristen sighed, got up, and went into the bathroom, shutting the door. Michael got up too, and heard the water running inside. He placed his hand on the doorknob, but changed his mind before he opened it and started looking for his clothes, which were scattered around the apartment. He collected the garments – black briefs, undershirt, button-down shirt, pants, belt, shoes. Then he noticed that he had never taken off his socks. As he started putting on his clothes, Kristen exited the bathroom wrapped in a white robe.

"What do you want from me, Michael?"

"I want a comment from you."

"What for?"

"I'm writing a story about your relationship with Dimmesdale."

"No you're not," she said. "There's nothing to write."

"Kristen, I spent the last few days getting witnesses to confirm your relationship with Dimmesdale. Other people know about it."

Kristen pulled open a drawer and pulled out a pair of underwear. She didn't break stride, or recoil as he had expected when he dropped that bomb. She sat at the edge of her bed and pulled the panties on. Michael suddenly doubted himself.

"What other people, Michael?" Kristen said as she pulled on her panties. "It sounds like someone's taking you for a ride."

Michael stepped forward aggressively.

"Cut the bullshit, Kristen. We're running with the story. This is a presidential campaign we're talking about. Dimmesdale is preaching about morals and Jesus, and he's carrying on an affair with you. That's newsworthy."

Kristen reached for the sweater she had been wearing earlier, and pulled it on again. Soon she was fully dressed, except for her shoes.

"It's not newsworthy if it isn't true," she said. "You've got no proof."

"Two witnesses," Michael said.

"Who are they?"

"They're solid. I promised one anonymity..."

Kristen suddenly seemed interested and looked up at Michael.

"Who's the other one?"

Michael took a deep breath.

"Dave," he said. "He's heard you in several motels."

"Clipper?" laughed Kristen. "Please! He's wound so tight he imagined the whole thing."

She got up as though the whole thing had been resolved, but Michael noticed that she kept her face turned away from his. Her movements became more rushed and random, rearranging a decoration here, looking under a pillow there, flipping on the television. Until finally she stopped and looked at Michael with the same severe face that she had been flashing him all week.

"Ok, Michael, if you are moving forward with a story, I have no comment because it is a fabrication. But I don't know what kind of story you can write without asking the governor himself. No editor in the world will run with a story like that without letting the accused at least respond."

"Kristen, I've done my due diligence on you too," Michael said. "I know you were arrested in Washington D.C. and that Frederick Newton was your lawyer."

That rattled her. Her entire tone changed: pure defensive, high pitched.

"What? You've been snooping around my background? How dare you? I've done nothing wrong."

"What happened in Washington?" Michael said.

Kristen walked calmly to the front door, opened it, and held it there for Michael.

"Please leave. I have nothing more to say."

As Michael passed her, they looked at each other. His eyes conveyed fear and uncertainty. Hers wore a slight smile.

Within two minutes of getting into his car, Michael's phone buzzed with a new Tweet from the Dimmesdale campaign. The governor's appearance at a house party that night had been canceled because the governor had an upset stomach. That was the last event that Michael had been counting on to get a comment from Dimmesdale. Kristen had been correct on that point. Without putting the question to the governor himself, there could be no story published.

Michael ran his hand roughly over his forehead and hair.

"What the fuck am I doing?" he said out loud in his car. He dialed his editor. Donald had been expecting his call and picked up.

"Donald, I talked to Kristen, but she denied the affair, even after I told her about the witnesses."

"How about Dimmesdale?"

"I couldn't get to Dimmesdale. I managed to yell out a question while he was jumping into his car that I needed to ask him about his relationship with Kristen, but he just slammed the car door and took off. I was planning on catching up with him tonight, but he canceled tonight's event two minutes after I questioned Kristen."

"God damn it!" Donald yelled. He was furious. "I already talked to Tindle Bailey big-wigs. They're expecting something tomorrow. Now they have time to change their minds."

The scandal would be contained another day.

CHAPTER 23

For what seemed like a long time, Michael sat on the edge of his bed, bent over, his head in his hands. His breathing became increasingly more shallow, as adrenaline rushed downriver in his veins. His eyes darted around the carpet. His face twitched. A deep breath invaded his lungs. He sat up and reached for the bible.

There: the book of Job. Satan had inflicted painful sores from head to toe on Job. Fuck Job. He tossed the bible on the bed and reached for his phone. The distraction seemed stale.

Michael turned on the television and scanned network and cable news outlets. They were all primary, all the time. Dimmesdale dominated the day's breaking news. His emphasis on religious rhetoric and moralizing was paying off.

CNT: George Dimmesdale is shooting up in the polls in early

primary states as potential voters respond to his new emphasis on moral values.

MSNBC: A new front-runner is emerging in the competitive Democratic presidential race. New polls show George Dimmesdale leading his rivals just a few weeks shy of the New Hampshire primary. The reason: moral values and his emphasis on the middle class.

BCN: The ever shifting ground in the democratic primary has shifted again, and the shake-up has Illinois Governor George Dimmesdale riding high atop the field. In just two short weeks he has jumped up two spots in New Hampshire from third to first. Pollsters say his new emphasis on religion and moral values are resonating with potential voters.

Michael scanned the websites of the major news outlets. They all carried headlines announcing Dimmesdale's momentum.

TNY: Dimmesdale moves up in polls

MH: Dimmesdale shoots past rivals!

FXN: Dimmesdale rises, but rivals pounce:

Even the satire website, CDD, piled on: God Thanks Dimmesdale after Dimmesdale Drugs Voters with God BS!

He checked twitter. Buzz @ #Dimmesdale. Good buzz. Ditto #georgeismore2015. Senior Dem operative @magsalore forewent discretion and declared victory was now imminent for Dimmesdale @ #DimWins. GOP gawkers and talkers countered that dems were undecided and divided @ #NoWinDim. Dimmesdale's campaign led the charge with @dimmesdale2015 declaring a sure victory when New Hampshirites voted #leadingthepack @CDDNews said: Dimmesdale's Viagra Use Paying Off! @ #DimsDong

Fuck, they were anointing the bastard already! They might as well skip the fucking primary and declare him the nominee already.

Adrenaline crash triggered a headache. Michael's hypothalamic-pituitary-adrenal axis secreted the battery acid named cortisol into his bloodstream. Nausea tickled his throat.

Michael went dark: doubts about his abilities, qualifications and competencies dominated all.

"What the fuck am I doing?" he said out loud. "I was so out of my league from the beginning in this job."

The phone buzzed in Michael's hand. Bianca, his wife, on the other end. He held the phone and stared at it. The rings cycled through. His breathing ticked up again. Heaves now. One after the other. Then a swift exhale and a sniffle. Michael's eyes watered. It was unfamiliar turf for him, sobbing.

But it didn't last long. The phone buzzed again. Michaels thumb twitched across the screen. Dimmesdale's daily calendar had been released. His first appearance: the foyer of a startup in Manchester called SignalTech at 7:30 am.

Michael stood up, quickly dressed himself, and headed to the lobby, where some fresh faces were waiting with the usual press corps members. Dave usually picked up the press corps around 7:15.

But it wasn't Dave. Some lad named McBride turned up instead in Dave's van.

"Where's Dave?" Whitney asked.

"Clipper's sick. I'm your driver today. Let's go."

The wary journalists piled in. Space was tight inside. The windows fogged up immediately.

"That's weird," Whitney said. "Dave's never sick."

They arrived at SignalTech just as Dimmesdale climbed the steps to the riser he was using as a stage. Kristen was standing at the bottom of the steps. The SignalTech offices were inside an old converted mill, and this was the open floor plan area that doubled as a grand lobby.

During Dimmesdale's speech, Michael jockeyed for position near the side of the riser. Kristen was just a few feet away. The same inflection points in Dimmesdale's speech hit the regular cycle of applause and cheers. The crowd in the room loved it. Michael could only note how false and shallow this whole business of running for president really was.

The speech ended. Dimmesdale smiled and raised his arms, basking in the admiring applause. Kristen made an unexpected move toward Michael and took him by the arm. He didn't resist. She unfolded her laptop on a windowsill, next to a curtain. The screen came to life. A video had been prompted. Kristen pressed play.

Upon seeing the first seconds of the footage Kristen urgently wanted to show him, Michael thought instinctively that she had recorded it for kicks. She had somehow captured yesterday's tryst on digital video. There he was on her laptop screen, debuting on amateur porn, hanging his head back as Kristen squatted before him, his pants sagging by his ankles.

"What...?" he said smiling nervously, turning the computer screen away from the people near them. "Not the appropriate place."

Guilt had already kept him awake half the night, tossing him about on his mattress with a head full of regret. Now his sin was on instant replay in public.

Kristen just stared at the screen:

Her breasts and long hair brush Michael's face; his hands massage her thighs, a flip-over, the beginning of a short missionary spasm. And there was sound too, just mumbles of pillow talk at this low volume.

He looked at Kristen, not sure what to think. He mumbled some words.

Kristen said "I own you." She gave him a flash drive and left him standing by the window, staring at the device in his hand.

He looked down at the palm of his hand, where this piece of modern technology harbored truths that he never intended to go beyond Kristen and God. Who else would receive a copy? His boss? His wife? Kristen hadn't gone deep into detail. For all Michael knew, the U.S. Postal Service was rushing copies to Miami and Washington, poised to deliver his ruin. Maybe it was just a matter of touching the "send" button with a link to the video on a server somewhere.

Michael's mind plunged into the clear waters of hindsight. He should have smelled a trap yesterday. Kristen had lured him to her apartment under the auspice of "clearing the air." She just wanted to have a relaxed conversation over a story Michael had been sniffing out for days. She'd been hard on him and wanted to bury the hatchet. A previous "miscommunication" needed to be cleared up. After two minutes soaking in her perfume and a couple of side-glances, she clocked him with a sob story about longing for tenderness. Her cleavage and perfume one-upped his moral defenses. What a fool!

Now she had digital video chronicling the romp. The footage had been shot from the left side of the bedroom, from the closet area if Michael recalled the layout of her boudoir correctly. Some recording device must have been stashed away discreetly among her LL Bean coats and J. Crew sweaters.

His mind raced. Is it even legal to film someone in New Hampshire without alerting them first? In Florida, his home state, someone couldn't record a conversation unless both parties were privy to it. It's a top ethics rule drilled into the minds of young journalists-to-be in Sunshine State universities.

But calling the police was not an option. Michael could only imagine the conversation: "Um, yes, 911, this is a journalist. I have a complaint about being filmed without permission. It's being used to blackmail me. Oh, the contents of the tape? Uh, well, it involves some graphic scenes of, ahem, carnal knowledge and fornication. No, mam, this is not a joke. Oh, you want to see the video? Um, well. And it becomes public record? Immediately?"

What if his pale backside appeared on Manchester billboards at the height of primary season? What if the bloggers got a hold of it? They'd mutilate his career like cyber piranhas. He'd be writing press releases for a mid-list PR firm before they finished hitting "tweet."

CHAPTER 24

Digital bells snapped Michael out of a nightmare involving a jaguar and a school bus. His mobile phone vibrated and lit up on the loose change Michael scattered on his bed table inside his hotel. It was 2 pm, earlier than his wife ever called before picking up the kids, dressing them and taking them to ballet and soccer. Michael reached for the phone and glanced at the screen: Donald, Editor.

"Hello," Michael said, trying to sound as awake as possible.

"Michael, it's Donald, we gotta talk."

"Ok," Michael said. "Hang on a second."

Michael had dozed off sometime after noon with a copy of the bible laying on his chest. He sat up on his bed, grabbed it, and put it back in the nightstand drawer.

"Ok, what's up?" Michael said.

"I just got off the phone with Jason Bryant from the Dimmesdale campaign," Donald said. "He told me that you and Kristen Dunlop slept together. I need to know what's going on."

Michael was silent as he passed his hand firmly from his forehead, over his eyes, and down around his chin. He took a deep breath. He didn't know what to say.

"Michael," Donald said. "If you slept with that woman, we obviously can't run your story."

"What did Jason say?" Michael asked.

"He told me that you and Kristen had been together a couple of times going back a few weeks."

"Anything else?" Michael said.

"He told me that I needed to ask you about it. So now I'm asking you about it. Is it true?"

Another long pause.

"This is bullshit," Michael said.

"God damn it!" Donald said. "Yes or no?"

Complete silence. Michael stared at the carpet.

"I'm sorry, Donald. I have to call you back."

"Sorry? You're sorry?"

"Yeah, I'm sorry. I stand by my story. I have to go. I will clear this up and call you back."

"You stand…ha!"

Tense and acrid laughter cackled over the receiver.

"Michael, there is no story," Donald said, raising his voice and speaking faster with each passing word. "In fact, as of right now, you are off this assignment and suspended from Tindle Bailey pending further review of this situation. I can't even express how I feel right now. Go home. I would fire you right now, but you don't officially work for me. You have flushed your fucking career down the toilet."

The line went dead.

Michael inhaled deeply.

CHAPTER 25

What the fuck was Lazaro's number?

The last Michael had heard from his eccentric childhood friend, he had moved to Spain to partner up with a colleague he met in college and tap into Barcelona's booming tech scene. That was 4 years ago.

Facebook had zilch on Lazaro. Nothing on any social media sites.

Michael called a couple of friends he and Lazaro had in common from high school. One of them said he heard a rumor that Lazaro had gone underground somewhere in Eastern Europe. They hadn't seen or heard from him in years. The only lead Michael had on Lazaro was in Miami, where Lazaro's father lived.

Miami. Until recently a place that harbored his happiness. Now a place he wasn't sure how to face.

Michael thought of his wife. He stared at the thumb drive with his amateur porn debut. He booked a flight to his hometown. His company card still worked.

Miami weather had morphed into paradise. The temperature was 75 degrees, the sky cloudless. Michael cabbed it to his house. It was empty. He figured his wife had taken the kids to eat dinner at her parents' house.

He went into his closet for clean clothes, and grabbed some fresh shirts, pants and underwear. He put everything into the trunk of his car and went back into the house. He walked around slowly, smelling every room, feeling every surface he passed. He stopped in his childrens' bedroom and sat on the chair Bianca used to nurse both her babies. The room smelled of violets and laundry.

The phone interrupted his reminiscing. It was his direct boss at the Miami Tribune.

"Hello."

"Michael, it's Harriett. Don't hang up."

"I won't."

"What's going on? I got a call from Donald in Washington."

"What did he say?"

"He said you slept with the campaign press secretary. Is it true?"

"Give me three days."

"Three days for what?" Harriet said, sounding incredulous. "It's a yes or no question. Did you sleep with her?"

Silence.

"Well, Michael? Donald wants me to get human resources involved right away. He wants me to cancel your corporate card, your phone. He wants you fired."

"Harriet," Michael said. "I love you. You're a great boss. But I need you to trust me on this. If you cancel my card and phone, I'm dead."

"What do you mean you're dead?" Harriet said. "What the hell is going on, Michael?"

"Tell Donald I haven't confessed to anything, and that if you fire me with only the word from a campaign staffer you will have a lawsuit from me on your hands."

"Michael, what the fuck are you talking about? I want to help you. Christ, I sent you on this assignment. But you're not making it easy for me."

"Look, let me call you back in an hour," Michael said. "I need to take care of something first."

He hung up on his editor and took the laptop out of his car. He booked a flight to Chicago, Manchester and back to Miami, with hotels and rental cars pre-paid at each destination, in case his employers nixed his Visa.

He left his house and drove to Hialeah, in the northwest section of

Miami, his trunk packed with extra clothes.

Memory guided him. Lazaro used to live off Red Road, down the street flanked by Rey's Pizza and El Rey De Las Fritas on opposite corners. The fritas joint was gone, but Rey's Pizza was still in the same place.

Lazaro's old house on the corner of 29th Street and Third Avenue looked the same, but the pink paint looked faded in the yellow glow of the sodium street lamp. Rust seeped from the white burglar bars. Michael parked his car. The chain link fence surrounding the house was unlocked. Michael opened it and walked up to the front door. He could see from a side window that a baseball game was on the TV inside. Before he knocked, he heard barking from inside. A big dog. The front door opened and a large pit bull lunged at Michael. The white metal gate blocked the dog. Michael looked up: it was a hollowed out version of Lazaro's dad, who he hadn't seen in a decade.

"*Que quieres?*" the man said in Spanish. *What do you want?*

"Anselmo, it's me, Michael Cervantes, remember me? Lazaro's friend."

Anselmo eyed Michael's face for a moment. Then quickly unlocked the gate and kicked the dog away.

"My God, Michael," Anselmo said in heavily accented English. "Come here, *hombre*, look at you."

He hugged Michael and invited him inside. The house looked the same as the last time Michael had seen it, including the furniture. The linoleum tiles, the signed portrait of Oscar De La Hoya hanging on the wall.

"What brings you by here? It has been a long time since I see you."

Anselmo reeked of rum.

"It's good to see you Anselmo," Michael said. "I'm trying to find Lazaro."

Anselmo's face grew serious and he nodded his head. He walked to his kitchen and scribbled something in a notepad, then handed it to Michael.

"Meet me at the Piernas Largas bakery in 10 minutes," the note said. "It's around the corner. Say nothing."

When Michael looked up from the note, Anselmo had his pointer finger extended over his lips in the universal sign of "hush".

Michael met Anselmo at the bakery a few minutes later.

"Sorry for the drama," Anselmo said, as they sat at a small table near the front door. "The Patriot Act *de mierda*. I can't even talk to my son on the phone from my house anymore."

"It's ok," Michael said. "Do you work at this bakery?"

"Here? Noooo. This place is pretty new. I still work at the Pinero Bakery. I'm head baker now."

"So Anselmo, I need to reach Lazaro. I need his help on

159

something."

"You need his help?" Anselmo said, laughing sarcastically. "I think he needs help more than you do. He's gone crazy. He's working with some secret group of these hackers or something. In Estonia."

"Estonia, the country?" Michael said. "Do you know how I can reach him?"

"Yes, he has an email that he checks. But look, I think he's in trouble. He came here about a year ago, but he left after a day because he said the FBI was looking for him. He told me never to talk about him in the house because the feds could be listening. The Patriot Act *de mierda*. He gave me instructions on how to reach him. You know Lazaro, very mysterious. I didn't even understand his instructions. I had to spend a whole day learning how to follow them."

"Lazaro's always had an adventurous spirit," Michael said, trying to lighten the conversation.

"Well, remember when he hacked into the MyFace pages of all those girls in Guadalupe High School. Do you remember that? Then he changed their photos around and put naked bodies on them? Remember?"

"Yes, I remember. That's why he got kicked out of Hamilton."

"Exactly. I thought he had flushed his life down the toilet. He lost his scholarship at Hamilton, and had to graduate from the public high school. Remember? Well, after high school, suddenly everyone wanted Lazaro to come work for them, the government, the universities, the tech companies. But Lazaro moved to Spain. He wanted to be a big shot entrepreneur. And now he's somewhere over there. I don't know exactly what he does, and I don't want to know."

Michael nodded sympathetically.

"So how do I reach him? Maybe we can help each other."

"Ok, by now I know this by heart," Anselmo said. "You might want to write this down. Use a public computer like in a library or a cafe. I use the one next door to my bakery in a cafe. Use a Tor browser. Create a temporary email address from one of those sites. I use anonymail.com. But there are others you can use. Then email him at goodwillhunted@yahoo.com"

Michael scribbled the notes on his notepad.

"Ok, this is great."

"You were always a good friend to him," Anselmo said. His voice went down a pitch. "He was always embarrassed by me. All of you other kids were from richer families. And I was a baker. I still am a baker. I'm poor. His mom left us when he was little. Lazaro hated that."

"Lazaro always loved you. He always loved the comic books."

Anselmo snorted. "Yes, the comic books. I used to give him one every birthday and every Christmas. I still have them. He left them in his room. I remember he told me what you did for him."

"What's that?"

"Lazaro told me about the fight, you know, before he got kicked out of school. He told me two boys stole his comic books, and when he tried to get them back, they started beating him up. Then you helped him and got his comic books back for him."

"Oh yeah, I remember that."

"He'll do anything for you," Anselmo said. "He loved you like a brother."

#

Michael parked himself in front of a computer at the Hialeah public library.

"Dear Laz, I know we haven't spoken in a long time, but I need your help. I was assigned to cover a presidential primary and now somebody on the campaign is blackmailing me with a video. I need to get the video back from their computer. If you see this in time, please meet me in Manchester, New Hampshire, two nights from now, at 8 am on January 10th at the lobby of the Garden Inn. You can email me at my same personal email address as when we were kids. Your friend in need,

M

Michael drove home and cut the lights when he pulled into his driveway. Bianca's car was there. She was home with the kids.

Michael called his wife from his phone. She answered after two rings.

"Hey B, it's me."

"Hi babe? Where've you been? The kids want to talk to you."

"Actually, I'm sitting outside," he said. "I need to talk to you."

"You're outside!?"

The phone went dead and a few seconds later, the front yard lights came on, and the door opened. The two kids sprinted out and grabbed Michael as he exited his car. His wife was close behind.

"Glory, Iggy, how are you kids?" Michael said, relishing what he thought could be the last time he was greeted this way at home. He kissed his wife.

"So what are you doing here?" she said. "What's going on?"

Michael stared at her with a nervous smile on his face. Then he pushed the childrens away gently and said: "kids, go inside a second. I need to talk to mommy."

They trudged reluctantly away.

"What is it?" Bianca said.

Michael waited until the children were inside. His wife's face had the look of frightened anticipation.

"I messed up, B," Michael said. "I messed up bad, and I don't know how to tell you."

"Tell me what? What happened?"

Michael folded his arms across his chest and lowered his head.

"I," he said. "I slept with Dimmesdale's press secretary."

His wife turned her face away and looked down at the front wheel of Michael's car. She closed her eyes and rubbed her eyelids. A heavy sigh escaped her mouth.

"There's more. She shot a video of it and she's using it to blackmail me."

Bianca looked up, fury in her eyes.

"You let her shoot video of you!?"

"I didn't know she was recording. She did it in secret."

Both of Bianca's hands rose to her forehead, as though holding her head up. She shook her head.

"I don't know what to tell you, Michael. You've been living in another world for weeks now."

Michael took a step toward her.

"I know. I am so sorry. She means nothing to me."

Bianca recoiled and took two steps back.

"I feel like an idiot," she said, tears in her eyes. "All this time, I'm worried that you're underdressed, that you're cold, that you aren't getting enough to eat. And now this. I don't even know you who you are. You have to leave right now. I don't want to see you around here."

Michael lowered himself into his car, reversed out of the driveway and drove straight to the airport.

CHAPTER 26

Michael spent a sleepless night in Chicago, tossing and turning in his hotel bed for a few hours before getting out of bed around 6 am. The drive north to Evanston was quiet, but even at this early hour there was traffic on North Lakeshore Drive.

He parked in front of Terry Gagnon's apartment building and stood out front, waiting for someone to open the door from the inside. Within a few minutes, a jogger decked out in cold weather running attire pushed the door open and let Michael in. There was a man in the building foyer who looked as though he were checking his mailbox. The man turned away from Michael as he passed.

Michael shot up the stairs and knocked on Terry Gagnon's door. He knocked two more times. Finally, he heard movement on the other side. The door opened a crack.

"Do you know what time it is," she said, eyeing Michael. "You're that reporter aren't you? What do you want?"

"I want to talk to you," Michael said. "You don't have to say anything. Just listen."

She unchained her door and opened it.

Michael heard footsteps on the stairs. He turned around and saw a man walking toward him. It was the man who had been checking mail. But he looked familiar. Where did he know him...Holy Shit! Ivan! The Chechnyan! Ivan reached into his coat. Ivan pulled something out. He heard a thud. The doorjamb next to Michael's face exploded into splinters.

Michael pushed Terry inside her apartment and slammed the door. Terry yelled. Michael grabbed a heavy bookcase near the door and tipped it over just as someone kicked the door. He slid a desk against the bookshelf, blocking the door. More thuds. Bullets pierced the wood.

Michael turned to Terry, her eyes frozen in panic. "Is there another way out of this apartment? Quick!"

She pointed to the back window.

"The fire escape," she said.

Heavy kicks pounded the door. The shelf and desk were giving. Michael grabbed Terry by the arm and headed to the window.

"Wait," she said, twisting her arm free. "My phone."

Terry snatched her phone from the kitchen counter, and suddenly dropped onto the floor as she ran back to Michael. Michael ran to her and helped her up. Blood gushed from her arm.

"We have to go right now," he said.

They climbed out the back window and down the fire escape. Terry held her arm. Michael had to help her down the last level. His arms were covered in blood. They ran to his car, got inside and peeled out down the street.

Michael raced down Dempster Street and hit I94. Not until Michael was sure they weren't being followed did he speak.

"Why are people shooting at us?" Michael said.

"You tell me," she said.

"That guy back there," Michael said. "He works for Newton."

"SilverLake," Terry whispered. "I knew it."

"We need to get you to a hospital," he said.

"No way," she said. "They'll find us."

Michael pulled his coat belt off and handed it to Terry.

"Tie this around your arm above the wound, very tightly."

Terry tied the tourniquet on her arm.

"My friend's a nurse," Terry said. "She can help me."

"Where?"

"Weiss Memorial, but I'll call her. We can't go there."

"Wait," Michael said. "Don't use your phone. They might have our phones tapped or under surveillance somehow. How else would they know where I was going to be? That guy was there when I walked into the building."

"If it's SilverLake, they won't just tap your phone. They'll tap your email, your credit cards, everything."

Michael looked over at her.

"What? Who are these people? I thought they were lobbyists."

"That's one way to describe them. They're more like extortionists. They persuade through any means necessary."

Headlights approached fast from behind. A Black SUV barreled toward the car. Michael didn't see it until the last second. The SUV slammed the rental car from behind.

"Fuck!" Terry yelled. "They're tracking us. We have to get rid of our phones."

Michael handed Terry his phone. She took both their phones and tossed them out the window onto the freezing asphalt. Michael cut between a tractor-trailer and another car. The SUV followed. A bullet hit the passenger side. Michael cut again across the truck, toward an exit and hit the brakes. The tractor blocked the SUV from view. Michael skidded across two lanes of busy highway and careened down the West Peterson Avenue exit. Michael gunned it down the exit, hopped the median to get past traffic and drove east on North Peterson Avenue.

The SUV didn't follow off the exit ramp.

Michael drove to the nearest big-box retailer. He removed his bloodied coat, went inside and bought two pre-paid cell phones and some alcohol and bandages. Terry dialed her friend and set up a meeting at her apartment, which was nearby.

Michael called his editor at the Miami Tribune, Harriet Spackler.

"Harriet, it's Michael."

"Michael, I've been trying to reach you since yesterday. What's going on?"

"I'm in Chicago. Someone just tried to kill me and the woman I was trying to interview."

"What?!" the concern in his editor's voice frightened him. "Who? Why? What do you mean?"

"Some guy with a fucking gun, Harriet," Michael said. "The guy works for Frederick Newton. I saw him just a few days ago with Newton."

"Michael, you need to go to the police right away," she said. "Are you safe?"

"I'm moving in my rental car. I had to toss my phone because they were using it to track my movements."

"Oh my god."

"Harriet, I need your help. I need you to make sure my wife and kids are safe. Do what you have to. Call the FBI, put them up somewhere. Whatever it takes. My wife doesn't want to hear from me right now. We're having a marital thing."

"Ok, I will get on that right away."

"I also need you to wire me $5,000 cash."

"What?"

"It's official business Harriet. The people that tried to kill me were tracking my phone, and I think they are also tracking my credit cards."

"Ok, where do I send it?"

"I will send you a Western Union address as soon as I can get to a phone book."

"Michael, I am very worried about you. Please get yourself somewhere safe and call me back."

Terry's friend, Chloe, agreed to meet them at her apartment. She had walked out of the hospital where she worked with everything she needed to treat Terry's gunshot wound: needles, sutures, bandages. Chloe created a triage area in her kitchen. She cleared an area of her bar for Terry to sit on so that the wound would be at a comfortable height to work on.

Terry removed all her clothes except her bra and panties. Michael stayed in the kitchen to help Chloe with whatever she needed. The bullet had torn through Terry's left tricep, shattering part of the bone. Fortunately, the bullet had exited without puncturing Terry's torso.

Chloe cleaned the wound and Terry's arm, and stitched it up. Not until Terry stood up, still in her bra, did Michael realize how attractive she was. Even pale from the injury, she had a tremendous presence. She reminded Michael of Kristen.

Chloe offered Terry some clothes from her closet. She told them they could stay as long as they needed then she headed back to work.

Michael was alone with Terry. She lied down on the couch, resting. Michael sat on a nearby chair.

"What a morning," he said.

She looked at him without smiling.

"Now you know why I didn't want to talk to you before," Terry said. "These are dangerous people."

"I see that. How are you feeling?"

"I'm ok. That oxycodone Chloe gave me is starting to kick in."

"So what exactly are we up against here?"

Terry caressed her arm.

"Are you still working on a story?" she said.

"Yes, and I think going public is the best way for you to stay safe. If you go public no one can touch you."

Terry shook her head.

"I can't believe this is happening. I thought my life would just return to normal after working for SilverLake. I should have known it wouldn't."

Michael removed the voice recorder from his pocket and placed it on the coffee table.

"Are you recording this?" she asked.

"I want to, yes," he said. "That way there's no confusion about anything you say. I want to make sure I get this right."

"I can't believe they tried to kill me," she said. "I took a huge hit for them. They said they would take care of me. Those fucking bastards."

Michael reached forward and hit record on the device.

"What are you talking about?" Michael said. "I'm confused."

Terry sat up on the couch.

"When I was in college at the University of Illinois, I lost my scholarship junior year. I started escorting to help me pay for school. I never meant to do it more than a few months."

Michael took out his notepad.

"Go on."

"I advertised on gregslist and blackpage. My street name was Gigi."

"What did your parents think of this?"

"You mean my mom? She didn't know. She was working two jobs. She was just glad I got into college. I didn't want to drop out."

"Ok, then what happened?"

"One night I respond to a call from a client. He wants to meet me at a hotel in downtown Chicago. I show up, the guy pays me, then every damn door in the room opens up, the closet door, the front door. Cops walk in with their guns out. It was a sting operation. The Chicago PD arrested me for solicitation of prostitution."

Michael stopped writing and looked at her.

"What did you do?"

"I didn't do anything. Next thing I know, the guard at the jail says someone bailed me out. I walk out of jail and there's Frederick Newton waiting for me with a limousine outside. He tells me that he wants to help me because one of my clients asked him to. But he never tells me which client. He just tells me that it has to remain anonymous."

"So Newton bailed you out. Was he a client of yours? Did you know him?"

"I had never seen him before."

"What did he tell you."

Terry nursed her arm. Her voice slowed.

167

"He told me that he could help me and get me a great job with a great firm. He told me he could get the charges dropped and make sure the University never found out about it so I wouldn't get expelled."

"What did you have to do?"

"He said he wanted me to sleep with certain men and get proof of the sex."

"Proof?" Michael said, light bulbs popping in his mind. "Like video and such?"

"Exactly," Terry said. "Newton was like 'look, you're already getting paid to sleep with men. This would be much fewer men, and for a lot more money.' I mean, the money was incredible. I hadn't even graduated from college and he was paying me $80,000 a year to work part time. They trained me for two months on tactics and roles…."

Michael stood up and swung his arm as though he were throwing a stone across a pond.

"God damnit," Michael yelled. "I should have fucking known!"

Terry looked startled.

"Known what?"

Michael shook his head. How could he have been so stupid.

"Were there other girls doing this for him?"

"I heard there were, but I never saw any. Why?"

"There's this woman. She's working for Dimmesdale, Kristen Dunlop. She's his press secretary."

"I don't know her," Terry said.

"I slept with her, and she recorded it. She's trying to blackmail me."

"Oh my God, for what?"

"I found out about her affair with Dimmesdale," Michael said. "She wants to stop me from reporting it."

"Dimmesdale's a creep," Terry said.

"What happened between you and Dimmesdale?" Michael asked.

"I had to sign a non-disclosure form about that lawsuit."

"I would say that attempted murder on your life nullifies that contract."

Terry swallowed hard. Michael brought her a glass of water.

"Yardley Stoops, the big oil company, wanted to start fracking in Illinois. I didn't even know what hydraulic fracturing was at the time. Dimmesdale came out against fracking. Newton had already placed me in his campaign. I had been fucking Dimmesdale for a couple of months and recording it."

"Do you have any copies of those videos?"

"No, I surrendered everything as part of the agreement."

"Go on."

"Newton tries to get Dimmesdale to change his mind on fracking, but the governor wouldn't budge. So Newton tells me I have to file a sexual harassment lawsuit against him. He said he would pay all the legal fees and pay me a lump sum of $100,000. So I filed the lawsuit."

Michael sighed heavily.

"And let me guess, Newton told the governor everything would go public if he didn't change his mind on fracking."

"Exactly," Terry said. "The governor caved. I got paid, signed a non-disclosure agreement and lived happily ever after. Until you showed up."

Michael sat down next to her on the couch.

"Wow," he said. "This is huge."

"That Kristen girl is probably working for Newton," Terry said.

Michael turned his head to look at her.

"I think you're right. But Dimmesdale hates Newton now," Michael said. "He wouldn't trust him again with one of his girls."

Terry shrugged.

"Maybe Newton didn't introduce them. Maybe this Kristen girl infiltrated the campaign through someone else."

Michael fell silent, rubbing his chin, staring straight ahead.

"Jason Bryant," Michael said. "Does that name ring a bell?"

"Yeah, I know Jason," Terry said. "He's the one who mentored me in Dimmesdale's office. I remember that I ran into him once as I was leaving the SilverLake offices. Jason was walking in. Why?"

"He's working for Dimmesdale's campaign."

"There it is." Terry said. "That's how she got in."

Michael stood up and paced the room a few times.

"Do you have somewhere safe to lay low?" Michael said.

"I'm staying put right here."

Michael went down to his rental car, and came back with a change of clothes. After he changed, he came out of the bathroom and walked toward the injured woman.

"I gotta go, Terry. I have some work to do. Thank you for sharing your story with me."

"Don't waste it."

He took down Terry's pre-paid phone number and walked outside to his rental car. He called Harriet and gave her a Western Union address to wire the cash. She insisted that he seek out the authorities immediately, but he demurred, saying he had to take care of some business. I94 led straight to Milwaukee. Michael didn't want to risk using his already-purchased ticket, with the threat of Newton's goons lingering. With the cash, he bought a ticket to Concord, departing at 10:30 pm that night.

CHAPTER 27

Michael's phone rang the moment he turned it on in Concord. He recognized the number: Donald, his Washington editor. Michael picked up.

"Michael, it's Donald, don't hang up, please."

"Why does everybody keep saying that?"

"Michael, I talked to Harriet. We're all worried sick about you. This is way out of your league. You need to get to the authorities immediately. You are not safe."

The passenger sitting next to Michael stood up to retrieve his carry-on bag from the overhead compartment. Michael turned away from the passenger and tried to whisper into the phone.

"Donald, go fuck yourself. I don't even trust you."

Michael kept his ear pressed to the phone waiting in silence for a full 10 seconds before Donald responded.

"I know I've been hard on you, Michael. But you're just a kid and I wanted you to learn while you're out there."

"They tried to fucking kill me Donald. Where's the story?"

"I know, I know. Look, our official position is you need to turn yourself in and seek out the authorities."

"I'm not going to do that Donald. I've got some unfinished business."

"Tell me what's going on?"

"What for?" Michael said. "The last time I gave you a scoop you sat on it."

Michael's voice grew agitated and he could tell he was attracting attention from other passengers, who were deplaning. Soon Michael was the last person left on the plane.

"I wanted Harriet to fire you," Donald said. "But she threatened to resign."

"You know why she threatened to resign? Because she knows me. She knows the work I do. She's a good journalist, Donald. She stands by her reporters, unlike you."

"None of us wants you to get hurt. Where are you? We can help."

"Donald, I will tell you what I told Harriet. Trust me. Now I gotta go."

"Wait, Michael, wait. Before you hang up. Look, I can help. We're well sourced all over, the FBI, the FEC, the FCC. We're still on the same side. God damn it, I'm a journalist too. If there's a story here, I want a piece of it."

"Donald, I'll get back to you."

Michael hung up. He walked off the plane alone and drove into Concord. He found a motel near the airport, paid for a room in cash and holed up until dawn.

#

The drive to Manchester took a little more than an hour. He guzzled gas station black coffee and ate a few Danishes on the way.

The Garden Inn was in downtown Manchester, away from the hotels near the airport usually occupied by the press corps and political operatives. The streets were desolate, the night still loosening its freezing grip on the city. Michael parked a block away from the hotel and watched the front approach. He sat there for half an hour, watching as the hotel came to life.

At 8 am, he exited the car, pulled a wool cap down on his forehead, and walked to the hotel. Once inside the small lobby, he said hello to the clerk, grabbed a Wall Street Journal and tucked himself into a chair in the far corner.

Two minutes later the clerk came around the desk and walked toward him.

"Are you Michael?" she said.

"Yes," Michael said, taken by surprise.

"You have a phone call at the front desk."

Michael walked to the front desk, took the phone and said "hello?" He eyed the lobby warily.

"It's me."

Michael cupped the receiver and turned his back away from the clerk.

"Laz?"

"Yes."

"Where are you?"

"I'm in your car."

"In my car outside?"

"Yes. Come over."

Michael reached over the counter, hung up the phone and smiled at the clerk. Back outside, he made out a figure in the passenger seat of his car. The figure remained seated even as Michael approached. Not until Michael tapped on the window did Laz open the door.

"How the hell did you get in here?" Michael said. "I just locked the door."

"Car locks are a joke," Laz said. "Now what the fuck am I doing here?"

"Good to see you too," Michael said, and walked around the car.

Inside, he looked over at his friend, who he hadn't seen in years. Laz had grown a grizzly beard. His jacket looked like some kind of military garb, but definitely not American. His hair was cut short, like a crew cut. But his eyes hadn't changed.

"Dude what POW camp did you just escape from?" Michael said.

"I found paradise," Laz said. "Estonia. The most beautiful women in the world. They're experiencing a sexual revolution, and the hottest bachelors in town are tech entrepreneurs and hackers."

Michael laughed.

"The hottest bachelors in this town are political ass kissers and hacks," Michael said.

Laz laughed, then took a deep breath.

"Seriously, what's going on? It wasn't easy for me to get here."

"I met with your dad a couple of days ago. That's how I got your contact information. He told me he thinks he's under FBI surveillance or something."

Laz shook his head.

"My dad's always been a little paranoid, but I was wanted for questioning by the feds."

"What the hell for, what did you do?"

Laz reached around to the back seat and pulled a bag forward.

"It's complicated. Can we just please drive?"

"Laz, things are bad," Michael said. "Someone tried to kill me yesterday. They shot the woman I was with. My company wants me to go the FBI."

"Fuck, and I thought Eastern Europe was bad. How did you get into this mess?"

Michael pulled away from the hotel and drove across Manchester to a diner at the outer edge of town, a spot Dimmesdale had visited a few weeks earlier that served great French toast and maple syrup. They stopped there and sat at a table in the corner. The place was jumping with the breakfast bustle, locals hypnotized by coffee steam, many of them reading physical newspapers.

Michael filled in Laz on the background of the situation.

"Does your wife know?" Laz said.

"Yes. I told her a couple of days ago. She didn't take it well."

"Of course she didn't take it well. How did you expect her to take it?"

"I made a mistake."

"Two mistakes. What I don't understand is why you fucked her again?"

"I couldn't help it. It was like watching myself in a slow motion car accident in a dream. I knew it was happening. I knew it was bad. But I couldn't stop it. I couldn't fucking stop it."

Laz let it sink in.

"Women," he said, a sly smile on his face.

"Women," answered Michael.

Laz pulled a tablet out of the bag he brought with him. But it looked different than anything Michael had seen.

"What is that thing?"

"My hackentab."

"Like an ipad?"

"If an ipad was a Somali refugee this tablet would be Arnold Schwarzenegger in Conan."

Laz powered up the tab.

"Ok, so you said this woman showed you a video of you and her fucking. Tell me about that. Where did she play the video?"

"She played it from her laptop."

"Ok, did she play it from a media player like QuickTime, or did she play it from a server like YouTube?"

Michael thought for a moment.

"God, I don't know. I didn't notice."

"At the event, was there Wi-Fi?"

"I don't think so, but I'm not sure."

"We gotta go back there."

"Where? SignalTech?"

"Yes, we have to find out if they have an open Wi-Fi server that anyone can use to access the web, or if they don't."

"I don't want to go back there."

"Why not? No one's going to be there from the campaign."

"Why is it so important?"

Laz changed his tone to that of a frustrated teacher.

"Look, if the video is on her laptop, then we have one set of solutions. If the video is on the cloud, we have another set of solutions."

"What solutions are you thinking of?" Michael said.

"We need to hack into her files to remove the video from the drive."

"How? Do you really know how to do that?"

Laz looked over his shoulder and lowered his voice.

"Here's what it boils down to. If that video is on her hard drive in her laptop, we're going to need to get our hands on that computer."

"You mean physically?"

"Yes, I mean we need that actual computer."

Michael leaned forward, with an agitated whisper.

"Why do we need her computer? Can't you hack in from the cloud or something? Isn't that what hackers do?"

Laz took a deep frustrated breath.

"Yes, we can hack in from the cloud. But it would take us a few days just to get the information we needed, like her IP and MAC addresses, her email addresses, her passwords. Then we'd have to wait for the laptop to be powered on for a prolonged period, and connected to the web. I don't envision this scenario playing out easily. At least not quickly. However, if we can get our hands on the laptop, we do a little surgery, and voila! We get access to everything."

Michael sat back on his seat and stared over the patrons' heads. His mind seemed to drift. His hand rose to rub the stubble on his chin with his knuckles.

"Steal her laptop?" Michael said, staring into Laz's eyes.

"Yes, steal her laptop," Laz said. "Or borrow it without permission, if you prefer."

Michael snapped out of his trance.

"Borrow it? Borrowing implies we will give it back."

"All I need with it is an hour. 90 minutes at most. Then we could give it back. She wouldn't even have to know."

"You just need an hour with it?"

"90 minutes at most."

Michael rubbed his head.

"Have you done this before?"

Laz shrugged.

"Look. That's what we do, we hack into people's emails. We monitor communications between high-level executives, government officials, diplomats. Sometimes we need to get our hands on actual computers. So..."

He shrugged again, hoping Michael would complete his thought.

"So you steal computers."

"Sometimes a little burglary is necessary."

"No wonder the feds want to talk to you."

"That's a whole other story my friend. Nail this story down first, then we'll get to that one."

"I'm trying to think of a way we can get near the laptop. Close enough to take it."

"Where does she take it?"

"Everywhere. At night, it's in her apartment. During the campaigning she brings it with her and leaves it in the car, which is always manned by a driver."

Laz rubbed his scraggly beard.

"I don't like the idea of an occupied burglary. Too risky."

"Wait a second!" Michael said. "Almost every Thursday and Friday she goes to the Wild Rover. She goes directly from the campaign office. Last time I saw her there, she didn't have a laptop with her in the bar, meaning she probably left it in her car while she was there."

"Ok, today is Thursday. Where is this Wild Rover?"

"Downtown Manchester."

"Ok, let's get out of here."

Michael and Laz drove to SignalTech and walked into the lobby where Kristen had shown Michael the video. Michael identified himself as a reporter, showed his ID card, and asked to speak to the manager. Laz tagged along, looking around him in awe, like a kid eyeing dinosaur fossils in the museum.

A young man with a shaved head and a red t-shirt appeared.

"Hi I'm Peter, what can I help you with?"

"Hi Peter, I'm Michael Cervantes from Tindle Bailey newspapers. I was here for the Dimmesdale event last week, and I have kind of a weird question. Was there an open Wi-Fi network here during that event?"

"Here? No. We have a secure Wi-Fi connection."

"Did anyone on the campaign ask for the password, or did you give it to anyone?"

Peter eyed Michael warily.

"Uh, no, but why? What's going on?"

"Oh, nothing," Michael said. "I'm just trying to gauge the level of online engagement from audience members at campaign events."

"Oh!" Peter said, apparently relieved. "Ok, thanks for stopping by."

Michael walked to Laz.

"So this is what my workplace would have looked like if I stayed here instead of moving to Europe," Laz said, his hands on his waist.

"I guess. So there was no open Wi-Fi for anyone at the event. Not even campaign staff."

Laz nodded.

"I didn't think so. This girl's got this video on her hard drive somewhere, and we need to get it."

CHAPTER 28

"I brought a few things I thought we might need," Laz said, reaching into his bag.

They were in the car, on their way to Concord, where Laz had located a spy shop that sold surveillance equipment.

"What?"

"There's this," Laz said, holding what looked like a prescription capsule between his fingers.

Michael glanced over.

"What is that?"

"It's a GPS tracker that you swallow."

"Does it work?"

"I've actually never used it before," Laz said. "I mean, I've tested the device, and I can track it from my tablet. But I've never swallowed it."

"But if you swallow it, don't you shit it out eventually?"

"You're supposed to give yourself an enema first."

"An enema? What the fuck?"

"This is a prototype. It was developed by some friends of mine in Estonia. They're marketing it for use with sick livestock. When a sick cow shits, they can find the shit in the fields."

Michael shook his head.

"There's a market out there for this kind of thing. Trust me."

"What else did you bring?"

"These," Laz said, holding up two SD-card sized chips. "They're magnetized trackers. They can attach to a car, or anything metal. Or just go in a pocket or something."

"All this tracking stuff. What's it for?"

"You never know."

They arrived at the detective store in Concord in the early afternoon. It was located in a strip mall near the airport. They knocked on the tinted glass door and were buzzed in after a few seconds. The morbidly obese man behind the counter pawed a bag of corn chips.

"Welcome. What can I do for you gentlemen?"

"We need a few things for a surveillance operation."

"Are you guys private I's," the man said. "We only sell to licensed private I's."

Michael took out his press id and showed it to the man. "I'm a reporter. We want to conduct an undercover operation."

The man's eyes opened wider, and he nodded his head. "Cool." He wiped his nacho-cheese powdered hands on his jeans.

"Alright. So what do you need?"

"We need two small wireless POV cams, a wireless body lavaliere with remote recording capabilities and an earpiece for two-way communication, a solid state drive with a SATA to Thunderbolt adapter and a Taser with two reload cartridges."

When Michael heard "Taser", he grabbed Laz by the arm and walked him to the end of the room.

"Why do we need a Taser?" he whispered. "You didn't mention that."

"Look, you never know with these things."

The clerk spoke up.

"The C2 Gold is our most popular model. But the X26 is on sale today. That'll knock out a rhino."

"We'll take it," Laz said.

Michael paid on his business credit card, which still had not been canceled. Next stop: a costume shop in downtown Concord.

"Are you sure this is necessary?" Michael said.

"How else are you gonna keep an eye on her? She could spot you."

The place was a teenage wonder store, filled with sexy costumes, magic tricks, a plethora of fake vomits and turds. Laz tried on a large afro. Michael tested a fake beard.

"You're clean shaven and your face is completely undecorated," Laz said. "We can busy it up."

The disguise came together: a light brown wig with a fashionable comb-over hairdo, thick black glasses, a bushy brown mustache and fake mutton chop sideburns that matched the wig color. They also bought a lumberjack-style plaid coat and a pair of jeans.

Their last stop on the shopping circuit was an auto parts store near the Manchester airport.

"I had no idea you could just walk into a store and buy a slim Jim," Michael said, as they walked back to the car.

"It's like the bong market. Most people buy them for nefarious purposes, but you can't ban a harmless object if some people use it for legitimate means."

CHAPTER 29

"I gotta check my email," said Michael once they got back in the car. "We have to find a public computer."

"You can check it here," Laz said, pulling out his hackentab. "It's equipped with a multi-carrier mi-fi system that disables the security pingback from the cell company."

"English, please."

"Basically, it's got the strongest cell connection money can buy, and it's free and anonymous," Laz said.

"I won't even ask if it's legal."

"Good."

Michael logged onto his email account from work. There was a message from Monique Goombley, the Tribune's researcher.

"Michael, I was asked to archive this recording of a conference call that Tribune editors had with Tindle-Bailey executives last night. It concerns you. Listen in. You didn't get it from me."

An audio file was attached. Michael downloaded it.

"Mind if we play this audio file while we drive?" he asked.

"Not at all," Laz said. "Let's Bluetooth it and play it on the car's audio system."

The audio file began playing. Michael heard the voice of Harriet, his editor.

Harriet: "Hi everyone. Thanks for joining us on this call."

A series of voices, both on location, and digitally transmitted over speakerphone, were heard sharing greetings and pleasantries.

Harriet: "So I don't know about you all, but I am extremely concerned about Michael Cervantes' safety. He asked me to move his family into a secure location. He says someone tried to kill him. This is a crisis in the making for this company. And a possible tragedy too. We need to do something."

"Let's take a step back for a second," said a voice that was apparently coming out of a speaker. It was Donald. "We don't know exactly what's going on. We don't know if Michael is telling the truth. I have a campaign executive telling me that he's romantically involved with a campaign staffer. That's a fireable offense. Then he tells us that someone tried to kill him. He won't go to the cops. He won't pick up his phone. He's…"

"Donald. Donald! stop right there."

It was Harriett, cutting him off.

"Let me stop you right there."

Her voice was rising in anger.

"First of all, a fireable offense? This young man's life could be in danger. He is worried about the safety of his family. He hasn't confessed to anything. Not to me. Not to you. If Michael Cervantes is in danger, we need to pull out any and all resources at our disposal as journalists to help him. And I mean anything. Call the FBI, call the police …"

"Harriet, Harriet. I hear you," said Donald, assuming a calm, assertive tone that a Kindergarten teacher would use with a misbehaving child. "But we're not going to get anywhere getting hysterical."

"No one is hysterical Donald," said Tom Johnson, the top editor at the Tribune and Harriet's boss.

"Let's start with what we know," Donald continued. "Michael supposedly had a scoop on a story about Dimmesdale having an affair with a campaign staffer."

Another speaker voice chimed in. It was the CEO of Tindle Bailey: "This is Donald Markerson. Hello everyone. We have a situation here, and it really isn't clear how we can handle it at this moment. So that's what we're discussing here. From what Donald tells me, this reporter appears to have gone rogue in the last day or so."

"Rogue?" Harriett said. "I spoke to Michael today and he is not rogue. He is scared. He is worried for his family. I have Helen Iguarte over at Michael's house right now talking to his wife, and trying to get them out of there. Michael doesn't know who to trust. The last conversations he had with Donald were about being fired, about his career being over. Then someone tries to assassinate him."

"Is that even true?" Donald Markerson said. "How can we confirm this? If this is the case, he should be with the authorities right now. But he isn't."

"I think he should be suspended immediately," Donald said. "We don't know what he is doing right now. We need to go into some sort of damage control until we get a handle on him."

"Damage control!?" Harriet yelled. "Don't you fucking pull this damage control shit on me Donald. This is the best reporter we have on our staff, and if he told me someone tried to kill him, then I believe it. If he told me to trust him, I'm going to trust him."

"I think we should suspend him immediately," Markerson said. "What if he does something to embarrass our organization?"

"I strongly disagree with suspending him immediately. We don't have all the facts about the romantic involvement case. When I spoke to Michael, he admitted to nothing, and he said that suspending or firing him on just the word of a campaign staffer could open us up to a lawsuit."

"He said that?" Markerson said. "A lawsuit? From who? Him? This doesn't sound like someone who is thinking clearly."

Tom Johnson put out an idea: "What if we write about what's going on? Put it out there. That way, we're transparent, we let readers and the public know what's going on. Maybe we give Michael a little cover."

"And write what?" Donald said. "There's no story right now. We have no on-the-record statement from the campaign. No authorities are involved. The call I received from the campaign was not an interview for publication. And how about Michael's wife and family? Do you think they'd appreciate a story about them in the paper right now."

"We can run a story based on what Michael has told us," Johnson said. "His tale is sourced. He has a staffer from the campaign on the record, plus a second source on background. He has his own account of what happened at the motel."

"Yeah, how about this decision not to run the story about Dimmesdale's affair with his staffer. Why didn't you run that story?"

"With something like that, we need it airtight." Donald said. "Too much at risk."

"I agree," said Markerson. "This is a young man, you said so Harriet."

"We've run a million stories that were less sourced!" Harriet said.

Everyone suddenly tried to talk at the same time, making it impossible to hear.

"Alright, alright," Markerson said. "We need to make a decision here. I think we suspend Michael Cervantes, redouble our efforts to locate and reach him, and bring him in. Then we can decide how to proceed in the long term."

"Donald, I sent that reporter to corporate in good faith. He is living away from his family. He is young. He has never covered a presidential campaign before. But he is a solid journalist. Michael Cervantes is in serious, life-threatening trouble. If we cut him off and something happens to him, we will all have blood on our hands."

"I think that's an exaggeration," Markerson said. "By keeping him on staff we are enabling him."

"Donald, Donald, I'm not cutting off my reporter."

There was a long silence in the room.

"Harriet, Tom, as of now, Michael Cervantes is suspended."

"No." Harriet said.

"I am the CEO of this company."

"You're not in charge of editorial," Harriett said. "We have to go through the proper channels at human resources to get a reporter suspended."

"These   are   the   proper   channels." Another silence.

"Donald, Donald, let me make it clear to you what will happen if you try to suspend Michael Cervantes," Harriet said.

She let it sink in.

"First of all, I will resign effective immediately. Second of all, I won't sit quietly by and watch Michael get killed. I will take all of the information I have and go to the Sun Standard, our competitor. I will give it to them. They will run a story about this, and I promise you that we will not come off looking good."

"I don't like threats."

"It's not a threat, Donald. You're not touching my reporter."

"God damn it Harriett, consider what you're saying here? You'd throw your career away over some dumb kid who's playing cloak and dagger while he's supposed to be covering a presidential campaign."

"I'm calling the FBI when we get off this call," Harriett said. "I'm also calling Dimmesdale's campaign. I'm calling Chicago PD. I'm calling everyone Donald. That's the right thing to do. You can either get on board with it, or fire me."

"I gotta say," chimed in Tom Johnson, "We should inform the authorities of what's going on at the very least. I still think a story would be a good way to go."

"No story," said Donald. "Don't even think about it."

A 7-second silence made Michael believe the call had ended.

"This is a mess," Markerson said finally. "Harriett, you leave me no choice but to accept your resignation."

A commotion could be heard in the room, a notebook flying, hitting a wall, a door slamming.

"She just stormed out," Tom said.

"Tom, can you carry out this order to suspend Michael Cervantes?"

"Reluctantly and over my objections," Tom said. "I will make sure he is suspended as soon as we can make it happen."

"Good," Markerson said. "Make it happen."

The recording ended. Michael took a deep breath in the car. He stared straight ahead.

"Fuck," he said. "That's my boss. She resigned over this."

"You have a good boss," Laz said.

"I had no idea."

"What are you going to do?"

"I don't know but I'm surprised my business card still works. It will probably get canceled soon."

"Why are you even doing this?" Laz said. "These fuckers obviously don't give a shit about you. You heard that guy. You're a dumb kid to them."

Michael shook his head, and shrugged.

"Because fuck them, that's why."

CHAPTER 30

By the time Michael and Laz pulled into a parallel parking spot near the front door of the Wild Rover, night had descended. The Rover was a stand-alone brick building, four stories tall. The first floor exterior was covered in wood paneling, all painted green. The letters were in gold. In warmer times, patrons gathered on the wide brick sidewalk out front. But in this freezing weather, people slipped into the warmth of the pub immediately.

They were parked in front of the three-story building across the street with a clear view of the front door. Around 5 pm, more people began to arrive at the bar, the happy hour crowd. Michael recognized a couple of campaign regulars.

"Ok," Michael said, adjusting a small device in his hear. "So you can hear me, and I can hear you."

"Right," Laz said.

"So what's the range on this thing?"

"Long enough."

Michael looked over at his friend. His look was tender, but in his disguise, it came off as comical.

"Thank you for doing this," Michael said.

"Don't thank me yet, bro," Laz said, chuckling.

"Is this crazy?" Michael said.

"Yeah, it's fucking crazy. But it's necessary."

Michael felt his stomach tense up.

"I don't know about this," he said. "Maybe we should just fucking forget it."

Laz took a packet of spicy mixed nuts out of his pocket. He had bought them at a gas station earlier.

"Look," he said. "I flew across the Atlantic ocean and snuck into my own country to come here and help you. Now man the fuck up, and get ready to do this."

"I look ridiculous."

"You look like a hipster channeling the working man."

Michael laughed.

"What do you think Bianca would say if she saw me now?"

"She wouldn't even recognize you. Your disguise is solid."

Michael grabbed the bag of spicy nuts and poured some into his mouth.

"When did you become this outlaw?" he said to Laz.

"I'm not an outlaw. Ok, maybe a little. But what I do isn't that different from what you do. I write code. You write articles. You use your job to expose and inform. I do the same. We just have different audiences."

"I don't know what the fuck I'm going to do."

"Worry about it tomorrow. Right now you have to focus on what we're doing."

"Ok, so you need an hour after you get her laptop."

"Once I get the laptop, I will know how exactly how much time I need. It depends on the size of her drive and the nature of it. Solid states copy faster. HDDs take more time."

Michael stared out the window.

"I have no right to expose Dimmesdale. I succumbed to the same temptation. I'm no better than he is."

"Don't cloud the mission, bro. Dimmesdale's a fucking hypocrite. He needs to go down. You think about these things too much."

"When Kristen handed me that thumb drive and told me she owned me, I've never felt weaker, more stupid, more vulnerable, more exposed. She's beautiful. It would be hard for any guy to resist her. Isn't that human?"

He looked over at Laz, who shrugged.

"Big deal, you fucked another woman. You're not running for president on a platform of religious virtues."

Michael eyed the front door of the Rover.

Laz continued, "this bullshit of punishing men for fucking women other than their wives is new. It's a result of the rise of feminism. But here in the United States, we mingled the feminism with religious values and all that crap. Women need something to hold over men. All they have is sex. It's their reward and their punishment."

"You want to hear something crazy?" Michael said. "I want to fuck her again. Even after all this. I want to fucking ravage her. It's like I'm a junky and she's my heroin."

Laz shook his head. "If she's as hot as you say she is, then it's not crazy. It's normal."

Michael adjusted a few hairs on his fake mustache, which were tickling his nose. A young patron who had parked somewhere behind them walked past the car and glanced inside. Michael recognized him as a junior staffer on the Dimmesdale campaign. Something suddenly caught the man's attention from behind. He turned around to face away from the bar and smiled at someone walking toward him. Michael turned around to look behind the car.

"That's her," he whispered to Laz.

Michael's hand instinctively shot up to cover part of his face as Kristen walked past the car. She greeted the man who had smiled at her, and they continued walking together toward the bar. She never looked toward the car.

"Wow," Laz said. "You were not exaggerating. She is hot."

"She's not carrying her laptop," Michael said. "That means it's almost certainly in her car."

Kristen and her friend crossed the street a few yards away and entered the pub.

"Ok, let's go," Laz said.

They stepped out of their rental car and walked in the direction from where Kristen had come.

"Let's find her car quick," Laz said.

Around the corner two blocks away, they located Kristen's Volvo parallel parked next to a three-story apartment building.

"This is it," Michael said.

Laz glanced around to make sure no one was watching. Shades were drawn on all the windows in the adjacent apartment building. A couple of lights cast their yellow glow over the ends of the street, but Kristen's car sat outside the penumbra. Using the flashlight app from his phone, Laz looked inside the car, checking the front seats first.

"Someone's coming," Michael said.

Laz stood up and lit a cigarette, which he had also bought earlier. He and Michael pretended to be having a conversation as they smoked outside. Only smokers had reason to linger outside in this weather. The pedestrian walked past them and turned the corner, heading toward the Rover. As soon as she was out of sight, Laz resumed looking into the car. His light shined upon something in the back seat.

"There's a lump under that blanket," he said.

Michael peaked inside at the lump on the floor of the back seat. He could make out a two-inch piece of strap from Kristen's laptop.

"That's it, I see the strap."

Laz moved toward the front passenger door and pulled the slim Jim from his jacket. He felt around with the device inside the door. A car turned the corner. Headlights shined directly on Laz and Michael. In a reflexive gesture, Michael pretended to be laughing joyously and slapped Laz on the back. Just then, Laz popped the lock on the passenger door, opened it and unlocked the back door. He put the slim Jim back in his coat, reached down, and grabbed the laptop.

Michael was standing on the corner, looking in the direction of the pub. Laz walked up to him.

"That's it. That's her laptop."

"Ok, you're on," Laz said. "Remember, stay a safe distance away from her."

Michael walked toward the pub. Laz returned to their rental car and went to work on Kristen's laptop.

"Can you hear me ok?" Michael said as he walked away.

"Loud and clear," Laz responded. "And you can hear me?"

"Loud and clear."

"Let's keep communication to an absolute minimum."

"Roger that."

The Black Keys on stereo and a blast of warm air greeted Michael as he opened the door to the Wild Rover. The pub had a vestibule at the front with a curtain intended to keep some of the heat from leaking out when people opened the door. It made for a good spot to scout the surrounding area. From there, Michael had a clear view of the bar area. Kristen wasn't at the bar or in the bar area. She had to be around the back side of the bar in the other room.

Someone entered the bar and bumped into Michael from behind. Michael turned around. Oh Fuck! Brian Petchell, Dimmesdale's campaign manager. Before Brian had a chance to look at his face, Michael spun around and walked to the far end of the bar. The place was not yet packed, so Michael was able to order a beer immediately. He kept his head down until the bartender delivered his beer. Brian walked past the bar and into the back room. Michael waited until Brian had turned the corner then sauntered across the bar and walked wide of the corner, glancing into the back room at an angle. Ever so slowly, he approached the threshold, tender steps. About a foot before he hit the threshold, Michael spotted Brian pulling a chair back from a table. Michael leaned forward. There! Kristen, sitting across the table from Brian. Michael pulled back. More people walked past him into the back room. He blinked a few times, debating in his mind how best to observe his target. Kristen was not wearing a jacket, meaning she had taken it off and placed it nearby. The jacket was a fuse with a 20-second warning before she walked out of the bar.

Michael walked around the bar to the far entrance of the back room. From there, he carefully peeked inside. Kristen had her back to him at this angle, and he could see her back, with all its blond locks, without exposing himself to Brian. A few sips from his beer later, a voice crackled in Michael's ear, startling him. Beer spilled. It was Laz.

"Michael, I've got the hard drive, and it's not encrypted, which is good news. Michael you there? Cough once if you can hear me."

Michael coughed and looked around self-consciously. His hand rose to his ear.

"Ok good. Look it's a half a terabyte. It's going to take about 50 minutes. Then I need another 5 minutes to put the laptop back together. So she's gotta stay there at least an hour."

Michael noted the antique clock on the wall at the Rover. 6:48 pm. The pub filled fast. Soon Michael's outpost at the far end of the bar became crowded. At 7:01, Brian stood up and began walking in Michael's direction. Michael turned his head, pretending to be listening to a conversation next to him, Brian continued past him to the bathroom. A minute later, he came back and grabbed his coat off the wall hanger next to him. It looked like he was telling Kristen goodbye. He left her sitting there with a near empty wine glass.

7:06, Kristen knocked back the last of her wine and stood up. She reached for her jacket. She was getting ready to leave.

"She's getting up to go," Michael said.

"What?" Laz said. "You gotta do something. I'm not ready."

Michael's heart sped up as Kristen pulled the ends of her blond hair from her coat and started toward the door. He placed his beer on the bar and followed her out of the pub. In the same vestibule he had used when he entered, he stripped off his wig, his mustache, his glasses. He opened the front door of the bar. Cold air gripped him. Kristen was already halfway down the block. Michael tossed the disguise on the sidewalk.

She had her back to him, walking away in the cold, quiet street. Her footsteps drummed on the sidewalk. He jogged toward her, closed the distance between them, and called out to her.

"Kristen," he said.

She turned around, a surprised look on her face.

"Michael? What are you doing here?" she said.

"I came here looking for you," he said. "I want to talk to you."

Much to his surprise, she walked in his direction, her hands in her pockets.

"I'm surprised to see you here," she said. "I thought you'd be out of New Hampshire by now."

Michael wasn't sure what to say. He had not planned on this conversation. Kristen yanked her hand out of her pocket and glanced down at her phone.

"Hold on," she said. "Just got a text from the boss."

She thumbed some words into her phone and put it back in her pocket. Then she turned her full attention to Michael. Slowly, they approached each other. For a few moments, they looked at each other in silence. Kristen touched Michael's jacket.

"What's with the lumberjack outfit?"

The touch proved tender enough to disarm Michael's wariness. Her eyes drifted upward from his jacket to Michael's eyes. Her hand stayed gently gripping his jacket. With the back of her hand, she rubbed Michael's chest. The intimate caress confused him. He raised a hand and pushed a blond strand of Kristen's hair away from her face.

"It's freezing out here," he said. "Let's go into the Rover."

Kristen obliged. They walked back to the pub side by side. He opened the door for her and she walked inside. They sat on a table at the far end of the room behind the bar, as cozy a spot as existed at the pub.

Michael kept his jacket on. He helped Kristen remove her coat and hung it on hook on the wall next to her.

"I'm going to get a beer. Can I get you anything?" Michael asked.

"I'll have a glass of red wine," she said.

Michael walked to the bar, noting the time on the clock, 7:14. Laz's voice crackled in his ear. "Cough once if you're alone."

Michael coughed.

"Good work on stalling her," Laz said. "I haven't been able to do any in-depth analyses, but I'm seeing a lot of video and audio files on her drive. I still need half an hour. Work your charm."

Michael navigated past clusters of congregating hipsters, carrying the drinks back to the table. Kristen had fluffed her hair. The soft tungsten lighting in the room seemed to make her hair glow. She smiled gently at him, almost submissively. Michael settled across the table from her and leaned in.

"I keep wondering what it would have been like to meet you under different circumstances," he said.

"I think we would have been lovers."

"We're already lovers."

"I mean lovers out in the open. The kind of lovers that make a U-turn on their way to meet friends because they got horny."

Her last word went straight below Michael's waist.

"I would have liked that," Michael said. "I can't get you out of my mind."

"Even after everything that's happened?" she said.

"What happened was circumstance. In a parallel universe," Michael said, pausing for effect, "I would have fallen in love with you."

"You're crazy," she said. "You don't want to fall in love with someone like me. I'm trouble."

"I know you're trouble. But I can see past it."

Kristen didn't interrupt him. She seemed eager to hear him speak about her.

"I should hate you right now," he continued. "You destroyed my life. But I don't hate you. I think you did what you had to do. I understand your position."

These words were difficult for Michael to say. He looked pained to say them. But he meant it.

"I think about you too," she said. "I think about that first night we hooked up after our dinner at Satin. I think about how you kept glancing over at me during dinner. I think about how I kept wanting you to look at me."

"I didn't want to leave town without seeing you. As messed up as things got, I still care about you."

"When are you leaving?" she asked.

"Tomorrow."

"I'm glad you came by. I like seeing you too."

A voice like a bucket of ice chimed into Michael's ear.

"Bro, holy shit, bro!" yelled an excited Laz. "Wait till you see what's in these videos!"

The interruption irritated Michael. He turned his head away from Kristen, pretended to scratch his ear, and pulled the listening device out. Laz's voice was gone from his head. He slipped the tiny speaker into his pocket. He didn't want any distractions. He felt his brain beginning to delegate judgment below his waist. And he liked it. He trusted it.

"I'm going to go use the restroom," Michael said.

The restroom visit took a couple of minutes. He noted the time at the bar on the way back: 7:32. Laz needed another 15 minutes. He sat down at the table and took a gulp from his beer.

"I'm gonna have to go soon," he said.

Her hand crept across the table and touched his. He looked down at it.

"Don't go yet," she said. "What's going to happen to you now?"

"I don't know," he said. "I guess find another job. Maybe another wife."

"Jesus," she said. "So many lives ruined by this."

"It's just my life ruined," he said. "I deserve it."

"And Dave's," she said.

The rock and roll cranking from the speakers in the bar seemed to slow down.

"Dave's?" he said

"Yeah, Dave. He was found dead in his apartment this morning. Haven't you heard?" Kristen said.

"Dave is dead?"

"Yes," Kristen said. "It's so sad. He took his own life, apparently."

"Jesus," Michael said.

"It's not your fault Michael," Kristen said. "He was really high strung."

Michael stood up, shaking his head.

"Oh my God," he said.

Kristen stood up and walked around the table. She placed an arm over his shoulder and whispered in his ear.

"I want to give you a proper send off," she said, taking his hand.

Michael couldn't tell if the news or the beers had clobbered him, but he felt unusually dizzy. Kristen's hand was warm and soft. They melted together through the happy hour throng. She opened the men's room door, waved hello to a man urinating, and led Michael into the handicapped stall at the end of the bathroom. The door closed behind them, and they grabbed each other, their lips locking. Tongues flicked into each other's mouths immediately. Her hand slithered to his crotch. His lips felt a little numb. She clutched his right hand forcefully and slid it under her shirt, under her bra.

But Michael found himself in a weird daze, where he couldn't move his hand across her chest. He had trouble kissing her. His mouth felt like it was filled with epoxy. A blurry film seemed to cover both his eyes. Her rubbed them with his free hand. Kristen took that hand and stuck it inside her pants, on her pussy. But he couldn't respond.

Something was wrong. He swayed and bumped against the tile wall. His pants were by his ankles. Kristen dropped to her knees, pulled down his underwear, and started sucking his dick. He tried to stop her, but found himself unable to maintain his balance. Kristen leaned back. Michael's back slid down the wall, until he was in a seating position, his back against the tiles. His dick was out, limp, but he couldn't cover himself up.

"I feel weird," he slurred. "I can't get up."

Kristen's demeanor changed instantly. She buttoned herself up and straightened out her clothes. He watched from his stupor as she opened the stall door and looked outside, making sure the coast was clear.

"That's because I drugged you," she said.

Michael tried to get up, but he had no motor skills. His attempted yell sounded like a weak groan. Kristen sat on the toilet, fully clothed and bent forward, resting her elbows on her knees. She shook her head.

"Pathetic," she said. "You don't learn do you?"

Michael tried to smile, but wasn't sure if it came out right.

"Did you really think I was going to let you just walk out of here?" she said. "We've been looking for you."

"You're evil," Michael managed to stammer.

"Evil?" she said. "Ha! I'm part of the system, Michael. Do you really think I liked fucking a 64-year-old tight-ass. I didn't. But I did it anyway because it was necessary. There's a lot of money riding on this election, Michael. Powerful interests see Dimmesdale taking the lead. He will most likely be the next president. And they want to have some insurance on him. Carbon tax my ass. We just need a little leverage to change his mind."

Kristen reached down and pulled Michael's underwear over his penis.

"Dimmesdale's a patsy. All I had to do was get him alone, flash a little cleavage, rub it against his arm a little and let his dick take over. You men are so predictable."

Kristen looked down at Michael's crotch.

"But you," she said, reaching down to rub his penis. Her tone softened. "I didn't plan for you. I admit I got carried away that first night."

She looked at Michael eyes and touched his face. She stood up in the stall, angry. "Then you showed up outside Dimmesdale's room that morning. What the fuck were you thinking Michael? You didn't belong there. And you must be an idiot to come back to Manchester and look for me."

The volume of music and people talking spiked as the bathroom door opened outside. Then it quieted down again as the bathroom door closed. From his sitting position, Michael saw feet approaching the stall. Someone knocked on the particleboard door. Kristen opened it. Ivan!

Michael was powerless as Ivan reached down and picked him up by the lapels. Kristen buttoned up Michael's pants. A huge wave of nausea came over Michael and he vomited on the wall in front of him. Some of it splashed on Kristen.

"You gave him too much," Ivan said. "We have to walk him out of here."

"We'll use the back exit. It's right next to the bathroom."

Kristen exited the stall. Ivan draped Michael's left arm over his massive shoulders and dragged him across the bathroom. Michael's legs were useless. He couldn't stand. He felt his shoes rub the floor as Ivan dragged him out of the bathroom. Outside the bathroom, a young woman shook her head as Ivan and Michael staggered by.

"Look at this dude. He's wasted!" the woman yelled.

Kristen pushed the back door open and Ivan followed. Soon the cold air seeped into Michael's neckline. Ivan dropped him next to a dumpster.

"Stay with him," he said. "I'm going to get my car."

Ivan walked away, leaving Michael alone with Kristen.

She bent down next to him and passed her hand over his hair. "Michael, if you don't want to die, you have to to tell us where to find Terry Gagnon. You got that? You want to live to see your kids again don't you?"

That's the last thing Michael heard before he passed out.

CHAPTER 31

A splash of cold water brought Michael to. The disorientation warped his perception of time. He looked around, at first thinking he had fallen asleep at the pub. But once his eyes found focus, extreme confusion set in. Duct tape bound his legs to the chair he was sitting on. More tape held his arms behind his back. A belt held him to the chair.

He shook off the water from his face and saw Ivan standing in front of him. Ivan's jacket was off, revealing a gun holster with a 9mm pistol. His sleeves were rolled up. Michael blinked through a wave of fear that nearly blinded him. He tapped all his strength to try to yank himself free, writhing in his chair until his face turned red. But the binds held. Just as he opened his mouth to yell, he felt the duct tape over his mouth.

"Hello pretty boy," Ivan said.

Another futile effort to free himself tired Michael. He panted through his nose. His eyes darted around the room. It looked like the cavernous interior of an abandoned textile mill on the Merrimack River, the type of mill that would eventually be acquired by a tech-startup and remodeled with glass, steel and LEDs. A single spotlight was shining on Michael from above.

Kristen stepped forward from one of the shadowy corners.

Ivan approached Michael. He crouched down until he was eye level with him.

"I'm going to remove the tape on your mouth," he said. "You scream, I hurt you. Understand?"

Michael nodded. Ivan peeled off the duct tape covering his mouth.

"What do you want?"

Ivan slapped Michael across his face with the back of his hand.

"We ask the questions, ok, pretty boy?"

Michael looked down and realized for the first time that he was still fully clothed.

"Where's Terry Gagnon?" Ivan asked.

"I have no idea."

Ivan grabbed Michael's hair and pushed his head back, exposing his neck. With his other hand, he gripped Michael's throat tightly. Kristen stepped forward and placed her hand on Ivan's shoulder. Ivan loosened his grip.

"Michael, there's two ways to do this," she said. "The easy way and the hard way."

"Why don't you just kill me and get it over with?"

Another man's voice emerged from beyond the glow of light.

"No one wants to kill you Michael," the man said. He stepped forward to let the light shine on his face. It was Newton.

"You?" Michael said.

"We're looking for Terry, Michael. Tell us where she is."

"Why, so you can kill her?" Michael said.

Ivan punched Michael square in the face. The pop sent blood gushing from Michael's nose.

"Not like this," Newton said. "Drown him."

"Is that what you did to Dave?" Michael said. "You drowned him?"

"Dave was easy," Ivan said. "We drugged him and hung him."

"Here's the thing Michael," Newton said. "At this point, no one will believe a fucking word you say. You're damaged goods as far as journalists go. And once you get arrested for rape, your life won't be worth a shit anyway."

Michael scrunched his face.

"Rape?" he said. "I never raped anyone."

Newton nodded to Ivan. Ivan clocked Kristen across the jaw, sending her tumbling to the floor.

"Once Ivan is done with Kristen here, she'll look like the poster child for a rape victim. She even has a little bit of your sperm sitting around somewhere."

Kristen spit out a mouthful of blood.

"Like I told you Michael, I own you."

Ivan walked to her calmly, grabbed her by her beautiful blond hair, pulled her face up and kneed her on the nose.

"Shit, Ivan, not the nose," Kristen said, clutching her face.

Ivan picked her up, straightened her out, then gave her a body blow that caused her to hunch forward.

"Leave her alone, you're going to kill her!" Michael yelled.

Kristen flashed Michael a bloody smile. "Aw!" she said. "You're so sweet."

Ivan took his 9 mm pistol and slammed it across Kristen's upper thighs.

"This is insane, you can't frame me for rape."

"Where's Terry Gagnon?" Newton said.

Michael stayed quiet. Ivan stood next to Kristen, who was curled in the fetal position on the concrete floor. Newton walked to him and whispered something in his ear. Ivan walked to Michael and dragged his chair a few feet back. With a kick, Ivan toppled the chair backwards. Michael's head slammed onto the floor. Ivan dragged Michael, still tied to the chair, across the floor. Michael's head was facing up, but suddenly the floor gave out, as though his head had reached the top of a staircase. Ivan put a cloth bag over Michael's head.

"Please, please don't," Michael said. "Please!"

Water pouring on the cloth bag pressed it against his face. Michael held his breath, but fear forced him to take a breath. He sucked in mostly water and gagged, coughing up inside the bag. A gargled yell escaped his throat. Terror seized Michael.

"No, No! Please!"

"Where's Terry Gagnon?" Newton repeated more sternly.

Michael choked on another mouthful of water and screamed hysterically. Wild, panicked sobs sucked the bag harder over his face.

"I hate stooping to this kind of thing, Michael," Newton said. "When I started my business after the military, I specialized in this kind of thing. My early clients were the mob. And they paid great. Those guys had everyone in their pocket. And do you know why? Because of me. I learned everything I needed to know back then. You know what the difference is between a president and a Mafioso? The title, Michael. That's it. It's the same human blood and weakness underneath. Now I'm going to ask you one more t….."

Michael heard Newton's voice trail off in what sounded like choking. Something hit the floor. The sound came from the direction where Newton was standing.

"Ivan!" Kristen yelled.

Michael heard Ivan's footsteps shuffle and run toward Newton's voice. Something zapped, followed by a second sound of something hitting the floor. Michael heard a brief scuffle. It sounded like Kristen. Then she went silent. A few footsteps sounded, followed by the sound of duct tape peeling from a roll. The sounds of tape continued for a few more seconds.

Then someone walked quickly in Michael's direction. The bag covering his face slipped off. Michael flinched then turned his head to see who it was.

"Laz!" he said, tears in his eyes.

"Let's get the fuck out of here," Laz said.

He cut the duct tape holding Michael to the chair and helped him to his feet. The Taser gun was hanging from Laz's waist, held there by a rope. Ivan, Newton and Kristen were all on the floor, their hands bound with tape behind their backs. Ivan tried to stand up. Michael kicked him hard across the face, knocking him back down.

"You're going down Michael," Kristen yelled as Michael ran behind Laz. "I own you!"

"Michael!" yelled Newton. "We'll find you!"

Outside, Michael ran to the rental car. Laz ran in the opposite direction.

"Where the hell are you going?" Michael yelled.

Laz sprinted to two more cars parked nearby and slashed all the tires with the same knife he had used to cut Michael's bonds. He ran back toward the rental car. He and Michael were climbing inside when gunshots pierced the quiet night. Passenger window glass shattered next to Michael. He ducked inside. Laz went in the other side. More bullets hit around them as Ivan emptied the clip. Laz gunned the car and fishtailed onto the main road, crouching down behind the wheel and glancing over the dashboard. The car careened wildly across all lanes of traffic, skidding across old snow on the shoulders.

After they had driven a few hundred yards, Laz and Michael straightened up in their seats.

"You ok?" Laz said.

Michael nodded. "Yeah, I'm ok. How about you?"

"I'm ok."

"Tell me you have some of this recorded," Michael said.

"I have it all," Laz said. "I thought shit was bad in Eastern Europe."

Michael exhaled.

"I thought I was dead," Michael said. "You saved my life."

"You would have done the same for me."

"I don't know how to thank you."

"Thank me by seeing this through. You have to expose this immediately. You need a story published tomorrow."

"No one will publish a story that I write, not with this kind of shit hanging over my head."

"Then what the fuck do we do?"

"We leak it."

"To who?" Laz said.

"To my competition."

CHAPTER 32

A fellow inmate at the Hillsborough County House of Corrections sat next to Michael and handed him a newspaper. His face was weathered and he had customized his county blues with pen drawings.

"That you?" he said.

Michael unfolded the paper. His mug shot graced the front page of that day's Manchester Herald. Headline: *Primary Sins! Journalist Arrested for Sex Assault on Campaign Staffer.*

"Yeah, that's me," he said. "I didn't do it."

Another inmate nearby laughed.

A day after he turned himself into authorities, Michael had been moved from the holding cell to the main jail. It wasn't as Michael had pictured it. There were no individual cells. Instead, he shared a large auditorium-size room with about 50 inmates. They slept on bunks on the mezzanine level. A guard manned a desk on the first level full-time.

Inmates played chess, checkers and other board games on tables. Michael continued reading.

> *By Jennifer Gordon*
> *A journalist for one of the biggest newspaper chains in the United States was arrested Saturday for allegedly raping a woman who worked for the campaign of George Dimmesdale, the leading Democratic candidate for the party nomination.*
>
> *Michael Cervantes, 29, a reporter for Tindle-Bailey Newspapers, pleaded not guilty at his arraignment early Sunday, and is being held on $500,000 bond at the Hillsborough County House of Corrections. Cervantes surrendered to authorities on Saturday after the woman reported the incident to Manchester police.*
>
> *The Herald is declining to identify the woman in adherence to this newspaper's long-standing policy of not identifying victims of sexual assault.*
>
> *Cervantes had been suspended earlier this week by his employer after allegations that he had a physical relationship with someone on Dimmesdale's campaign, creating a conflict of interest, according to Tindle Bailey CEO Donald Markerson.*
>
> *"We are shocked and saddened by this turn of events," Markerson said in a written statement. "Tindle Bailey is committed to the highest-level of journalism and service. We will reserve further comment until all the facts are in."*
>
> *Tindle Bailey is the second largest newspaper chain in the United States, with more than 30 newspapers across the country, including The Miami Tribune. Cervantes, who is from Miami and works for the Tribune, declined to comment at his brief court appearance Sunday.*
>
> *The Associated News reported that Cervantes is married and has two young children. His family lives in Miami and his wife could not be reached for comment. No one answered the door at his Miami home, and there didn't appear to be anyone at home.*
>
> *Dimmesdale continued campaigning Sunday, and briefly spoke to the media during a campaign stop in Concord.*
>
> *"My campaign has been successful because of my wonderful staff, who I consider my family," Dimmesdale said. "An assault on one is an assault on all of us. My thoughts and prayers go out to the victim, who is a decent, hard working woman. I only hope that this disturbed young man can do no further harm to anyone else."*
>
> *Dimmesdale said the victim had taken a leave of absence from the campaign.*
>
> *Police said the victim showed extensive signs of trauma, including cuts and bruises to her face and body. Cervantes allegedly visited her apartment in Manchester Thursday evening, after he had been suspended from his job. The*

victim reported the crime Friday, and Manchester police issued an all points bulletin for Cervantes.

The assault charges come a few days after another campaign staffer for Dimmesdale, Dave Myrtle, was found dead of an apparent suicide in his apartment.

Cervantes began his career working for Newstime in New York, and was a rising star in journalism, according to his Linkr profile. A search revealed that he had been filing stories about Dimmesdale's campaign for more than four months.

Cervantes is best known for his work in exposing corruption in an obscure department in Miami City Hall, where a city commissioner had been siphoning millions intended to help the poor into his own pockets through an elaborate kickback network. He graduated Summa Cum Laude from Florida University with a degree in journalism.

No one at Dimmesdale's campaign headquarters would comment on the incident, referring all questions to the national campaign headquarters in Washington.

Dimmesdale has shot ahead of the pack of contenders for the Democratic nomination for president in the last few weeks, mostly on a message filled with religious overtones that focuses on morals and values.

"So many problems in our society are rooted in a lack of values," Dimmesdale said, when asked about Cervantes. "We need to return to our roots of hard work, decency and strong morals. Only then will this country move forward. Only then will be able to overcome the challenges that lay before us as a nation."

The Associated News contributed to this report

Michael placed the newspaper down on the table where he was sitting and looked up. Four large flat-screen televisions were set up on the mezzanine balcony on the four sides of the room. They were tuned in to whatever sports or news was broadcasting at the time.

"Sounds like you tuned her up pretty good," said the inmate who handed the paper to Michael. "You a fucking celebrity in here."

While Michael had been reading the paper, other inmates had congregated around him.

"I didn't get no picture in the paper when they threw me in here," said another inmate with his arms tattooed top to bottom. "They didn't even mention me."

"Yeah, college boy," said another inmate. "How come you're so lucky? What the fuck makes you so special. I beat my bitch up ten times worse and never got no picture in the paper either."

Michael stood up. He couldn't tell if their comments were threatening or funny. He bumped into another inmate behind him, who pushed him back down to the table. More inmates noticed and walked over. The guard at the desk ignored the group. Michael wasn't sure what to say, so he asked the first questions that popped into his head.

"Do you guys vote?" he said. He noticed his heart beating fast.

"No we don't vote. Cause in New Hampshire, we can't vote even after we serve our time," said an inmate who had walked over. He was older than the rest, and wore wire-rimmed glasses. "Now, you're a journalist. Why don't you write about that?"

"I actually wrote a story once that exposed the unjust policy of prohibiting former felons from voting," Michael said. "It has an adverse effect on the electorate."

A couple of inmates chuckled.

"You talk pretty," said one.

"He's right," said the old inmate. "The fact that we can't vote means our voices can never be heard again in the democratic process."

As a conversation on the topic arose around the inmates, Michael noticed the guard stand up with a remote control in his hand and aim it up at one of the televisions behind Michael.

"Check it out," the guard said.

Michael looked up. The volume on the television went up. It was still the early afternoon, but a television anchor on ABC was on the screen with a photo of Dimmesdale superimposed over his shoulder. It was Mafikwa's station.

The inmates around Michael quieted down and looked at the television.

"I'm Brian Topping. We interrupt this programming to bring you some breaking news," said the anchor on the television. "A series of graphic sex videos have surfaced in the last few hours showing Democratic front runner George Dimmesdale having sex with one of his campaign staffers."

"ABC news did the best they could to blur out some of the most flagrant images and language. But viewer discretion is advised."

Michael walked to the television. It felt as though a cloud were lifting him toward the screen. The station cut to a video of Dimmesdale with his shirt unbuttoned, but his tie still on, embracing Kristen in her apartment bedroom in Manchester. Kristen's set-up to record Dimmesdale was exactly like the one she used to record Michael, with a hidden camera bundled among her sweaters and cardigans. In the video, Kristen fumbles past his belt, dropping Dimmesdale's pants. A circular blur effect popped up on the screen just as Dimmesdale's pants slid down.

A jump cut later, Dimmesdale is positioned behind Kristen, getting ready to pump her from behind. The entire middle of the screen was blurred out. But Kristen's face was clear and visible. She was turning toward

Dimmesdale. Her blond hair loose and wild.

"Is this what you want, George?" Kristen could be heard saying.

"That's it right there," Dimmesdale said, approaching her from behind. "Oh, God, look at that. That's a beautiful sight."

A couple of the inmates around Michael whooped.

"Yeah boy, look at that shit!"

"That's some presidential shit right there," said another.

The news segment cut back to the anchor.

"The videos first appeared a few hours ago, after several political bloggers received an email from the woman in the videos, who is described as Kristen Dunlop, the New Hampshire press secretary for Dimmesdale's presidential campaign," the anchor said.

The image switched to Mafikwa, standing outside of Dimmesdale's apartment, holding a microphone.

"Our correspondent in New Hampshire, Mafikwa Coleman, is with us live from Manchester. Mafikwa is joining us from the apartment complex where Dimmesdale has taken up residence. Mafikwa, what can you tell us?"

The network must have been desperate to put Mafikwa on the air. As good a journalist as she was, they had only used her to file feeds. Until today. She looked beautiful, all made up and decked out for her debut on ABC.

"Hi Brian, I'm standing here outside of George Dimmesdale's Manchester residence where Governor Dimmesdale has taken refuge from the media after abruptly canceling all of his campaign appearances for the rest of the day. Dimmesdale has not yet made any statements about the videos. His campaign has not returned phone calls seeking comment."

Now the network split the screen so that the anchor was on the left, and Mafikwa on the right. Typical Q & A setup.

"How about the woman in the videos, Mafikwa? Have we heard anything from her?"

"Not yet Brian," Mafikwa said. "The woman in the videos is the same woman who accused Tindle-Bailey journalist Michael Cervantes of rape a few days ago. Now, there is evidence emerging that casts doubt on the legitimacy of that accusation against Cervantes."

The older inmate with the glasses grabbed Michael arm tightly, and shook it lightly. It was not a threatening grip, but more like a hug.

"You really don't belong here do you?" the man said, laughing.

Michael shook his head. The guard changed the channel on the other televisions in the jail. The faces of his competitors graced two others, each one of them almost unrecognizable in their makeup and hairdos. Rachel's heavy Brooklyn accent was lost in her assertive reportage. Although Michael had never found her attractive, she seemed angelic on

CBS, a white silk scarf around her neck and her hair pushed behind one ear.

"This appears to be the makings of a sex scandal for Dimmesdale just on the eve of the primaries," Rachel said in her report. "With New Hampshire set to vote in 5 days, this will clearly factor in to the race."

Audra had never looked as authoritative and confident as she did on the big flatscreen, with the MSNBC logo emblazoned on the lower third showing her name.

"Dimmesdale's aggressive move to paint himself as the candidate of morals and values has now been turned on its head, as these videos showing him en flagrante in an extra-marital affair threaten to unravel his hopes of becoming president."

Audra appeared to hear a noise behind her and turned around in the middle of the broadcast. The microphone pressed back up to her mouth as she turned to walk to the right of the screen.

"It appears as though Shirley Dimmesdale, the candidate's wife, has just slammed the door and stormed out of the apartment she shares with Dimmesdale."

The cameraman followed Audra, shaking up the footage as he jogged to keep up. The other televisions in the jail soon revealed similar shots in their reports. The unplanned pan across the scene revealed a small crowd of reporters clustered near the front door of Dimmesdale's apartment. A campaign staffer was edging his way past the crowd with Shirley behind him, but the reporters closed in around them, blocking off an easy exit. They strafed her with questions.

"Mrs. Dimmesdale, have you seen the videos?"

"Mrs. Dimmesdale, are you quarreling with your husband over this?"

"What do you think about these videos?"

"Did you know your husband was having an affair?"

"What are you going to do now?"

"Will you get a divorce?"

"Is he still a worthy candidate."

"Do you feel deceived?"

She ignored all the questions and pushed aggressively against a cameraman holding a Panasonic in her face.

"Fuck off!" she yelled.

The Dimmesdale staffer urged the reporters to respect her privacy.

"Please," he said. "We have no comment. Please make room for her to pass."

The questions continued as Shirley Dimmesdale and her escort made their way to a nearby Ford, got in and drove off.

CHAPTER 33

The guard called out to Michael.

"Hey Cervantes, you have a visitor."

Michael followed the guard to a closed door. Another guard on the other side buzzed them through. The guard led Cervantes to a room with three booths. Glass panels divided the booths from another room they faced, and telephones hung on the side of each. Whitney from the New York Herald was sitting behind the glass on the left booth. She stood up when she saw Michael.

He smiled and signaled with his hands for her to sit down. He picked up the phone, and Whitney did the same.

"Michael, you look an absolute mess," she said.

"Grooming options are limited in here," he said. "How's the campaign?"

"Well, I'm sure you've seen what's going on with the Dimmesdale campaign."

He nodded.

"Yes, we actually have television in here."

"Well, I'm working on a story," she said. "It's running tomorrow. I know this goes deeper than Kristen."

"What do you know?" he said.

"I know you don't belong in here," she said. "Michael, I have the recordings that you made of you and Kristen."

Michael didn't respond.

"I'm sorry you had to go through all of that," she said. "But you're part of the story."

"Do you think it's any coincidence that you have those recordings?"

"What do you mean?"

"I made sure those recordings went to you. You're the best reporter I know. I knew that you would know what to do with the information."

"Well, we're running the story," she said. "Tomorrow. One thing I don't understand is why you're in here if you had those recordings proving your innocence."

"They said they didn't want to hear it. They said the proof was overwhelming that I had raped Kristen. That a jury would decide."

"Did they even hear the recordings?" she said, surprised.

"They wouldn't even listen to them."

"Michael what happened to you out there?" she said.

"Are you asking me as a reporter or as a friend?"

"I'm here as a reporter. For the story. This is an interview."

"I made a mistake with Kristen," Michael said, pausing to let Whitney write down her notes. "It was an error of judgment. I have no excuse for that. And it's something I will have to make right with my family. But I didn't rape her, and these recordings prove that. I was drugged at the Wild Rover and kidnapped by her and by the head of security for Frederick Newton, a man named Ivan. They tortured me to try to get me to tell them the location of Terry Gagnon because she had given me incriminating information about Newton's shakedown racket."

"How long have you known about Dimmesdale and Kristen?"

"For almost two weeks," he said.

"How did you find out about them?"

Michael smiled shyly.

"When you scooped me on that story about Dimmesdale's new emphasis on morals and values, remember that? My editors came down hard on me to interview him exclusively. So I woke up early that day we spent the night in Berlin and sat outside his hotel room. I heard him and Kristen going at it inside their room. Then I saw Kristen walk out and watched them make out in front of me."

"Why didn't you run a story."

"I wanted to run a story, but my editors didn't think I had enough evidence."

"Even though you had seem them kissing on the mouth and heard them?"

"That's right."

Whitney shook her head. "Wow. Unbelievable. What happened in Chicago?"

"I went looking for Terry Gagnon, who had worked for Newton in the same kind of operation. Ivan tried to kill us. We got away."

"Why didn't you go to the authorities?"

"I didn't think I could trust anyone."

"Where's Terry Gagnon?"

"In Chicago, staying with her friend. Here's the address."

Michael wrote it down for Whitney.

"Needless to say, don't share this with anyone."

"Don't worry, we have a correspondent in Chicago. He's very good. We'll get him over there to talk to her and say that you shared her contact information."

"What's going on with you and your family?"

"I love my family. I'll do everything I can to regain their love and trust."

Michael answered the rest of Whitney's questions as best he could. When she had exhausted all her curiosity, she sat back on her chair and sighed, looking Michael directly in the eyes.

"Michael, this is your story. It should be your byline on it."

Michael shrugged.

"Now it's your story Whitney," he said. "Now get out of here and go win a Pulitzer."

On the morning of the fifth day of his captivity, a guard approached Michael unceremoniously.

"Cervantes, you're out of here," he said.

"Bail?" Michael said.

"No, all charges against you have been dismissed."

Michael changed back into his civilian clothes, and walked out to the jail waiting area. Harriet, his Miami editor, saw him walk out and called to him.

"Michael!"

He turned to see her.

"Harriet? What are you doing here."

She clutched a folded up newspaper in her right hand.

"I flew in yesterday. I've been waiting out here since last night. Michael I am so sorry."

She hugged Michael. His arms hung limply by his side at first. Then his right arm made its way up and around her back.

"I wanted to be here when you got out. I'm so sorry about everything."

"Harriet, I just want to go home."

She held up the newspaper. "When this thing hit the media in the New York Herald, it was like a torpedo. Donald Jenkins resigned last night. Donald Markerson is expected to resign today. The board of directors at Tindle Bailey went nuts when they heard what happened."

"How about Dimmesdale?"

"Nothing yet. But Frederick Newton and Ivan Javonavich were arrested this morning. Kristen Dunlop is now a fugitive."

"They haven't caught her yet?"

"She's gone. But they'll find her."

Harriet put her hands on Michael's shoulders and looked him in the eye.

"Now, are you ready for this?"

"For what?"

"There's a hoard of media outside. They've been arriving since last night."

Michael walked to the window and looked outside. It looked like the media turnout at a space shuttle launch, tripods, cameras, cables, lights; correspondents bundled up and space heaters glowing.

"I'm doing everything I can to get you back on the job," she said. "I think we can do it."

"I'm not so sure I want to go back," Michael said. "Not after all this."

"We can have this conversation later. For now, we gotta walk the gauntlet. You ready?"

"Aren't you going to prep me or something?"

She shook her head.

"I'd stick to the facts, that's pretty much it."

"You mean the truth," Michael said, a defeated smirk on his face.

"What's the difference?" she said.

"The facts were misinterpreted and I ended up in jail," he said. "The truth is why I'm walking out."

CHAPTER 34

Dusk settled over Miami, flattening the vibrant colors of lush foliage into a pastel wonderland. Airplanes flying overhead basked in the glitter of a million windows reflecting sunbursts skyward. Tourists napped in palm shade on sand dunes. Rush hour rendered the 836 a time bandit. Reporters at the Miami Tribune cranked copy on deadline. Strippers slapped hands backstage for the shift change. Bars lured Happy Hour fiends with mojito specials. Central American laborers clogged bus stops. Windshields glared in the falling light on westbound Calle Ocho. Another cycle of daylight faded at the tip of the continent.

Leaving Miami International Airport, Michael headed for his old house. The house was dark outside, as the front yard lights had not yet come on for the night. Bianca's car wasn't there. The lawn looked a bit more overgrown than usual. The front door was ajar. He stepped inside into an empty living room. He suddenly remembered this was no longer his home.

In his absence, Bianca had taken on the entire burden of moving houses. She hadn't complained. But Michael hadn't looked at any of the texts she had sent of their new place. He jogged back to his car and peeled out of his driveway, eager to get to his family.

He pulled into a street he had only seen once at dusk. This was his new street, but it felt alien and hostile. Michael stood in front of his new house, gazing at the begonias that lined the front wall. The sun had dipped behind his house, casting a long shadow that shrouded Michael. He approached the door, as though he were a guest, and rang the bell, his suitcase in tow.

Someone yanked open the venetian blinds at the window near the front door. He heard yelling from inside. It was his older son Iggy.

"Mom, it's pap pap!"

The door swung open. Iggy shot out and wrapped his arms around his father's waist. Bianca stepped out behind him, followed by their little one, Glory, who timidly approached him. He bent down, picked her up and embraced her.

"Hi kids, I missed you so much!"

"I missed you so much pap pap!" Iggy said. "I can't wait to show you my drawing I did yesterday in school! It's of you flying in an airplane and us and mom and a park."

Bianca crossed her arms. No hint of a smile escaped her face. She had kept a cordial distance.

"I went to your parents' house first, thinking you were there," Michael told her. "But they told me you moved back in here today."

Bianca waited for Michael to put down Glory and for Iggy to release him from his bear hug.

"Kids, go inside, mom and dad need to talk," she said, corralling the kids back into the house.

She closed the door behind them, crossed her arms and stepped closer to Michael. To Michael, she had never looked more beautiful.

"You can't stay here," she said. "You don't deserve to step into that house."

"Bianca, I'm so sorry, about everything. Things got so…"

Bianca cut him off.

"'Things', you love to blame your mistakes on 'things'."

"I need my family, Bianca. I need you."

"You don't care about me, Michael. You humiliated me. You made a fool of me. The whole world saw what you did. I don't even know if I love you anymore. I hope she was worth it."

"I will do whatever I have to do to win back your trust, Bianca. I will wait as long as I have to. I made a terrible mistake that I will regret for the rest of my life. But I love you. I have always loved you, and I will always love you."

Bianca sighed and shook her head. She looked away, across the street.

"I'm glad you're out of jail," she said, "for the kids' sake."

"Me too," he said.

"Look, go stay at your parents' house. I need time to decide what I'm going to do. At this point, I don't know if I want to stay married to you."

Michael hung his head.

"Okay," he said. "I understand. Can I come by and see the kids after school tomorrow?"

"I'll think about it."

Michael turned to walk away.

"Wait," Bianca said. "I have something for you."

She went back into the house and returned with a small parcel postmarked in Canada.

"I found this in the mailbox here when I got here today."

CHAPTER 35

Alfredo Cervantes dragged his oxygen tank to the door. He opened it and regarded his son for a moment before starting to laugh, which quickly crescendoed into a coughing fit. Michael walked in and kissed his father on the cheek.

"*Hola papi*," he said.

"Is that Michael?" his mother yelled from the kitchen. "*Dios mio, mijo*. Come here, let me look at you."

His mother, Gladys, pulled down his head and embraced him, planting a warm kiss on his cheek.

"Are you ok? *Papi* and I have been worried sick."

"Yeah, I'm ok mom. I'm fine. Bianca...she..."

"Let me guess, she doesn't want you to stay there."

Michael nodded sheepishly. "Yeah."

"I don't blame her Michael. I don't blame her at all."

"Can I stay here?"

"Of course," Alfredo said. "Of course you can."

"*Claro, mijo*," said his mother.

Alfredo walked to his favorite armchair and settled in. His mother went back to the kitchen. The television was on in seconds. Michael sat on the couch next to his father.

"I told you not to get involved in politics, Michael, but you didn't listen to me," Alfredo said. "Politics is vile, no matter where you live. Now look at the mess you've gotten yourself into. It's just like in Cuba, when Castro took over the whole political system. You don't think a bunch of journalists got taken down? That's the first thing he did. He took them down so he could control the media. So he could control the people."

Michael's mother brought Alfredo a cup of water and two white pills. Without taking his eyes off the television, he took the pills and swallowed them in a gulp.

"How are you doing dad? How're the lungs?" Michael asked.

"He's better," Gladys said.

"Ha!" Alfredo said. "You try hauling this tank around everywhere. After a while you don't want to go anywhere. Ah, here we go!"

Alfredo boosted the volume on his television. An ABC anchor prepped the audience for a news conference.

"Just in time Michael. Look at this."

The anchor on the television said: "And we are expecting an announcement any minute now from Governor George Dimmesdale, who has kept quiet for days about the sex scandal that has engulfed his campaign in controversy. With the New Hampshire primaries just days away, the world is tuning in to see what the Democratic front runner is going to do. Now let's tune in to the ballroom of the Chicago Grand Hotel, where Dimmesdale is expected to appear at a press conference in just a few moments. Let's turn to our correspondent in Chicago, Mafikwa Coleman. Mafikwa, what's the scene like over there."

The shot cut to Mafikwa. Michael chuckled.

"I know her," he said to his dad.

"The mood in the room is rather somber," Mafikwa said. "Dimmesdale hasn't been seen in public since the videos of his liaison became public, and there has been little indication of what he will say or do today. One thing is certain. It will be difficult if not impossible for him to recover his standing in the campaign. And...oh, oh yes, here we go. Dimmesdale is now entering the room."

The camera switched to a wide shot from a tripod positioned at the back of the hall. There seemed to be more media than supporters there. No one was holding up poster boards or cheering as Dimmesdale entered the hall. His wife, Shirley, was absent. Dimmesdale approached the podium. For once, Dimmesdale didn't have to raise his hands to acknowledge adulation and jockey for a moment to speak. His face was serious.

"Thank you all for coming here today," Dimmesdale began. "We've come a long way in this campaign. We started off with little more than hope and a few people who believed in us. And we rose to the front of the pack in a race against worthy and able opponents. I'm proud of what we did. I'm proud of my campaign staff and their wonderful dedication. Our supporters are second to none, and I want to thank you all for standing by us during these last few months. Thank you from the bottom of my heart."

Expecting some sort of applause, Dimmesdale paused. But the audience was quiet.

"You probably noticed that my wife is not standing with me today. She usually is at these things, standing right here. She's always been my biggest supporter."

Dimmesdale looked to his right, and gestured with his hand at the empty space next to him.

"The fact that my wife is not here says it all. Without her endorsement, I cannot continue in this race. I hereby officially withdraw my candidacy for the Democratic nomination for president of the United States, effective immediately."

Now a buzz arose in the crowd.

"I will use the next few weeks and months to try to mend the damage I have done to my family and to my country. I apologize to anyone I may have hurt, but especially my wife Shirley. There is no excuse for my behavior, so I won't give you one. The only thing I can say is that sometimes the devil shines brighter than the Lord and we are drawn to that foul light, only to be fooled by its luster."

"Working toward better values in this country means that people need to take responsibility for their words and actions. And so today, I take responsibility for my actions. Thank you, God Bless you, and God bless the United States of America."

Dimmesdale ditched the podium and walked to the far end of the riser, where reporters swarmed to him and shouted questions.

Suddenly the buzz around Dimmesdale fell silent. The cameraman focused on a point in the crowd, jerking the camera around. People parted like sardines around a shark to reveal a woman standing in the center. It was Kristen. Michael jumped up from the couch. Mafikwa's voice came through the television.

"Oh, my God, it's Kristen Dunlop. She's here with her hands in her pockets, here at the press conference. She has just appeared in the crowd. Kristen Dunlop is the woman in the middle of this controversy. She is currently wanted by police. She has been a fugitive the last few days."

Michael shook his head. "No way! I can't believe it. What the hell is she doing there?"

All eyes in the room were fixed on Kristen. A couple of guards skirted the edge, their hands on their waists, gripping guns or radios. The cameras at the scene remained focused on Kristen. For once, her blond hair was pulled back in a ponytail, keeping it out of her face. She slowly walked to Dimmesdale and grabbed him by the shirt. Dimmesdale raised his hands in a gesture of surrender. The room went quiet.

"Please, Kristen, don't do anything crazy. It's over."

Kristen kissed Dimmesdale on the lips. He flinched his head back, but didn't turn it to avoid the kiss.

"Don't I get a turn in front of the cameras George?" Kristen said. "You get to walk into the sunset now and work a cushy job as a lobbyist. And what do I get? Jail? I don't think so."

"Kristen, it doesn't have to be that way," Dimmesdale said, trying to strike a soothing tone.

"I have a question for you Kristen," yelled Mafikwa. "What would you like to say right now?"

Kristen jammed a hand in her pocket and turned to Mafikwa. A woman in the crowd yelled: "She's going for something in her pocket!"

"Oh my god," someone else yelled, "Is it a gun?"

"Please, Kristen," Mafikwa said. "If you have something to say, now's your chance. Why are you here today?"

Kristen wrapped her left arm around Dimmesdale's shoulder. Her right hand remained jammed in her pocket. She squeezed Dimmesdale's shoulder, shaking him. Dimmesdale tried to pull away, but she yanked him back.

"You're going to be a daddy," she said to him.

"What?" Dimmesdale said, his face oozing incredulity.

"You heard me George. I'm carrying your baby."

"That's…what? How is that possible?"

Armed police officers ran into the room and started shouting orders. They pushed the press back, shaking the camera that was broadcasting the feed. Mafikwa kept the microphone close to her mouth.

"Chicago police are on the scene now," Mafikwa reported. "They have their weapons drawn and are approaching Kristen Dunlop slowly."

The next few moments unfolded quickly. Cops shouted at Kristen.

"Mam, remove your hand from your pocket and put it above your head!"

Kristen looked around at the press corps and shouted.

"Stay back! I'm not done yet. I want to hear what George has to say."

"Mam, take your hand out of your pocket!"

Kristen, in a swift movement, pulled something long and slender from her pocket and held it up in front of Dimmesdale's face.

"Knife!" yelled one of the police officers.

"No!" Dimmesdale yelled.

Dimmesdale embraced Kristen and spun her around just at two shots rang out.

People screamed and ran in different directions.

Dimmesdale dropped to the floor. A shocked Kristen stepped back from Dimmesdale. Police knocked her to the floor, next to Dimmesdale, as he lay clutching his stomach. Police wrestled the object free from her hand. The cameras zoomed in. It was a pregnancy test. A light-colored plus sign filled the box.

"It's a pregnancy test, you idiots!" Kristen yelled. "I wanted him to be the first to know, since he is the father."

Mafikwa's cameraman jerked his Panasonic violently. Kristen groaned. The camera steadied again. Mafikwa's face was stunned on television, but she raised the microphone to her mouth.

"It appears that George Dimmesdale has been shot by Chicago police," Mafikwa said. "Kristen Dunlop has been arrested. Dimmesdale is conscious and alive."

Dimmesdale, who had two police officers crouching over him trying to stem the bleeding, mouthed words.

"He's gasping for air, but I think he's trying to talk," Mafikwa said.

Mafikwa walked toward Dimmesdale, two other police officers were trying to form a space around him, but Mafikwa and her cameraman managed to squeeze between them and shine the light on his face. He had tears in his eyes. The camera zoomed in on his face. Mafikwa put the microphone up to his mouth.

"It's not mine," he stammered.

"What isn't yours Governor?"

"The baby," he exhaled then took another few seconds. "It isn't mine."

Mafikwa turned to her cameraman. "Are you getting this?" she could be heard saying.

The cameraman flashed a thumbs up.

"I…" Dimmesdale said. "I had a vasectomy."

Michael sat back on the couch and pondered these words, which had been whispered by the injured candidate live on national television. Was he the father? Was Dimmesdale lying? Would he even live? His father looked over at him.

"Damn son," he said. "This is better than your mom's *telenovelas*."

Michael watched the news until the late hours of the night, until long after his parents had gone to bed. He imagined reporters were trying to reach him, but without a new cell phone and away from his old house, their searches would likely turn up empty. The report later on from the hospital was that Dimmesdale was in critical but stable condition, and was sequestered in a secure wing under police watch. Cops took Kristen into custody and had her on suicide watch at the Cook County Jail.

Michael finally went to the guest room at his parents' house and unpacked his suitcase. He picked up the parcel that his wife had given him and opened it. Inside there was a hard drive and a typed letter from Laz.

"Dear Michael, I hope you're reading this from the comforts of your own home. I've been thinking a lot about what we did, and the only conclusion I can come to is that it was necessary. Who the fuck are we if we don't push back? We pulled some militant shit to expose bad people, and the world is better for it. Someone tried to destroy you and you didn't take it lying down. We fought back.

"I wanted you to have this duplicate of Kristen's hard drive, which is the best treasure I've ever looted. Who could have guessed that she recorded all her conversations with Newton about the oil companies and their fixation on Dimmesdale? And that she kept her recordings on the hard drive. When I saw that first video of her and Dimmesdale fucking, I knew it was game over. Then we got her emails, and Newton's emails, and all the recordings during your kidnapping. This is real journalism. Exposing evil people using the same tools and techniques that they use to lie, cheat and steal. It almost makes me want to move back home and do this full time. What do you think, bro? You don't need some company to call you a journalist to be one. Hit me up if you're looking for a partner."

"Your friend, Laz."

ACKNOWLEDGMENTS

Thank you to all who made this book possible, including but not limited to my wife, my kids, my dog, my old bosses, my family and friends, and those great members from my book club who volunteered to read this book and provide valuable feedback for the humble wage of beer.

ABOUT THE AUTHOR

Oscar Corral, a former award-winning journalist for some of the largest newspapers in the United States, has covered several presidential primaries around the country. His experience living in New Hampshire and traveling through other early primary states as a political correspondent for the second-largest newspaper chain in the United States is forever frozen into his memory. His other Michael Cervantes novel, *Keep Her Contained*, is about a modern day mummy discovered underneath a Long Island mansion and the police investigation that ensues. Corral has also directed and produced several documentaries, including *Tom Wolfe Gets Back to Blood*, *Exotic Invaders: Pythons in the Everglades*, and the Emmy-nominated *The Crossfire Kids*. He lives in Miami with his wife, Cecile, his two daughters and his pound mutt Cleo.